Dylan Stone's Journal

W. D. Nelson

Stone Lake Publishing

Dedication

For Wesley and Damon—the original backpackers.

Chapter 1

Pelekas Beach

Corfu, Greece

June 29, 1983

WHEN DYLAN STONE WOKE up that morning, he never thought this could be the last day of his life.

As the sunlight peered through a crack in the curtains and crawled down the wall above his head, he rose quickly from his bed. Reaching under his shirt, he checked his money belt-passport, travelers' checks, return airline tickets, Eurail Pass, and now...a small envelope with a poetic verse handwritten across the back. Next, he confirmed he'd stashed his journal in his backpack, then glimpsed his guitar case leaning against the wall below the window. He unzipped his money belt and pulled out the envelope. He could feel the skeleton key inside. He looked around the hotel room. There was no movement from the others. He placed the envelope inside the guitar and closed its case.

Dylan had woken early, as he always did. As a young boy, his dad would coax him out of bed to go for runs well before dawn in the hills of central Texas. That routine somehow stuck, and now he just couldn't sleep in. Besides, it was a tiny coffin of a bed, and he was ready to check out Pelekas Beach, which he'd heard so much about.

Tanned and fit with sandy brown hair and a slightly crooked but welcoming smile, Dylan's most striking feature was his eyes. Due to an elbow to the face during a pick-up basketball game a few years earlier, the left pupil was permanently dilated, making the eye appear to be black, while the right eye was pale green. The doctor had told him that he had anisocoria, and then he winked and whispered to Dylan, "You look like David Bowie, pretty cool." Though his eyes were different colors, they were expressive and kind.

He was about a month into an eight-week backpacking trip across Europe with his best friend, Bull Eastland. They had started their odyssey in Ireland the day after their high school graduation ceremony for the class of '83. After hitchhiking across the island, they took a ferry to France and began their journey, mainly by train, across the continent before finally reaching the island of Corfu, Greece. They were ready for a break from nonstop traveling and sightseeing. Dylan wanted to lie on the beach and read a book, explore the island by motorbike, and if he was lucky, run into the pretty American girl he had met in Florence. However, he had found it difficult to enjoy the trip ever since someone had started following him. He was fairly certain he knew the reason and hoped to resolve the issue here in Corfu so that they could enjoy the rest of their trip.

Across the room, Bull lay asleep in the other bunk, snoring like a drunk lion. He looked like he was pressed into a child's bed, his enormous feet jutting out from beneath the sheet and extending half a foot beyond the mattress. He was a night owl and hated mornings. But once he got going, he was non-stop energy.

Bull and Dylan had been friends since first grade. Bull's given name was Mark, but he got his nickname in the fifth grade, when he scored a touchdown in his first football game of the season by mowing down nearly every defensive player on a sixty-yard run. His coach had shouted "Go Bull!" and the nickname had stuck. On the surface, the friends seemed like an unlikely pair. Standing at six feet four inches with jet-black hair, a muscular build, and a five-o'clock shadow, Bull had been an all-district offensive and defensive lineman on the high school football team. He didn't just walk, he pounded the ground so hard that plates vibrated on nearby tables. He was loud, witty, and driven.

In comparison, Dylan was a wiry distance runner, standing five feet ten inches on his tiptoes. He moved silently, like a leopard gliding through the forest. He was more introspective but clever, with a dry sense of humor. A talented writer and musician, he was a bit of a loner, and he saw Bull as his protector from the chaos of high school. Together, they shared the same taste in books and music and loved debating—whether it was politics, philosophy, or whose mother was the best cook. Both of them had an insatiable desire to learn as much as possible and to experience life to the fullest.

As Dylan tiptoed across the room, he tripped over a figure lying under a blanket between the two beds. He heard a soft grunt. The lumpy shape twitched, and an arm slipped out from under the sheet. Then it went still and quiet.

Now Dylan remembered. It was Nels. He was a Norwegian guy Dylan had met at the ferry terminal in Corfu Old Town the previous day while waiting for Bull to arrive. After a late dinner, they had made their way through the town's historic streets to a hotel on Pelekas Beach, situated on the opposite side of the island. He'd first heard about this infamous beachfront property from a drunk Irish girl he met after a John Mayall concert in Reims, France. Then, the next day, during a conversation with two German backpackers on an overnight train, tales about the same hotel came up again. A few days later, in a bar in Blanes, Spain, Dylan and Bull overheard some locals speaking in Spanish, laughing and gesturing wildly as they discussed the very same location. Dylan asked them about the beach and hotel in his broken Spanish, and their story matched the others they had heard: when you get to Corfu, take the bus to Pelekas Beach and stay at the hotel there. It's the only one. It's impossible to miss. "It's cheap. It's on the most popular beach on the island; the girls are beautiful, and bathing suits are optional." Well, what eighteen-year-old guy could resist that?

Nels seemed nice, though a little serious, and Dylan and Bull had invited him to stay with them during their time in Corfu. He was tall and slim, with long blond hair. He appeared to be in his early twenties. He traveled with a small backpack. That was it. And it was half full of books. He told Dylan and Bull that he traveled for a month each summer and had become very efficient at packing light. He would bring several paperbacks along for the trip and then leave them on trains or park benches as he finished reading them. This summer, he was traveling solo across Greece and was excited to have some company. Plus, he was low on funds, so sleeping on the hotel floor for free was a great deal for him.

They had arrived well past midnight. They stepped into the small, gloomy lobby of Hotel Nikos and tapped the bell to summon the innkeeper, hoping someone would be around at 2 a.m. That was when they knew they'd found the right place. An ancient, arched wooden door creaked open from behind the green linoleum front desk, and the most beautiful girl Dylan and Bull had seen on the entire trip meandered to the desk, frowning. Her tousled "beach blonde" (as

Dylan called it) hair framed her bronzed face and flowed halfway down her back. She looked like she might be Swedish or Finnish. Her eyes were cat-like and piercing blue as she stared at them. Dylan couldn't help but notice her form-fitting T-shirt and shorts; it was clear that there were no tan lines.

Bull, who had memorized a few phrases in Greek, attempted to ask her if a room was available, but he was so flustered that the words just wouldn't come out. Dylan began to give it a try, when she looked at them both blankly and said in clear English, with an accent they couldn't place, "We have one room left. Next time, try to get here earlier..." She tossed the key at Dylan and pointed down the narrow hallway. She then clearly cursed in some language they didn't recognize and slinked back to her lair.

A brief screech escaped as Dylan opened the hotel room door. He tried not to wake Bull and Nels as he slipped outside. As he stepped onto the cool sand, he was blinded by the sunrise. Waves crashed in the distance and seagulls chirped shrilly around him.

"Hey, stranger."

A slight Yankee accent drew Dylan's gaze around the corner of the building to a guy standing in front of an outdoor grill situated in front of the hotel, the postcard-beautiful beach in the background. A powerful wave of translucent blue water pelted the white powder sand just feet away from where he was standing. Then it receded, only to repeat the process every few seconds, as if the ocean was calmly breathing in and out. Dylan stood still for a second and soaked it in before replying. It was mesmerizing, the water sometimes blue, sometimes pale green, and completely transparent.

He then smelled fresh coffee.

"Good morning," Dylan said.

Mr. New England didn't fit the stereotype of a Yank; he looked like he spent most of his time on a surfboard: tall, bronze, and athletic, with rock-star-length sun-bleached hair under a Boston Red Sox cap. But there was something in his eyes that conflicted with his friendly smile, making Dylan uneasy. He looked familiar.

"My name's Julian. Welcome to the Hotel Nikos... once you settle in, you'll never want to leave," he said with a half-smile as he held a mug to his mouth and blew on it. "Cup of coffee?"

Dylan raised an eyebrow. "Nice to meet you. I'm Dylan. I'd love some coffee. Black." He had never had a cup of coffee until he arrived in France less than a month ago, and now he was hooked.

"How long are you staying?" Julian asked as he poured the coffee into a chipped ceramic mug with a picture of a seashell on one side and the word Corfu in rainbow-colored letters on the other.

"Not sure. We've been traveling hard and want to relax for a few days, so we're keeping it flexible. I'm looking forward to not even thinking about a museum or a cathedral for a bit. How about you?" Dylan eyed the bacon, realizing that he was starving.

"I'll be here through Friday. I'm meeting some college buddies in Athens this weekend." Julian placed his coffee cup on a small three-legged table next to the grill.

"Where do you go to school?" Dylan asked.

"Charlottesville. I'm studying art history at UVA. I've been traveling by myself for a few weeks, mainly in France, and I'll spend the rest of the summer with two frat brothers, exploring Greece and Italy. How about you?"

"I'm traveling with my friend Bull from home, and a Norwegian guy we met yesterday, Nels. I'll be attending UT in Austin next fall, and Bull will play football at LSU." Dylan didn't mention the puzzling and even near-death experiences he had encountered along the way. "We only have a month left. It's going too fast."

"It's heaven over here. What's your plan today?" Julian asked.

Dylan got the impression he was looking for some company. But something about Julian made him uncomfortable. *Could he be the guy who's been following us?*

"No plan yet," Dylan responded. "We need to go to the bank and exchange some travelers' checks for Greek drachma. All we have is some Italian lira and a few francs left over from France, and I don't think many people here will accept that. Other than that, I'm not sure. We got here late last night."

"That was you? I heard you all come in. That was late. I'm surprised anyone was up to let you in."

"I'm pretty sure we woke the hotel clerk up. She wasn't happy," Dylan said with a smile.

"That's Ingrid. She's never happy. But it's hard to take your eyes off of her, isn't it?" He winked. "Hey, I've been in Corfu for a week. If you'd like, I could show you all around."

"Sounds great!" Bull exclaimed as he barreled through the door, much to Dylan's surprise, Nels following, trying hard to keep up.

He extended his hand towards Julian. "My name's Bull," he said. "This is Nels. Nice to meet ya! It would be great to get some advice from an expert."

Julian shook Bull's hand, then turned to Nels. The two studied each other for a moment, briefly shook hands, and then looked away from each other. *It's as if they know each other*, Dylan thought. Julian regained his composure. "Name's Julian. Coffee? Breakfast?"

"Hell yeah!" Bull exclaimed. "I'm starving."

"I'll tell you what—after we eat, I'll give you a tour of the island," Julian said as he poured some eggs into the pan. As Bull, Nels, and

Dylan walked out to survey the famous beach, Dylan glanced back and noticed Julian studying them carefully.

Chapter 2

Hamer

Friday, June 20, 2025

WHAT A STRANGE DAY it's been, Floyd Stone thought as he left the bank in downtown Hamer, Texas, *if you can call that one-stoplight intersection a downtown.* After a sharp ninety-degree turn onto No Name Drive, he steered the old Jeep up the winding trail to the bungalow he had loved visiting as a child. *It's a good thing this Jeep has four-wheel drive,* he thought as the vehicle strained to reach the peak of a steep hill. With wavy ash-brown hair, flecked with gray, and standing six feet tall with a few extra pounds around the middle, Floyd could be considered attractive if he ate a little better, exercised a little more, and drank a little less. He hadn't been to this house in twenty-five years, and now... it was his.

He opened the front door and peered inside. This had been his grandparents' house when he was a child. It brought back great memories of Nana's baked cookies, late-night movies in the "kid room," Easter egg hunts in the woods, and Christmas mornings spent around a tree on the back deck. In the corner of the kitchen, he saw the smiley face he had scratched onto the wall with the handmade pocket knife his father gave him after he won a spelling contest in fifth grade. When his grandfather saw the damaged wall, instead of getting angry, he looked at Floyd and said, "I think it's a masterpiece. We'll keep it!" Then he fashioned a small frame and placed it around the etching.

Floyd winced when he recalled the horrible weekend of his tenth birthday later that same year. The whole family had gathered at the lake house to celebrate. He remembered walking through the nearby trails with Papa, searching for hummingbirds and baby deer, when Papa stopped and looked down at him and said, "Floyd, I've been watching you your whole life. You are very talented. The sky is the limit for you. Keep working hard. You will be something special." And at that moment, Floyd felt he could be something special. Yet later that same night, his world turned upside down.

He wedged in between Nana and Papa as they watched *The Princess Bride*, an annual tradition. Floyd could think of no better place to be. During the famous sword-fighting scene between Inigo Montoya and the Man in Black, Inigo stated the famous line in his melodic Spanish accent, "My name is Inigo Montoya. You killed my father, prepare to die." Floyd and Papa then sang the phrase along with the swashbuckler and laughed and laughed.

Then it happened. Papa gasped and held his chest. Floyd thought he was kidding and chuckled. It was their favorite part of the movie, and Papa was a joker. But Papa wasn't joking. Suddenly, Nana started screaming. His mom and dad appeared out of nowhere, their faces etched with concern. Everything became a blur. Mom was crying, and paramedics showed up and pushed Floyd out of the way as they raced to assist Papa. And then everyone had gone to the hospital except for his dad and him. Floyd remembered coming out of a fog and seeing Miracle Max (Billy Crystal) gazing out from the TV screen, saying,

"There's a big difference between being mostly dead and all dead. Mostly dead is slightly alive." Unfortunately, unlike the character in the movie, Papa was all dead.

Floyd was crushed. Birthdays were never the same. Nana imploded with grief and only lived a year or so longer, and Floyd never returned to the lake house again. He always figured it had been sold after Nana passed. He was amazed it had somehow stayed in the family.

Floyd glanced inside the fridge. It was empty, except for half of a twelve-pack of Shiner Bock, perched on the top shelf, and an expired carton of milk and some fuzzy cheese in the door. A small marble dining counter separated the kitchen from the living room. The room was bare, except for a large, well-worn recliner facing what must be an 85-inch big-screen television mounted on the wall. A framed picture of a young man belly-laughing while holding a bandana in front of the midsection of Michelangelo's *David* was displayed next to the TV. Floyd knew the picture well. It was the last known photo of his Uncle Dylan, and it had been on this wall as far back as he could remember. Uncle Dylan mysteriously disappeared not long after this picture was taken during a trip to Europe in the 1980s. His uncle's old acoustic guitar from that ill-fated trip hung in a wall mount next to the photograph. A perfectly maintained 1980s stereo system, complete with a turntable, equalizer, and stereo speakers the size of a small car, sat on a table below the guitar.

An album whose center label displayed an unmistakable triangular prism set against a black background with a ray of light refracting through it lay on the turntable. *Dark Side of the Moon* was one of Uncle Dylan's favorites. Which meant it was one of Floyd's father's favorite albums as well. He smiled. As the story went, when Dylan was a teenager, he announced to anyone who would listen that he would name his children Pink and Floyd. Everyone figured it was a joke.

However, after his disappearance, Dylan's younger brother, Robert, decided that if he had a son, he would name him Floyd. And, years later, much to his ex-wife's chagrin, that's what he did.

Next to the stereo system were three crates filled with the best music collection known to man (according to his father). It had belonged to Uncle Dylan but eventually became his father's. *Blonde on Blonde* was protruding out of the first crate.

The coffee table in the corner of the room was bare except for one postcard-sized picture frame. Floyd walked over to look at it more closely and found that it was a photo of his mother, father, and himself from an Easter morning at this house, probably twenty-five years ago.

He grabbed a beer and headed out onto the back deck, which was the highlight of the old house his grandfather had built in the 1970s. It extended twenty feet from the back of the house, with a view straight down to the rocky shore of Lake Hamer, more than one hundred feet below. His grandfather had been so proud of this panorama of the locally famous lake, which had been named after the retired Texas Ranger who had killed Bonnie and Clyde back in the 1930s.

It wasn't until this morning that Floyd realized his father had been living here for the last few years. He sat down on a wooden deck chair and absentmindedly watched an eagle glide through the sky, then swoop down and snatch a smallmouth bass from just beneath the lake's surface, as he thought about the day.

He'd gotten up early this morning, even though he didn't need to. He didn't have a job or a wife anymore. He had been laid off a month earlier, and his wife had left him the week before Christmas. He couldn't blame her; he'd have done the same if he were her. He couldn't keep a job, he drank too much, and he just felt directionless. She kept the house and he moved to a cheap hotel in south Austin, the kind where you park your car right outside your front door and hope it's still there the next morning. Of course, it didn't matter since his car had been inoperable for several weeks. If someone wanted to steal it, they'd need a wrecker. Plus, he wasn't going to be able to afford to live there much longer, the way things were going.

Just when he thought things couldn't get worse, he'd received a certified letter from a law firm. Opening it, he'd been shocked to learn that his father had recently died. Even though Floyd hadn't seen his dad in years, it still felt like a punch to the gut. After overcoming the initial shock, he realized that the letter was an invitation for him to attend a reading of his father's Last Will and Testament today at noon in Hamer, Texas, a town halfway between Austin and San Antonio.

Since his car was on the fritz, he was forced to take the one bus that went through Hamer as it meandered through the Hill Country between the two larger cities. What should have taken an hour took two and a half, due to the number of local stops in the small towns that appeared along the winding roads. He quickly hopped off the bus at the only stoplight on Hamer's Main Street. Before he had taken a step, the bus abruptly accelerated and continued its trek towards San Antonio. Floyd threw his backpack over his shoulder and headed to the most prominent building on the street, a retrofitted post office with a sign that read: Law Offices of Frank Wilder, Esquire. It was sandwiched between Bob's BBQ—with a line of people waiting to enter, sweating in the Texas summer heat—and Franklin's Funeral Home. There was no line there, he observed with a smile. Across the street was a saloon, with luxury apartments located on the second floor above it.

Frank Wilder fit the stereotype of a small-town Texas attorney. Tall and lean, aside from a basketball-sized belly straining his light blue seersucker suit, he had stern eyes and lips that drooped downwards as if his face had forgotten how to smile.

"Good day, Mr. Stone. Please have a seat. I'm sorry for your loss," Mr. Wilder stated dourly as he placed his cattleman crease cowboy hat on a small end table to his right, then placed a vintage clay pipe between his lips and inhaled.

This guy looks like he's from the 1800s, Floyd thought, and then he responded, "Thanks, but you know I haven't seen my father for several years. He sort of disappeared."

Floyd looked around the office. Frank Wilder sat behind a prominent rustic desk in a cowhide executive leather chair. *Quite the throne*, Floyd thought. The desk was completely bare, except for a manila envelope with the words Last Will and Testament of Robert Stone typed across the front and an ashtray made from an ostrich egg. On the wall behind him were the trophy head of a nilgai, the largest antelope in Asia, framed diplomas from Texas A&M University and the University of Oklahoma College of Law, and a large Remington painting of a cowboy riding a horse, holding a six-shooter in one hand and a rifle in the other. A short-legged wooden chair was placed directly across from the immense desk, facing Mr. Wilder. Floyd squeezed between the armrests, knees almost touching his chest, and put his backpack on the ground below him. He looked up at the lawyer, feeling like a second-grader who had been sent to the principal's office.

"Well, Mr. Stone..." the lawyer said in a serious tone.

"Please, call me Floyd."

"Of course, Floyd. Well, let's get to it. I don't like to waste time. Your father's will is straightforward. You are his sole heir, and his assets will pass directly to you. This includes his house out by the lake here in Hamer, his old Jeep, his retirement savings of about $90,000, and the contents of a safe deposit box. Here are the keys to the house, car, and safe deposit box. We will need to address some probate issues, but it should be simple. Do you have any questions?"

"What can you tell me about his death? I knew nothing about it until I got your letter."

"As far as I know, it was a heart attack. He'd become reclusive over the last few years. He would come to town occasionally to have a meal at Bob's BBQ next door, and we chatted a few times."

Floyd fidgeted in the too-small chair. "What did you talk about? I haven't heard from him since Christmas seven years ago. That was when he left my mom—and me, for that matter."

"We would usually chat about politics, the weather, that sort of stuff. But he did seem preoccupied with his brother's disappearance forty years ago. For some reason, that had become an obsession. I'll tell you what. After you've gone through his belongings, if you want to discuss it further, I'll try to answer your questions. We can meet next door and talk over some brisket. It's the best in Texas, and they let me in the back door so I can avoid the line." Mr. Wilder put down his pipe. "Unfortunately, I have a meeting across the street, and I need to head out. Please call my office if you'd like to talk further. Have a good day." He stood up abruptly, grabbed his hat, and left Floyd sitting by himself in the office. No handshake, no nothing. Floyd picked up the keys and the copy of the will, placed them in his backpack, and let himself out.

Five minutes later, he was at the Hamer Federal Credit Union just down the street, where the local bank manager opened his father's safe deposit box and left the room. Floyd was alone in a small windowless cell, with a card table and two metal chairs. If he didn't know he was in a bank, he would have thought he'd just been incarcerated. Floyd studied the box; it was of medium size, about two feet long, ten inches wide, and maybe five inches tall. He reached in, and the first thing he found was an old journal, filled with receipts, brochures, postcards, and other loose papers. It had seen better days. It appeared to have water damage, and some of the pages were defaced, making them hard to read.

The front cover was decorated with a bumper sticker emblazoned with the call letters KLBJ FM 94 in yellow letters on a black background. There were three smaller stickers on the back cover—the logos for Led Zeppelin, Rush, and The Beatles—and a song lyric about kissing paradise goodbye written across the top of the back cover. Floyd wondered if this was just typical teenage musing or whether perhaps it had a deeper meaning. The inside cover was emblazoned with the name Dylan Stone in cursive, along with an address and telephone number. Floyd leafed through the fragile pages. It didn't appear to be anything more than the journal of the teenager's trip to Europe. The first page listed each place they'd stayed throughout the journey. It began when they left Texas on May 27th, 1983, and the last entry was made in Corfu, Greece, on June 27th.

Floyd put the journal aside. He found the deed for the bungalow, the title to the Jeep, a wallet, and some bank statements. Reaching inside the box again, he pulled out an old, water-stained money belt. He tried to open the zipper, but it was stuck. After shaking the box to make sure there was nothing else in it, he placed all the items in his backpack and left the dungeon. He needed to breathe some fresh air.

As he exited the bank, backpack over his left shoulder, he headed to the parking garage across the street to find his father's Jeep. It was time for a ride to the old lake house to check out his new digs.

Chapter 3

Lift Off

2025

Floyd sat on the back deck and watched the sky transform from a still blackness into evolving shades of orange as the sapphire lake sparkled under a peaceful sunrise. A cardinal stared down at him and chirped excitedly from a tree limb that reached out over the railing. It was Floyd's favorite time of the day at Lake Hamer. As a child, he would sit here next to Papa while everyone else slept, and they would watch the first light together. Papa would sip coffee out of his special tin coffee cup he'd picked up on a vacation in Italy, and he would invent stories with the local animals as characters. Bucky and Buttercup were young deer who would go on exciting adventures with their best friend, Wendy, the fox. They rescued lost children and battled villains all over the world. Floyd recalled years later that Papa had told him he and Uncle Dylan had the same routine when Dylan was young.

He picked up Dylan's journal, swigged some coffee from Papa's old Italian mug, and opened it to the first entry. Handwritten in blue ink, he could sense his uncle's enthusiasm as he began to read the words of an eighteen-year-old boy, written on an airplane a month before his disappearance, forty-two years before.

Friday, May 27, 1983

Finally, the day has come. I got a total of three hours' sleep last night and was well-prepared for today. Left the house at 8:32 a.m. and finally got to the airport by 9:45, thanks to Bull's older brother. After sitting around in the airport for almost two hours, we finally got to board the plane. Luckily, Bull and I got to sit together. The weather was ideal for me (sitting next to the window) to see the cities and countryside, the lakes and the oceans.

Hmm, Floyd thought. He tried to imagine his Uncle Dylan leaving home for the first time, heading into an unknown world, with a backpack, a money belt, and a guitar in hand. This was before cell phones, personal computers, and email were commonplace. He would be on his own and inaccessible. It must have been exciting and a little scary. He read the next entry.

Saturday, May 28, 1983

The sun came up, and Ireland appeared out of the window. What a sight! Never have I seen such green land. It was beautiful! Everything was so vibrant and lush. After collecting our bags and my guitar, we went outside to wait for the bus to Limerick and were surprised to find it was 46 degrees, yet we were dressed for the Texas summer. We have plans to go to Bunratty Castle tonight, and we have a room at some nice lady's home for 7.5 pounds.

Dylan's opening entries chronicled his first experience in a bed and breakfast, a feast at a castle, the challenges of hitchhiking across Ireland with backpacks and a guitar, and finally boarding a ferry to France. He also made passing comments about the Troubles and an unusual woman they had met on the ship. At the end of the entry was a lyric by Paul and Linda McCartney, from their song "Give Ireland Back to the Irish," which was written in a different color ink, as though it had been added later.

Chapter 4

Hitchhiking

1983

DYLAN WALKED ALONG THE road just outside of Cork, thumb extended. As he looked forward, he observed the gray ribbon winding its way through rolling hills until it disappeared. He was struck by the lack of trees. There was a steady light rain, and despite the gloomy sky, he was amazed by the depth of the green everywhere. *Now I know why they call it the Emerald Isle*, he thought.

He and Bull had decided to hitchhike separately from Cork to Rosslare Harbour, as there was no train available and the small cars couldn't accommodate both of them with their baggage. Bull had been picked up within five minutes. As the car pulled away, the passenger window rolled down, and Bull gave Dylan the one-finger salute. He laughed and yelled, "I'll beat you to the harbor!"

Dylan was not an attractive target for the local drivers due to the fact that he carried a bulky backpack and a guitar. Most of the vehicles he saw were tiny, at least compared to what he was used to in Texas. After one minuscule car drove by, Dylan thought, *I could put that in the bed of my dad's pick-up truck.* He decided to mentally attack the hike as if he were running a marathon. He had no idea how long he would be out there before he got picked up, so he focused on short-term goals. He set his sights on the next curve in the road. Once he arrived at the turn, he would find another target and work his way towards it. It became a game.

After two hours of hiking in the drizzle, the game was starting to get old. The guitar case was getting heavy, and his hands were beginning to blister. Dylan paused for a moment, put his gear down, and stretched his arms. A truck came along, loudly braked, and stopped just in front of him. An arm slowly extended out of the window and waved him to the passenger side. Dylan climbed in and threw his backpack and guitar behind the seat.

"It looks like you're not from these parts," the trucker said with a strong Irish accent. "Where are you headed?"

He was a short, stout man with a speckled gray beard, and hair that looked like it was once red, along with clear, friendly eyes. When he spoke, you could hear his smile.

"Thanks for stopping," said Dylan. "I'd been out there for a while. I'm headed to Rosslare Harbour, or as close as I can get. I'm catching a ship there tomorrow, hopefully."

"Well, I'm glad I came along and found you. I can get you about twenty miles past Waterford, then I must head north."

"That would be great. Thank you very much. My name's Dylan."

"Finn. Good to meet you. I notice an accent, and it isn't from around here."

"Yeah. I'm from the States. Texas, actually."

"Oh, really? Is it anything like the TV show *Dallas*? My wife and I watch it every week."

"Not where I come from. But I do ride a horse to school every day…" Dylan paused and looked at Finn with a smile. "Just kidding."

Finn laughed. *A hearty laugh, like Santa Claus*, Dylan thought. "This sure is a beautiful country," he continued.

"You should see it when it's sunny. There's no place more beautiful."

They drove along narrow roads, not wide enough for two vehicles. Dylan had a hard time getting used to sitting on the left side of the car as a passenger.

"Where are you visiting in Ireland?" Finn asked.

"We landed in Shannon and stayed in Limerick and Cork. Now we're heading to the coast to catch a ship to France. So, a pretty quick trip, unfortunately."

"You're missing out. Dingle, Kilkenny, Dublin, the Cliffs of Moher—so many great places to visit. It's the greatest country in the world, with a fascinating history. And then there's Northern Ireland. A beautiful place, but a lot of tension there."

Dylan settled back into his seat as Finn gave him a short history lesson.

"You see, the Troubles—it's been a heartbreak, truly. It's mostly up in the north, in Northern Ireland, but of course, it's on all our minds down here too. You can't help but feel it every time you turn on the radio or pick up the paper."

"Tell me more," Dylan said, intrigued.

"To put it simply, it's a terrible conflict mostly between the nationalists, who are mostly Catholic and want Northern Ireland to reunite with the rest of Ireland, and the unionists, who are mainly Protestant and want to stay part of the United Kingdom. It's political, but it's religious too, and it's about history, land, and power. It goes back centuries, to when the Brits colonized Ireland.

"In the north now, it's not just protests or politics anymore—it's bombs and shootings. The British Army's been over there since '69, trying to keep order, but a lot of people down here feel like they're only making things worse. Groups like the IRA say they're fighting a war of liberation. But you know, a lot of us down here don't want violence."

"Northern Ireland isn't far away, is it?" Dylan asked.

"Not at all. Maybe a four-hour drive from here."

That's like driving from Dallas to Houston.

Finn continued, "Every so often, there'll be a bomb in Belfast, or worse, and the news is just full of grief. We worry about it spilling down here, but for the most part, the Republic has stayed peaceful. Still, the Troubles hang over everything—our politics, our conversations, even our sense of who we are."

"That's terrible," Dylan said. He'd had no idea it was so bad.

A flock of sheep plodded across the road in front of them, and Finn had to hit the brakes.

"Yeah," Finn responded, as he honked his horn and cursed some words that Dylan didn't recognize. "We're hoping, praying really, that someday there'll be a peaceful solution. That somehow, the north will find a way to move forward without all the killing. But for now, it's like a sore that won't heal—and every month it seems to get worse."

"That's tough. I wasn't aware of all that," Dylan said as the last sheep vacated the road, and Finn put the truck back in gear.

"Yeah," Finn said. "My brother and his family live in Belfast. They worry every day about their children walking to and from school. I'll only drive my truck in the Republic of Ireland. Too dangerous across the border."

Neither Dylan nor Finn spoke for a while. Dylan looked out the window as the rolling hills and the lush countryside rushed by.

Finn piped back in and said, "So, tell me about what school is like in Texas. My kids attend primary school in Dublin. I'd like to compare notes."

For the next two hours, they talked about school, weather, their parents, their religions… Suddenly, Finn slowed down the truck and said, "Well, Texas, this is where I head north." He pulled over onto the shoulder amid a sea of green. "I hope you find a way to spend more time in Ireland someday. It's a great place. And don't waste your time in England. Nothing to see there," he said with a wink. "Enjoyed talking to you."

"Thanks, Finn." Dylan shook his hand and stepped out of the truck into the rain, guitar in one hand and backpack in the other. He was in a small town he had never heard of called New Ross.

It was late, so he decided to give up hitchhiking and find a place to stay for the night. He would need to figure out a way to get to the port the next day and hopefully meet Bull there. As he walked down South Street looking for a cheap hotel or B&B, he heard a voice shouting at him.

"Dylan!" Bull stuck his head out the door of the Theatre Tavern and motioned for him to come in. Dylan dropped his pack and guitar inside the front door and walked to the bar where Bull was engaged in a lively conversation with an older couple, each with a Guinness in their hand.

Bull looked over to Dylan and said, "I was wondering if I would see you today. I caught six different rides and couldn't get any further than here. Then I ran into the O'Malleys and decided to stay here for the night. They helped me get a room at Mrs. Kavanaugh's B&B. Only seven quid, and she owns a bakery down the street. We're set. So glad I saw you. I've been keeping an eye out the window all afternoon, hoping you'd happen to walk by."

A hand was thrust Dylan's way.

"Liam O'Malley," said a portly man with curly red hair and a double chin, as he crushed Dylan's fingers with a warm handclasp. "And this is my wife, Molly. Molly O'Malley. Has a nice ring to it, don't ya think?"

Molly could have been Liam's twin, short and squat with frizzy ginger hair.

"Name's Dylan. Nice to meet you both. I hope Bull hasn't bored you too much," he said with a half-smile.

"Ha! Not at all. Bull here is a nice fella. He hasn't stopped talking since we met. We've been arguing about Reagan and football, and I've learned how to say 'y'all' like a Texan."

"You have fascinating eyes, Dylan. Has anyone ever told you that?" Molly said as she studied Dylan positioning himself at the bar.

"I've heard lots of comments—fascinating is a first," Dylan said as he grabbed a newspaper placed in front of him. The headline screamed, 'New Clues About The Missing Crown Jewels!'

Dylan turned to Liam and asked, "What's this all about?"

Liam looked at Molly and then turned back to Dylan and said, "Yeah. I hadn't thought of that in a long time. There are lots of rumors—that it may be found, that it may be hidden, that some of the jewelry is way more valuable than originally thought, that important people don't want it found for some secret reason..."

"I'm not familiar with the story. Can you tell us about it?" Bull asked, as he caught the bartender's attention with a wave and motioned for him to bring a Guinness to Dylan.

Liam smiled and his eyes sparkled as he began, "Ah, the missing Irish Crown Jewels—now *that's* a story! And not just any story, but one with mystery and scandal. And I love to tell stories.

"It started a long time ago, back in 1907, when we were still under British rule. The British had this order called the Order of St. Patrick. It was their fancy way of knighting Irish aristocrats and showing off the whole imperial power business. Well, they had a set of jewels for it—rubies, sapphires, diamonds—the works. They were kept in Dublin Castle, in a safe in the Office of Arms. Very secure, you'd think.

"Then one day—*poof*—they were gone, just like that. No break-in, no busted locks, just vanished. And this was just before the king himself was due to come over and present them at some ceremony. Terrible embarrassment for the Crown."

"Wow," Dylan exclaimed as he and Bull exchanged glances. "I can't believe I've never heard this before."

"Yeah. It's a big deal here. Officially, the case has never been solved. But there were rumors—oh, *loads* of rumors. Some said it was an inside job. Others blamed the British themselves, trying to cover up some scandal. There were even rumors about secret lovers and blackmail... This was Victorian society, remember, and full of closets with skeletons and people who liked to keep things hidden.

"We love a good yarn, and the story has never quite gone away. Every so often, someone will claim to know where they are, buried under the floorboards of some big house in Cork, smuggled to the Continent, or kept quiet in London all these years. But officially? Still missing. And now, suddenly, it's in the news again. I've even heard they're going to tear out some walls in the castle to search for them."

"Hmm," Dylan commented. "I wonder why it's grabbing headlines now, almost eighty years later."

Liam placed his mug on the bar and thought for a second. "I think there's more to it," he whispered and looked around. "I've been hearing rumors as well. Something's up."

Chapter 5

Lisa

2025

Floyd placed the journal in his lap and stared at the lake, deep in thought. A sailboat glided by in the distance. The familiar riff of "Sweet Home Alabama" snaked its way up the cliff and struck Floyd just as the boat disappeared around the bend.

He had only read through the first few entries of his Uncle Dylan's journal, but he was hooked and wanted—needed—to learn more.

It didn't take long to inventory his current situation. No job. No personal obligations. He now had some cash, a house, and a car. He had time on his hands. He thought to himself, *Why not pull this thread and see where it takes me?*

He opened the sliding glass door and entered the cabin, then lifted the guitar off its wall mount. It was clear the instrument hadn't been touched in decades. He grabbed a washrag and wiped off the dust. It was a beautiful Martin D-28 with a solid spruce top and East Indian rosewood back and sides. It had several scrapes, as expected, since it had traveled through Europe with a teenager forty years ago, but it was still in excellent shape. Floyd carefully tuned the strings as best he could. They needed to be replaced, but they were good enough for him to play a few songs, he figured.

He strummed it. Something was off. Floyd had played a similar Martin for years, and he could tell that something was affecting the sound. He looked at the front and back and then shook the guitar to see if there was an errant item inside, the way he'd done before when trying to fish out a pick he had accidentally dropped into the soundhole. Something was flapping inside. Then an envelope slid through the strings and fell onto the floor at his feet. It was smaller than a postcard and looked like it hadn't been opened in decades. Floyd picked it up and studied it. Across the back, hand-written in blue ink was a lyric, or maybe a line from a poem: "Where sun dies soft in Ionian blue, / The crowned heart waits beneath the view."

He took the pocketknife that his father had given him, which he carried everywhere, and carefully slit open the envelope. A two-inch-long brass skeleton key was inside. It looked like it might be used to wind a hundred-year-old grandfather clock or to open an old storage chest. *This might be important...* He carefully put the key back in the envelope and zipped it inside a compartment in his backpack.

Floyd then walked over to the kitchen table and picked up his dad's wallet. He fished out the small piece of paper he'd noticed when he first opened it at the bank. It had a name and a phone number. He decided it was time to take this to the next step and picked up the receiver of the avocado-colored telephone hanging on the kitchen wall.

"Hello?" a female voice answered after three rings.

Floyd was puzzled. "Hello," he responded, "my name is Floyd Stone. I'm looking for Bull Eastland. My uncle, Dylan Stone, was friends with him a long time ago. They traveled to Europe together as teenagers. This was the number I found in my dad's wallet."

"Uh…well, this is Bull Eastland's daughter, Lisa Eastland. I'm sorry to inform you that he passed away about five years ago," she said with a catch in her voice.

"I'm so sorry," Floyd said.

"Thanks. I'm glad you called. My dad had such kind things to say about your uncle. His disappearance affected my dad for the rest of his life. I also remember your father visiting with my dad a couple of times, not long before he passed away."

"I hope this isn't presumptuous, but could I meet with you and talk about this further? I'd like to hear more. Plus, I have my uncle's journal, and it has some fascinating stories from their trip. You might find it interesting."

"I'd like that. I visit my parents' house in Boerne regularly and spend time with my mom. She's retired now, and I like to see her as much as I can. That's how I got your call. Where would you like to meet?"

"I don't live too far away…in Hamer. How about we meet at Black Rifle Coffee on South Main tomorrow at 10 a.m.?"

"That sounds good. I look forward to seeing you, Floyd."

Chapter 6

Regrets

2025

Floyd Stone... That's a surprise, she thought. He obviously didn't remember, but they had met once before.

Petite, raven-haired, and athletic, Lisa could take care of herself. The only daughter of a former professional football player father and a successful business executive mother, she had always participated in many sports and was also an excellent student. Her first love was softball, but her small stature became a disadvantage during the college recruiting process. Instead of pursuing the college athlete route, she'd decided to focus on her studies and enjoy her time at Texas State University in San Marcos, Texas while studying to be an elementary school teacher. She'd always participated in sports and lifted weights at the gym, so she needed a new outlet. She decided to take a Krav Maga class with some sorority sisters. She wanted to be able to defend herself, whether it was from a drunk frat guy or a man in the shadows who attempted to attack her while running. She thrived in the class. Within three months, she was the only one of her friends who'd stuck it out in the martial art, and she continued to train throughout college and beyond, eventually earning a black belt.

One Saturday in the fall of her junior year of college, she attended a University of Texas football game with some girlfriends. UT was only a thirty-minute drive from her apartment in San Marcos, and they piled into her best friend's hand-me-down minivan for the trip. It was a perfect college football Saturday in Austin. Sunny, with clear skies and a crispness in the air. It was a sold-out game, and the good guys won. Afterwards, they walked through the hilly campus with 50,000 of their best friends and finally ended up at an off-campus frat party. It was there that she met Floyd Stone...and she also met her future husband. What started as an ordinary day turned into one that changed her life forever.

It was your typical wannabe *Animal House* frat party. Lisa didn't drink alcohol, so she figured she wouldn't stay long. She found a spot at a backyard patio bar where she could watch TV, while her friends disappeared into the throng of dancing bodies by an outdoor stage. She had loved football ever since watching her dad play in the NFL, and she knew the West Coast games would still be on. Stanford was playing at UCLA, and it was a close game. The Stanford safety appeared out of nowhere, intercepted the ball, and ran it back fifty yards for a touchdown. Lisa jumped out of her seat and screamed. The guy sitting next to her smiled and stuck his hand up in the air, and she high-fived him.

"Impressive!" He laughed as he shook his stunned hand. "I don't know many girls who get that excited about college football...or hit that hard!"

"I love football: high school, college, pro...I love it all. And this is a good game. A guy from my high school plays for Stanford."

"Cool," he said, looking down at her. "My name's Floyd."

He was roughly six feet tall, athletic, with a shock of light brown hair and blue eyes. She was probably a foot shorter than him. "Lisa," she responded and reached out her hand.

"Are you gonna hit me again?" he said, playfully holding his hand as if it were numb. She smiled. "Do you go to UT?" he asked.

"Texas State. Education major. But I come to every UT football game I can. They've been my second-favorite team my whole life."

"Second favorite? Hey. Who's your favorite?"

"LSU. But it's only because my dad played there." Then she changed the subject. "Floyd... That's an interesting name."

"Ha ha. It's a long story, but it all starts with a rock band that was a big deal in the 1970s," he said with a wink.

"Pink Floyd! My dad is a huge Pink Floyd fan. He told me stories of listening to them with his best friend back in high school."

"Your dad sounds like an interesting guy...a college football player and music lover. My dad is a huge Floyd fan as well, though he didn't play any college sports..."

He suddenly noticed how attractive she was as she looked up at him, eyes sparkling, and a smile that made his heart miss a beat. Dressed in tight blue jean shorts, cowboy boots, and a loose-fitting vintage white and orange football jersey with the name CAMPBELL on the back, she stood out from the other girls at the party.

At that moment, a half-drunk frat guy plopped down next to them. Slightly taller than Floyd, he wore khaki pants, Top-Siders, a white button-down shirt, and a cap emblazoned with the words TPC Sawgrass on the front.

"Floyd, hit the road," he said.

Rob Darling was the president of the fraternity, and his word was law. He exchanged glances with Floyd, making it clear that Lisa was now his target and that Floyd should move on.

Floyd turned to her and said, "It was nice to meet you, Lisa. I hope we meet again. I'll keep an eye out for you at the football games." He smiled, shook her hand, and disappeared into the crowd of sweaty co-eds standing by the pool like penguins on the edge of an iceberg.

"I like baseball too..." she yelled after him and then looked into the eyes of the man who would eventually become her husband. She often thought back to this night and wondered what would have happened if it had turned out differently.

Rob seemed like a good guy: attractive, smart, and wealthy (she thought). She didn't realize at the time, but he had a flaw—a big one. He was allergic to the truth.

They got married the month after graduation. They eloped and celebrated their honeymoon in Cancun, Mexico. Things started well. They moved into a small rental house to save money and, hopefully, someday, buy their own home. Lisa taught first grade, and Rob left early for work every day and came home late at night. He was always evasive when she asked him about his job and why he worked so many hours.

One evening, Lisa finished a tough four-mile run at the end of her street and started walking toward her house as she cooled down. She noticed Rob's car in the driveway. She could see movement inside. She took off her headphones and quietly approached the vehicle thinking she'd surprise him with a kiss when he opened the car door. However, when she got close, she saw Rob in the backseat changing his clothes. She knocked on the window. When he looked up and realized she had seen him, he deflated like a child who'd disappointed his mother. He slowly opened the door and stepped out. He was barefoot, wearing unzipped suit pants and a grease-streaked Bill Miller Toyota work shirt.

"What the...?" Lisa exclaimed.

Rob looked at his feet and then back at her. She could see tears.

"I'm sorry, Lisa. I'm a horrible person," Rob said. He couldn't look her in the eyes.

"What is going on?" She spoke sharply as sweat dripped down her back.

"Okay. Okay. I'm a failure. I'm not a financial analyst at Wilson Brothers Financial Group. I'm a mechanic at Bill Miller Toyota in Round Rock. I purposefully chose that location, hoping I wouldn't ever see you there."

"I don't understand. Did you get fired? You just graduated from UT."

"Look. I'm really sorry. I love you, and I was just so afraid to lose you. I failed out of college. I figured I could somehow make it work and finish my degree and get it fixed before you found out."

Lisa didn't know what to think. She was in shock. And she was mad. She couldn't think of anything to say that she wouldn't regret later, so she abruptly turned around and walked through the front door, slamming it behind her. A few minutes later, shoulders hunched, and carrying his extra clothes and fake briefcase, he followed her inside.

They tried to make their marriage work. A few months later, she became pregnant. They were both excited. Rob was acting unusually pleasant. He told her that he was "doing well at work" and they would be able to buy a house the next year. However, when she finally got a peek at the bank statements, which he had hidden from her, it was apparent that their meager savings were declining monthly, and the credit card balances were going in the opposite direction.

Two months later, he committed the unforgivable. It was a random Tuesday morning. Her morning sickness was so severe that she'd left her job and come home to sleep it off. As she walked up the stairs, she noticed that the master bedroom door was closed, and she heard Rob's voice...and a female laugh.

Within a month, it was all over. Rob was gone forever. And...so was the baby. Lisa felt like she was at the bottom of a dark well, and the water was slowly swallowing her.

That was when her father saved her.

Chapter 7

Walking Death

2025

FLOYD SAT AT AN outside table in a large, shaded patio behind Bob's BBQ. It had been years since he last ate there. He had been thinking about this ever since he got off the bus and saw the line of sweaty, hungry people stretching along the sidewalk, patiently waiting for their turn to get in. He looked down at the butcher paper in front of him, piled high with moist brisket, jalapeno cheddar sausage, a pork rib, and some cowboy beans. Bob's, cooked with brisket, were hands down the best beans in Texas. He sipped iced tea, grabbed a rib with one hand, and turned to the next page in Dylan's journal.

Wednesday, June 1, 1983

Yesterday, Bull and I boarded a big, beautiful ship of the Irish Continental Line so we could get from Ireland to France using our Eurail pass. We woke up at 6:30 (yuck), had a fantastic breakfast, served personally by Mrs. Kavanaugh of the bakery-down-the-street fame, and we caught the 7:30 bus to Rosslare Harbour. Once we got there, we had time to kill before the ship departed, so we asked a lady at a bed and breakfast if she could open the gift shop next door a day early, and she did gladly. We got T-shirts. I decided on the Guinness one, and Bull got a Séamus Darby jersey (he's a famous local Irish Gaelic football player).

Finally, we boarded the huge ferry for the twenty-two-hour trip to Le Havre, France. It started out pretty boring. We couldn't afford rooms, so we found some deck chairs and made them our home base. Then we explored the ship. First, we found the buffet, which reminded us of our high school cafeteria, except we didn't recognize most of the food. Breakfast with beans? Next door was the bar. Bull ordered a Guinness, and I had a George Killian's Irish Red. Nice splurge, but we couldn't afford to spend too much time there. Eventually, we tried to sleep. Bull fell asleep fast, but I couldn't, so I decided to walk around and hopefully tire myself out.

As I gazed out over the rail and watched the waves in the darkness, a woman with sunken, dark eyes and long, messy black hair appeared next to me. She said she was a professor from UCLA. She told me I had kind eyes, and she knew she could trust me. Weird. She started talking and wouldn't stop—about philosophy, history, missing treasures, politics. She also told me she thought she was being followed. I tried to excuse myself politely, but she just stayed with me, even finding a nearby deck chair when I went back to try to sleep. At one point, we had a peculiar conversation in the ship's restaurant. Then she gave me an envelope and asked me to keep it for her until she could find me again. Despite it being a weird request, I didn't see the harm in it, so I took it.

The next morning, she stayed close to Bull and me. Bull pulled me aside and said, "What's with Walking Death?" (a perfectly appropriate name, I thought; she looked to be on her last legs). I told him that she wouldn't leave me alone. So, we crafted a plan to ditch her. After we departed the ship, we jumped on the first train leaving the local station, before Walking Death could catch up with us. What a relief. I thought she was going to try to stay with us indefinitely.

Once we were safely on our way, I pulled out the envelope. On the back, written in blue ink, were the words, "Where sun dies soft in Ionian blue, / The crowned heart waits beneath the view." Strange. I opened the envelope and found an old skeleton key. And I mean old. She'd said something about a key, missing Irish jewels, and being followed by a blond-haired guy. Hmm. I put everything back in my money belt. I think she's a crackpot, but who knows? Maybe I'll run into her again.

Well, it looks like the next major train stop will be Rouen. Bull and I decided we would spend the night there. So, we pulled out our Let's Go Europe *books and started researching Rouen. Looks like a great place.*

Chapter 8

A Chance Meeting

1983

DR. ALEXANDRA MORANA STROLLED along the ferry's promenade deck, frequently glancing behind her. She could sense someone was following her. Or was it in her head? No, it was real. Someone was after her. How did he find out? Who was he?

She was getting towards the end of her academic sabbatical. Alexandra had spent the last month in Ireland, starting her search at University College in Cork, then the National University of Ireland in Galway. No luck. She then moved onward to Dublin, more specifically, the library of Trinity College, which was established in 1592, and was known for its extensive collection of letters, journals, and manuscripts. Unbelievably, it only took her two days searching in the old library amid its floor-to-ceiling bookshelves to find the key to everything, hidden in the back of a diary that had been written seventy-five years ago. Literally, a skeleton key and a cryptic note about a location.

Since that pivotal moment, Alexandra's life had been hell. She apparently wasn't the only person looking for the key and someone was now pursuing her. It was clear she had to leave Ireland, but she couldn't use the standard transportation for fear of being overtaken. So she hiked for miles, took two buses and a train, and finally boarded the ship to France. She thought she had made it without being followed and hoped she'd be free if she could only get to the mainland. She was exhausted and hungry.

Finding a chair in a corner of the promenade deck with its back against the wall, she sat there and tried not to fall asleep as the waves gently rocked the ship, crawling its way to France.

Her quest had started when she'd read an obscure article about the first female students at Trinity College in Dublin. The article had inspired her. Less than ten years before they were admitted, the former provost of Trinity College Dublin, George Salmon, had stated, "Over my dead body will women enter this college." The first women had been admitted the year that he died. Alexandra loved that.

Three women had been admitted in 1904, sixteen years before Oxford and Harvard had admitted women. Then, later that year, forty-seven more women joined the ranks. It wasn't easy for these women. They were subject to strict regulations. Except during lectures and exams, female students were required to be separated from male students at all times. Additionally, women were not permitted to eat in the dining hall, they were required to wear formal attire, and had to leave the campus by 6 p.m.

As Alexandra researched further, she became fascinated by the story of Molly O'Leary, one of the first fifty women to be admitted, enrolling at the age of seventeen. A year before graduation, in

1907, Molly had gone missing. In addition to her interest in Molly's disappearance, Alexandra became intrigued by the rumors she had gleaned from reading the diaries and letters of her classmates. Molly, it seemed, had been quite the rascal. Classmate Sophie Bryant wrote in her journal, "Molly worries me so. She considers all the rules to be optional. The men fancy her, and she likes the attention." Another classmate commented, "Molly may get us all expelled."

However, the note that caught Dr. Morana's interest most was a letter from a student named Sally Sheeran, written to her brother, Ed, and dated July 6, 1907. Sally wrote, "Last night I saw Molly by St. Stephen's Green. She was in a hurry. She told me she was going to the castle to see Arthur. I didn't think much of it. However, no one has seen her since. There has been a search for her today, but she is nowhere to be found."

Through other research, Alexandra discovered that on the same day, July 6, 1907, the trunk containing the Crown Jewels of Ireland was found to be missing. The person responsible for its protection was Sir Arthur Vicars, the Ulster King of Arms. Was this the "Arthur" Molly had been on her way to see? Alexandra developed a theory that Molly O'Leary may have been involved in the disappearance of the jewels, and she'd come to Ireland to solve the mystery.

She got up from her seat, leaned over the ship's rail and studied the waves, so hypnotic and comforting. She didn't know how long she stood there. Maybe five minutes? She was tired. Slowly, the trance lifted, and she noticed a slender man with long blond hair pulled back in a ponytail under a ball cap. He was leaning against the rail about twenty yards away, his hands thrust in his pockets. Dark, serious eyes studied her and then quickly averted when she looked his way.

Alexandra walked about twenty feet away from him, stopped, and looked back. The man's cap was now on backwards, and he was slowly heading towards her, an intense look on his face. He pulled his hand out of his pocket, and she saw something glimmer. Was it a knife? Was she just paranoid? As she edged further along the railing, running out of room, she clearly heard him say, "You will give me that key." Her heart raced.

It was then that she saw the young man walk up and lean over the rail a few steps away, gazing out into the ocean, seemingly lost in thought. She quickly scanned him. Blue jeans, a Guinness T-shirt, and an orange baseball cap. Young, American, and non-threatening. Dr. Morana turned around and saw that the mysterious blond man had stopped his approach. He was now leaning against a wall, watching her intently.

Alexandra gently bumped up against Dylan to get his attention. "Hello," she said.

"Hi," he responded, his eyes moving to her hair and her wrinkled blouse.

He *was* American. Then it struck her how horrible she must look. She hadn't slept in two days, and she had been wearing the same clothes since she left Dublin.

"I noticed you here alone. I'm Alexandra." She tried to smile, but a grimace was all she could muster. She hoped it didn't come across as a pick-up line. It would probably scare him away.

"I'm Dylan. Are you okay?"

"I'm okay. A little tired; I've been traveling by myself. And I haven't talked to anyone in a couple of days. Where are you headed?"

"Not sure. My buddy and I are going to figure it out when we land in Le Havre. We'll definitely spend some time in France before moving on. How about you?" He turned to face her.

"I've been in Ireland for a month or so. I was doing some research. I'm a history professor at UCLA, and I was sort of on a mission. I'll be returning to California soon."

"Were you successful?" he asked with interest.

"You could say that. I found what I was looking for. Unfortunately, it opened Pandora's Box." She looked over Dylan's shoulder towards where the blond man had been standing. He was gone. She decided at that moment that she was going to stay as close to Dylan as she could for the duration of the ferry trip.

"I'm gonna get a Coke. Wanna come?" he asked with a hint of hesitation in his voice.

"That would be great," she said in relief. There was something about Dylan. She could sense that he was a trustworthy person. It was a gut feeling. As they walked towards the all-night buffet, Alex convinced herself that the mysterious man was following her because she had the key. Before they disembarked, it would be in Dylan's possession. She would figure out a way to get it back from him at a later time, she hoped. Right now, she just wanted to get home.

Chapter 9

The Hand-Off

1983

Dylan strolled toward the ship's restaurant. He glanced over his left shoulder at the woman walking with him—Alexandra. There was something strange about her. She seemed scared. She kept looking around, as if someone was following her. And her eyes looked like they were painted with the eye black that baseball players use, except it wasn't makeup. Her hair was a bird's nest, with its black strands sticking out in all directions, and it looked like she had been sleeping in her clothes for days. She said she was a professor, but he wondered if maybe she was a homeless woman who'd stowed away on the ship.

Though he didn't have much money, he figured the right thing to do was to buy her a drink or something to eat. It was the middle of the night, and the buffet was sparse.

"Are you hungry?" he asked, hoping she didn't have expensive taste.

"Just a cup of coffee. That would be great. Would you join me?" Her eyes pleaded with him.

"Okay," he replied slowly. It couldn't hurt to talk to her for a little while. Besides, he didn't have anything else to do.

They sat down at a table in the restaurant next to a circular window overlooking the ocean. It was still dark outside, and the window was simply one of many opaque black dots on the curved wall. He could smell Alexandra's coffee as he sipped on a Coke. He hadn't acquired a taste for coffee yet, but he planned to try it as he worked his way through France and Italy.

"Have you ever heard of the Irish Crown Jewels?" she blurted in a whisper.

"Funny you should ask. I saw a story about it in the newspaper the other night in a pub in New Ross. And I got a short history lesson from a local guy who'd had a few too many Guinnesses. Pretty cool story. Not sure how much of it is true. I'd never heard of it before." Dylan leaned toward her, intrigued at where this conversation was going.

"Yeah. It's been a mystery for almost eighty years." She looked around, grabbed his hands, pulled him close, and whispered, "I know we don't know each other, but I'm going to tell you a secret and trust you. The Irish Crown Jewels are believed to be hidden in a trunk somewhere in Europe. This is the key."

She pulled out an envelope the size of an index card and quickly put it in Dylan's hand, then carefully scanned the restaurant. Not knowing quite how to react, he closed his hand around it.

"I'm still working on the location," she whispered, "but I think it's in a cave, or on an island—or maybe both. Here. Look." She pointed to a short phrase on the envelope. "I'm convinced this...this poem maybe...is a clue to where the treasure is hidden, but I haven't figured it out."

Dylan quickly placed the envelope in his pocket.

"That seems far-fetched. And why are you telling me?" he asked.

"I'm not sure, but something tells me I can trust you. On the ferry, a man... He's been following me, and I hope he will leave me alone once he realizes I don't have it. So be careful. Try not to let anyone find out about this."

"I've got to tell my buddy, Bull. I tell him everything."

"Okay, but please keep it to yourselves," she said with a serious face. "I have to get back to California." She reached into her pocket, pulled out a small card, and handed it to him. "When you return home from your trip, give me a call, and we can figure out a way that you can return it to me."

Dylan studied it. It read, "Dr. Alexandra Morana, PhD., Professor of History, UCLA" and listed her address and telephone number. *So she really is a professor.* He pocketed the card as she sat back, looking relieved.

"Be careful, Dylan. That's why the Crown Jewels story has been in the news lately. Sometimes, the people searching for things like that have hidden motives. Hey, maybe you and your friend can figure out where the treasure is hidden. I'd love that."

Dylan didn't know what to believe. It all seemed so improbable. He was just a kid backpacking through Europe. What were the chances he'd get caught up in an international incident? If any of what she'd said was even true. Maybe she was just a paranoid woman losing her mind.

"So, do you have a girlfriend?" She was trying to make small talk. Dylan responded awkwardly, "Uh, not really." There was a girl back home that he liked, but he didn't think that was any business of hers. He was getting uncomfortable again. This lady was just strange. After they finished their drinks, she stayed close to him as they walked out of the restaurant and up the stairs to the promenade deck, where Bull was sleeping.

"I'm going to try to get some shut-eye at least for a bit," Dylan said, sitting in his deck chair. His backpack and guitar were at Bull's feet.

Alexandra took the seat on the other side of Dylan. "Sounds good; I'll do the same."

She instantly fell asleep. Dylan hoped they would head in different directions once the ferry docked.

He looked around. Across the deck, among a dozen chairs filled with sleeping travelers, Dylan noticed a slender man with golden hair staring at him. Dylan stood up to get a better look, and the man was gone.

The Art Collector

1983

Julian Marks calmly observed the professor and her two new friends as they stirred in their deck chairs, after two hours of interrupted sleep. He had been following Dr. Alexandra Morana since she'd arrived in Ireland a month ago.

Two years ago, he'd written a term paper about the missing Irish Crown Jewels in a European history class he took at UVA. He had been obsessed with the topic for several years and was determined to be the one to discover this long-lost treasure. Two months ago, he'd obtained a copy of a paper that Dr. Morana had published, which offered some clues about her search for the same jewels. He'd been impressed with her research and could tell she knew more than she'd revealed in the paper. He decided to learn more about this professor from California.

Through his research, he found Dr. Alexandra Morana to be a highly respected expert on Irish history. She was deeply interested in women's rights and the long history of conflicts between England and Ireland. It was clear she was also passionate about the story of the missing Irish Crown Jewels, and she was making progress in her investigation. He learned that she had arranged a trip to Ireland in May of 1983, and he planned to follow her and gather information so he could find the jewels first.

Julian had been born on New Year's Day, 1960, to Frank and Joan Marks. His father Frank was a successful Wall Street financier who led two separate lives. During the week, he lived in an NYC penthouse, which he shared with his latest local conquest, while he spent the weekends at his estate in Southampton Village with his wife, Joan.

Joan and her five siblings had grown up in a two-bedroom shack in the hills of West Virginia, but her stunning beauty had enabled her to make a living as a model before she'd met and wed Frank, fifteen years her senior. Once she joined the "club" of the wealthy elite in New York, her focus was on playing the part of a rich and famous socialite. Neither Frank nor Joan had any interest in having children, and when Julian was born, he was raised by a nanny in a separate wing of the estate from where his parents lived. By age four, he was a proficient reader and played and composed music on the piano, but his parents neither noticed nor cared.

Frank Marks's only passion besides making money and bedding beautiful women was collecting rare works of art. He would travel the world, acquiring museum-quality pieces, which occupied a wing of his estate. Young Julian, desperate for his father's attention, became fascinated with the art collection as he grew up. He would study each piece carefully and then have his nanny take him to the local library so he could read everything he could find about the artist and the work's significance. Frank was impressed with Julian's knowledge of art history, and it became their one common interest. That meant the world to young Julian.

At age seven, Julian was sent to the Institut auf dem Rosenberg in St. Gallen, Switzerland, the most expensive and prestigious boarding school his parents could find. Plus, it was 4,000 miles away, which allowed them to enjoy their opulent lifestyle, one that had no room for a precocious child. Populated with the offspring of the brilliant and wealthy from all over the world, Julian thrived there, though he primarily kept to himself. He immersed himself in European history and art. Not only did he excel scholastically, but he also took every opportunity to travel throughout Europe on school trips, while most of his peers chose ski vacations or trips home. He spent hours in the world's greatest museums—the Louvre, the Uffizi, the Vatican, the Rijksmuseum, as well as the many smaller ones scattered across the European countryside. He also toured castles and churches throughout the UK, France, and Germany, and visited famous European battlefields. Each year, he would focus on learning a foreign language, which eventually enabled him to read academic texts in their original German, Italian, and French.

Julian believed that art should be adored, appreciated, touched. To him, museums were like prisons for art. On an eighth-grade school trip, he visited the Basilique Saint-Julien in Brioude, France, a medieval church with a polychrome bell tower and red stone façade that could be seen from miles away. While touring the basilica's interior, he observed a temporary exhibit of Roman coins. When he saw them, he knew he must have one. He would appreciate it more than the traveling exhibitors, who simply packed them up and displayed them without valuing their unique qualities.

It was easy; he leaned down to tie his shoe, and when the group of students moved further into the church, a two-thousand-year-old silver coin with a profile of Pompey the Great on one side and what appeared to be horses on the other rested safely in his pocket.

He kept the coin in a shoebox under his bed. Every night, he would take it out and study it. No one could love that coin more than he did. It belonged with him.

Over the next year, the Roman coin was joined by a sixteenth-century belt buckle and a piece of ancient pottery. But Julian decided he needed to be more strategic about his acquisitions. He didn't want to have an ad hoc collection of miscellaneous pieces; he wanted to curate a selection of quality artifacts that rivaled the best museums in the world—and, most importantly, exceeded his father's collection.

After returning from Christmas break in the Hamptons during his tenth-grade year, Julian met his classmate, Günter Müller, the son of a German billionaire, for a cup of coffee. Six feet tall, slender and handsome, with blond hair like Julian's, Günter shared Julian's interest in history and art. It was a joke in the school that Julian and Günter could be brothers, they looked so much alike.

Günter had a devious side, which was what had first attracted the attention-starved Julian to him.

"Remember when we went to Naples and toured Pompeii?" Günter said with a glint in his eye.

"Yeah. That was a great trip," Julian said. "It was like going back in time two thousand years. And I'll never forget those bodies encased in ash."

Günter looked around and, satisfied that no one was listening, said, "Have you seen that red-glazed terracotta bowl in a glass case in my room, by the bookshelf? I got it in Pompeii."

"Yeah. I always figured it was a replica...or something," Julian said, feeling a rush of excitement and jealousy travel up his spine.

"No. It's the real thing. I took it from an exhibit there. Just stuck it in my backpack and no one ever noticed." He smiled mischievously. "I also took a clay tablet when I toured Jerusalem last year. There's a black market for this kind of stuff, you know. I'm going to make a fortune."

Julian was stunned. First, he couldn't believe someone else was taking art. But mostly, he was repulsed at the idea of simply selling these incredible pieces of history to the highest bidder. It was sacrilege.

"How could you do that? These are priceless pieces of our past," Julian said.

"Don't get your panties in a bunch. This kind of thing happens all the time. I learned in my art history class last semester that antiquities theft is one of the highest-grossing criminal trades. I can always use some cash. I hate asking my father for money. He always makes me feel guilty," Günter said seriously.

Julian thought about this. It was not acceptable for someone who didn't appreciate the art to be doing this. He had to stop it.

The following week, because of an "anonymous tip," Günter had been expelled from school, accused of stealing a clay tablet from Jerusalem. School security took Günter directly from the classroom. It was a walk of shame, intentionally done to leave an impression on the other students and to show that this kind of behavior would not be tolerated. Julian saw Günter as he left the room. There was something in Günter's eyes. Just as the door closed, the class heard Günter yell, "Julian, you'll pay for this!"

Meanwhile, Julian's shoebox welcomed a piece of Pompeian pottery.

During a senior year lecture in an advanced art history class, Julian's favorite teacher, Professor Merced, sparked his interest when he casually mentioned the missing Florentine Diamond.

Julian raised his hand. "Professor, can you tell us a little more about the Florentine Diamond? I'm intrigued."

Dr. Merced, excited that a student had expressed interest in the topic, enthusiastically responded, "Yes, it was a massive yellow diamond, shaped like a lemon, which was originally mined in India. There are several stories about how it ended up in European hands and whose hands held it in the 1500s. It appears that somehow it ended up in Bruges, Belgium, where a famous Flemish gem cutter transformed the rough stone into a polished 137-carat diamond. Yeah, 137 carats! It's said to have been lost in a battle and subsequently bought and sold a few times before coming into the possession of the Medici family. You remember the Medicis, right? They ruled Florence from the 1430s through the 1730s and were incredible patrons of the arts, sponsoring artists such as Michelangelo and Leonardo da Vinci, among many others. Anyway, after the Medicis died out, it ended up in the Habsburg Imperial Treasury in Vienna, Austria, until 1918. However, it disappeared when the Habsburgs were toppled during World War I. Most people believe the last imperial couple took it with them when they fled. Maybe they put it in a Swiss safe deposit box. Some people believe it was stolen from them, or that they sold it because they had lost all their wealth during the war. I think with the proper research, it could be tracked down."

Julian was enchanted. He decided at that moment to conduct his own research. Maybe he could track down the diamond if he tried hard enough. It was just the kind of historical artifact he wanted for his collection. The fact it was highly sought after made it even more special.

"Can you tell us about any other missing treasures?" Julian asked.

Professor Merced responded, "Well, Julian, that could be an entire class. However, I will mention a few that you can research on your own. Do you have a notebook ready?"

Julian answered immediately, "Ready!" Pen in hand, he listened intently.

"Okay. Study the Amber Room. Briefly, it was a room made of amber, gold leaf, and mirrors. It changed hands several times and spent a couple of hundred years in a palace in Russia. The Nazis then disassembled it, crated it, and relocated it to Germany during World War II. They're said to have hidden it as the Allies approached. It's never been found. It included more than six tons of amber. For that matter, research Nazi plundering in general if you're interested. They stole countless works of art and artifacts during World War II, and many are still missing."

"Fascinating. What else?" Julian asked as he immediately tried to think where the amber room could possibly be hidden.

"The missing Fabergé eggs. Fabergé is considered one of the greatest jewelers of all time. He created fifty-two jeweled eggs for the Russian Imperial family. Six are missing. They are incredible works of art. Each egg is completely different and took more than a year to make. For example, one of the eggs, the Gatchina Palace egg, is covered in gold, enamel, diamonds, and pearls. When you open the egg, you find a detailed gold replica of the palace."

Julian scribbled away as Professor Merced continued speaking. He was getting more and more animated, raising his voice in excitement.

"Let's move away from Russia," he said. "The Irish Crown Jewels disappeared from Dublin Castle in 1907 and have never been seen since. It's probably one of my favorite stories. Check it out.

"One more—a panel from Jan and Hubert van Eyck's fourteenth-century polyptych, a painting called the Ghent Altarpiece, was stolen from the Cathedral of St. Bavo in Ghent, Belgium, in 1934. It's still missing.

"Seriously, I could talk all day about these and more. There are hundreds of missing pieces of art and cultural artifacts. Some are lost, and many have been stolen."

That one lecture changed Julian's life forever. He'd found his life's mission.

***

After boarding school, Julian moved back to America and attended the University of Virginia. He grew several inches during college and became very fit due to years of skiing, horseback riding, and fencing, to the point where he would be almost unrecognizable to his schoolmates back in Switzerland. He had become an impressive figure, marked by his dark blue eyes, handsome face, and long blond hair. It was clear he'd inherited the attractive genes from his mother.

He found that the college curriculum required much less effort than boarding school had, so he used his spare time to research the art and treasures he sought. He intended to obtain a PhD in art history. While serving as an assistant professor in an introductory course on the art of the Renaissance, he met Adriana, who would become the next most important thing in his life.

His primary objective in life had been to collect priceless art and cultural artifacts. In an air-conditioned storage unit a mile from campus, he created an assemblage of "missing" Renaissance paintings, as well as jewelry, ancient pottery, and some gold coins from an obscure pirate's lair he had found referenced in an obscure journal buried in the Yale library.

However, his obsession was to obtain the missing Irish Crown Jewels. Dr. Morana, the UCLA professor, was on to something, and he knew he was on the right track to follow her. He built a perfectly-sized jewelry box in his storage unit museum to house the heavily jeweled diamond star and badge that had been created in 1831 for the Grand Master of St. Patrick, an order of knighthood established by King George III. The jewelry box stood out in its emptiness. His collection would never be complete without them.

Chapter 11

The Plan

2025

IT WAS A RARE breezy and overcast summer day in Texas Hill Country, which made it possible to sit outside at the coffee shop located on the corner of San Antonio and Main Street in Boerne. Typically, on a summer day, the outdoor tables were vacant due to the unbearable heat. Lisa sipped her vanilla latte and watched a flock of bridesmaids giggle their way into the Christmas Shoppe across the street, where the sign over its door proudly declared: We are open 364 days per year—every day except Christmas! She returned her attention to Floyd, who sat across from her, sipping from a cup of plain black coffee. He had the same friendly eyes, the same genuine smile. His hair showed whisps of gray, he'd put on some weight, and he had a few worry lines. But there was something about him that made her feel safe.

"We met once before," she said. Floyd looked at her intently, as if trying to place her. "It was at a frat party after a UT football ga—"

"High-five, college football girl! Now I remember you! Yeah, we were having a nice talk, and then that loser Darling pulled his power move. I never liked that guy. Well, it's great to meet you again."

"Yeah, it's been a long time."

"Time has been good to you. You look great," he said as he looked her over.

"Thanks, but I've had my ups and downs, for sure. So, are you married?" she asked.

"Not anymore. It just didn't work out. Mostly my fault, if I'm honest. Hasn't been that long either. Still getting used to it. How about you?"

"Same. I was married briefly... Believe it or not, it was to Rob."

"Rob Darling! I'm sorry. I wish we'd talked longer that day. I could have told you that guy was a dog who couldn't be trusted."

She saw concern in his eyes.

Floyd regrouped and continued, "Anyway, thanks for meeting today, and on short notice. Let me give you a little background. As I mentioned on the phone, my dad recently died..."

"Yeah, I'm sorry to hear that," Lisa said.

"Thanks. We hadn't seen each other in years. Turns out that since I was his only heir, I'm now the proud owner of a cottage in Hamer, along with my dad's other belongings."

"Well, that's kinda nice, isn't it?" Lisa said, hoping the comment didn't come across the wrong way.

"Yeah. I know what you mean. I feel fortunate and sad, all at the same time. Though I hadn't seen my dad in a long time, I have good memories from my youth, and I wish he was still around." He stared out at the street for a moment. "Anyway, you're probably wondering how this involves you."

"Yeah, but I'm patient," Lisa said with a wide smile.

"Well, I found out that my dad had become obsessed with the disappearance of his older brother, Dylan."

"Dylan... I know a little about him," she said. "My dad talked about him often. I think that trip to Europe with Dylan was the best time of his life, until...it became the worst time of his life."

"Well, my dad kept Dylan's journal in a safe deposit box. I started reading it, and I think Dylan got involved in something serious—and he didn't realize how serious it was until it was too late." She was following his every word. "Then I found an envelope and an old key stashed in his guitar, which confirmed a passage in his journal where a traveling professor gave those very items to him, and she said people had been following her because of it. Anyway, I have time on my hands now, and I want to see where this goes. Your dad was the first person I wanted to talk to for obvious reasons."

"He would have loved to talk to you. He was a great guy. He told me stories of his adventures with Dylan, but when the conversation got to the end of their trip, he couldn't talk about it. I do know that when he returned from Europe, he went straight to college and focused all his energy on football. As you probably know, he was really good—one of the best defensive linemen in LSU history. I think football was his therapy. He played for a few years in the NFL but retired early due to chronic knee injuries. Afterwards, he got a law degree and focused most of his energy on helping young professional athletes manage their finances. He had some good friends from college who had made millions of dollars and were bankrupt as soon as they stopped playing professionally. He was determined not to let that happen to as many athletes as possible."

"That's honorable."

"That's a good word to describe him. He was an inspiring man. He also traveled extensively throughout the US and the world, giving motivational speeches about the importance of having a purpose in life, and following a passion, but also how to be financially successful."

She toyed with her coffee cup for a moment and continued, "After my divorce, he saved me. I was devastated and humiliated. The depression contributed to a miscarriage, I'm convinced. I thought my life was over."

Lisa looked down and paused, then slowly looked into Floyd's eyes. They showed compassion. In her experience, unlike most men, he didn't speak or offer her advice at this moment; he listened.

"My dad dropped everything and came to my house and took care of me. My mom actually came for a bit as well. She was very supportive—I'm fortunate to have great parents—but she had to be in Paris for work. My dad's work schedule was flexible, though, so he was able to move in and be there for me. He listened to me. He let me vent. He let me cry. He never questioned any of my earlier decisions. Eventually, he tricked me into going to the gym with him to 'help him with his rehab.' I later figured out that he planned to get me to exercise with him because he knew it would help me feel better about myself. And over time, it worked. Eventually, I became a personal trainer, and now I help others who struggle with various demons—alcohol, drugs, depression, whatever. It's funny, if you think about it, he dedicated his life to helping athletes improve their personal lives, and I use physical fitness to help people improve their personal lives as well."

"Well, you and your father make me feel like a sluggish oaf! I used to be a pretty good athlete. I was a competitive swimmer in high school. But I haven't swum a lap or lifted a weight in probably five years, maybe more. If I'm honest with myself, I've been treading water—no pun intended—over the last few years." Floyd chuckled at his own joke, and then he turned serious, "But, weirdly, now that my dad died, I feel that I have a mission. I want to figure out what happened with

Dylan. I also might even pull out the gym membership," he said with a smile.

Lisa kept a straight face and continued, "Eventually, my dad got cancer. Since I had become self-employed, I was able to take time off and be there with him, helping him face it with dignity. I feel fortunate to have had that chance. As it was nearing the end, he became a little loopy and didn't always make sense. But one day he said, 'I should have listened to Dylan. He tried to tell me...' I asked him what he meant, but he just repeated, 'I should have listened. Maybe I could have saved him.' And then he never talked about it again. It's been on my mind for five years. So, when you called, I wanted to meet with you. I also want to know what happened."

Floyd unzipped his backpack, pulled out a beat-up old journal with a bumper sticker across the front, and handed it to her. "Take a look," he said.

Lisa carefully opened it up, noticing that some loose items had slipped between the pages. She opened a random entry and began reading.

Thursday, June 16, 1983; Cassis, France

Woke up, got out of bed, pulled a comb across my head, went the way downstairs and had a piss, somebody screamed, and I ran into a wall—ah ah. Had some coffee and bread and butter and jelly—an excellent French breakfast with Shannon, who is the granddaughter of the Kellys, who own the B&B.

Dylan is clever, she thought. She was glad that her dad had introduced her to the Beatles and *Sgt. Pepper's*, so she understood the reference. She kept reading.

After breakfast, Bull and I headed up into the mountains. Shannon pointed us in the right direction. We walked for a long time, then Bull headed one way to start climbing, and I went another way to go for a run. I started running up a very steep trail. I finally found a rocky path that went up the mountain and hiked and ran that for a long while. Eventually, I came to the sheer cliffs that overlook the ocean. I lay down so my body was on the edge with my head extended over, and I looked down over the sea, hundreds of feet below (this deserves a few blank lines because there is no way to describe what I saw, really...)

I could see for miles in every direction. I could see the mountains, the ocean, the horizon, the beaches, tiny boats, even a few minuscule topless sunbathers (I think)—it was amazing. I was so high and free. After a dangerous but exciting run down the rocky trail, I got back to the hotel to shower and change clothes. My body was wrecked (and felt great). But Bull was nowhere to be seen. The afternoon went by and he didn't show. I started to get worried. What if he fell off the cliff? I surely didn't want to have to call his parents to tell them that their son had died.

Finally, right before dusk, Bull dragged himself into our hotel room. His clothes were ripped, he had several bloody scratches, and he was smiling from ear to ear. He clapped me on the back and said, "Let's get cleaned up and go meet Shannon for a beer. I have to tell you all about my close call with death! It scared the shit out of me!" He was smiling as he said this. I was actually a little pissed. I had really been worried. Plus, he just doesn't believe me that there may be more to it than just an exciting adventure on a cliff overlooking the Mediterranean.

"Have you read this entire journal?" Lisa asked. "I picked a random entry, but I'm fascinated already. What happened to my dad on this day? What was the near-death experience? Dylan doesn't give us any more info about what happened."

"I've read the first few entries. I feel like it's important to understand what happened from start to finish," he said, and then he looked straight at her. "I have this crazy idea."

"What are you thinking?"

"I want to retrace their steps and try to figure out what happened."

Lisa thought about this for about two seconds. "I think that's a great idea. I'm in."

"Are you serious? I never expected that. When I reached out to you, I just wanted to learn anything I could from your dad's perspective."

"Something weighed on my dad. I'm in a place where I can take some time and do this. If you're okay with it, I'll join you."

She observed Floyd study his coffee cup, deep in thought.

With a serious tone, he continued, "I assumed I'd take on this crazy adventure alone. You know, clear my head, get my life back on track. But, as I think about it, it would be nice to have someone to bounce ideas off of and talk to along the way. Plus, you deserve answers as well. And heck, it could be a lot of fun. I'd love it if you came."

Before she could say anything, he put his coffee cup down and said, "Are you sure? I'm starting right away."

"I'm ready."

"Okay. Believe it or not, our first stop is 1,200 miles in the wrong direction."

"What? I don't understand."

"I have an appointment with a retired history professor from UCLA."

Chapter 12

Rouen

1983

"THIS IS THE BEST éclair I've ever had," Bull said as he licked his fingers.

Dylan grunted in agreement as he took a bite of a croissant and then sipped his first-ever cup of coffee, the bitterness hitting his throat. "I'm in love. I've never tasted food like this. Maybe we should just stay in France for the whole trip," he said as he placed his coffee cup on the table.

They sat at a small table outside the patisserie, watching the cars and bicycles meander through the cobblestone street inches from their feet. It was their first morning in France. The sky was the clear blue of an impressionist painting. Excited to experience Rouen, they had left their hotel early in the morning, stopping at the first patisserie they found. They could smell it from a block away. The counter clerk spoke no English, so they ordered by pointing and handed over cash, hoping that the change they received was correct.

"Okay, we have three objectives today: tour the Notre-Dame Cathedral, find a food market, and get lost," Dylan said with a smile.

Bull nodded, and they stood up from the table.

Over the roof of the building across the street, Dylan could see the spires of the cathedral in the distance. It was impressive, even from where they were—wherever that was. He pointed in that direction and said, "Onward!"

After strolling through a maze of narrow streets, carefully observing the shops and people, they turned a corner and entered a plaza the size of a football field, and were struck by the massive cathedral towering over them.

"Whoa!" Dylan said. "I knew it would be impressive, but wow."

The front of the cathedral was divided into three grand towers, each decorated with statues and carvings. The central tower was the most impressive, showcasing biblical scenes of angels, saints, and other figures carved into the stone with delicate precision. Above the doors, tremendous stained-glass windows glowed in many hues.

"It's weird how it's not symmetrical. I read that it was built over several hundred years, but geez. Let's go in and check it out," Bull said.

Once their eyes had adjusted to the cavernous room, they were fascinated by the intricate detail everywhere.

"Look. That's a tourist group getting ready for a lecture. Let's join," Bull said with a wink as he nonchalantly strolled up to a group of middle-aged folks encircling a man with his hand in the air, motioning them towards him. Dylan quickly joined Bull and tried not to make eye contact with any of the tourists.

The tour guide began his spiel. "Welcome to the Cathédrale de Notre-Dame de Rouen, one of the most remarkable Gothic cathedrals in France! This awe-inspiring structure has stood as a symbol of Rouen for centuries, serving as a testament to the city's rich history.

The cathedral's construction began in the twelfth century, but its most iconic features were added later, with significant work occurring in the thirteenth and fourteenth centuries. The stunning façade, a masterpiece of Gothic architecture, is adorned with sculptures depicting biblical scenes and saints. Its towering spire, which once stood as the tallest in France, reaches a height of 151 meters. That's 495 feet for you Americans."

Bull leaned toward Dylan and whispered, "This guy may look like Benny Hill, but he's pretty interesting."

Dylan chuckled, thinking of watching the zany *Benny Hill Show* with Bull late on Saturday nights after *Monty Python's Flying Circus*.

"Benny" continued, "During this tour, you'll find an impressive blend of art and architecture. The cathedral's nave stretches more than 137 meters, creating a sense of openness and grandeur. The stained-glass windows, some of which date back to the thirteenth century, cast beautiful colors across the interior, enhancing the spiritual atmosphere. Notably, the cathedral houses the tomb of Richard the Lionheart, King of England, who died in 1199.

Dylan whispered to Bull, "Richard the Lionheart was the king that went to fight in the crusades during the time of Robin Hood, according to legend."

Bull smiled. "That insane Dylan Stone memory—always astounds me."

An older woman gave them the evil eye and put her finger to her mouth to shush them. They looked back at "Benny".

"The Cathédrale de Notre-Dame de Rouen is also famous for its connection to Joan of Arc. In 1431, the young French heroine was tried and condemned here, before being burned at the stake in the Old Market Square. Today, a plaque inside the cathedral commemorates her presence. Another fascinating aspect of this cathedral is its artistic history. The renowned painter Claude Monet captured it in a series of paintings, highlighting the play of light on its façade at different times of day, adding another layer of cultural significance. Do you have any questions before we move on?"

A gray-haired man said in a shaky voice, "I was over here in World War II. Was this church damaged?"

The tour guide responded, "Unfortunately, yes. In 1944, the British Royal Air Force struck the church with seven bombs, and the US Air Force hit it again a few months later. There was significant damage from the bombs and related fires as well. Fortunately, earlier in the war, the local townspeople had surrounded the church with sandbags and moved the stained glass to a location far outside the city. The church was closed for a decade, and various restorations took place over several decades. They did an excellent job."

Bull backed away, and Dylan followed. They shared a high five, grabbed a brochure, dropped a franc in a jar, and began their own tour.

"Fascinating," Bull said excitedly. "It's hard to believe this place was bombed less than forty years ago. It looks amazing. Let's head up to the choir area. I read that it's one of a kind." At that, Bull was gone, almost at a jog.

Dylan walked down the center aisle, following Bull, but trying to take in the sights along the way. He walked through the nave, the area where churchgoers assemble for a service. Tourists were sitting like random pieces on a checkerboard. Some were admiring the beauty of the church, with their heads up and rotating slowly. Some were looking down, praying. A few stared ahead dully, as if they were waiting for a friend to finish exploring the church so they could find an outdoor café to enjoy some cheese and wine. Out of the corner of Dylan's eye, he glimpsed a blond-haired man sitting a couple of rows back, studying him intently. Dylan turned. The person was now looking the other way. He quickly glanced forward to locate Bull, and when he looked back, the man was gone. Was it the guy from the ship? The one Walking Death had described? Or was it nothing? Maybe it was someone staring at his unusual eyes, which happened frequently. Dylan scanned the entire church unsuccessfully, decided to get on with his tour, and rushed to catch up with Bull.

"Remember when we were on the ship and Walking Death was following me around?" he asked Bull as they walked down Place de la Pucelle, looking for a food market where they could buy bread, cheese, and meat to make their own incredible, yet inexpensive, sandwiches. Their twenty-five-dollar daily budget was a challenge, but they were determined to make it work. They had to. They only had a set amount of money in traveler's checks to last them for the entire trip. The key was to find a cheap hotel and limit meals to two per day. They were already getting good at it.

"Yeah. She gave me the creeps," Bull said.

"Did you happen to see anyone watching us when she sat by us on the deck?"

"No. But I wasn't paying attention to that. Why?"

"Remember when I told you she gave me an envelope?"

"Yeah. That was weird. What are you going to do with it?"

"I'm holding on to it. She said it was important. She caught me off guard when she gave it to me, and I guess I thought I was helping her out by taking it. Anyway, she told me she was being followed by someone who wanted that envelope," Dylan said.

"You think she was paranoid?" Bull asked as he turned left on the next street.

Dylan felt like they were accomplishing goal number three for the day: they were getting lost.

"I don't know. She told me about a guy with blond hair and said he'd been following her," Dylan said as he hurried to catch up with Bull's pace. "I think I saw him in the cathedral."

"What? That's crazy. I think you let her get to you. I wouldn't worry about it. It's just an envelope. Besides, how could he have followed us? We've been bouncing all over the place." He turned down another street and then said, "Aha! The market!"

"How did you do that?" Dylan asked, staring at the bustling crowd before them.

"I have my ways." He smiled. "And I studied a map I saw on the side of a building earlier. My two years of high school French apparently paid off."

Late that night, as Dylan and Bull lay in their hotel beds, sweating and listening to the next-door neighbors scream at each other through wafer-thin walls in a language they didn't recognize, Dylan wrote in his journal, detailing the day's events. Before he set the book down on the small table between their beds, he recalled the song "Sorrow" by David Bowie, which had been recorded just sixty miles away in Hérouville, France, in 1973, where he referenced a person with long blond hair who only brought him sorrow. After concluding the journal entry with the song lyric, one of hundreds he had memorized, he closed the book and went to sleep.

Chapter 13

Dr. Alexandra Morana

2025

FLOYD AND LISA STOOD on the balcony of a ninth-floor high-rise apartment on Ocean Avenue in Santa Monica, gazing out at the Pacific Ocean while sipping iced tea. He looked down at the beach, filled with sunbathers, and then watched a surfer riding a wave in the distance, while wondering how a college professor could afford such an incredible beachfront property. He expected a movie star to walk by at any moment.

Dr. Alexandra Morana opened the sliding glass door from her apartment, stepped onto the balcony carrying a charcuterie board, and said, "Please sit down."

She was slender and tan, with shoulder-length gray hair in a ponytail. She wore shorts, sandals, and a sleeveless blouse. Floyd guessed she must be around seventy years old, but she could easily pass for someone in her fifties. "Dr. Morana, thank you for meeting with us,"

Floyd began. "I mentioned to you on the phone that my uncle had interacted with you on a trip to Europe in 1983. You are so nice to take some time to talk."

Dr. Morana interjected, "I remember your uncle clearly. I've thought about him many times over the years and wondered what happened to him. He was very kind to me. Over the years, I've tried to locate him with no success, because I only knew him as 'Dylan from Texas.' That's a big state with a lot of Dylans. I gave him something very important. I was in a bad way at the time and not thinking very clearly."

Floyd put his drink down, looked at Lisa, and then at the professor, "Lisa's father—his nickname was Bull—traveled with Dylan on that trip."

"Bull! I met him. I don't think he thought too highly of me at the time, though I can't blame him. He seemed like a great guy."

Lisa smiled. "I'd love to hear more about my dad from back then if we have time."

Floyd brought the conversation back to the topic at hand. "I don't know if you're aware, but Dylan never made it back from that trip."

"Wait...what?" Dr. Morana's face turned ashen. "What happened?"

"We don't know what happened to him," Floyd said. "I have his journal, and he wrote about meeting you, and you handing him an envelope. He also said he felt he was being followed. We were hoping you might be able to give us some information. We're on a mission to figure out what happened to him on that trip." Floyd put his glass down on the small dining table. "Lisa and I are heading to Europe next. We're going to retrace his trip and try to make sense of everything."

Dr. Morana stood up, walked to the railing, and looked blankly in the direction of the ocean for several moments. She fidgeted with a button on her blouse, then turned to them with a serious look.

"I believe I can help. And I'd like to accompany you, if you'll have me. I'm retired, widowed, and frankly, a little bored. A person can only play so much pickleball. Plus, this would allow me to solve one of the greatest mysteries of my lifetime."

After talking it over with Lisa in the exquisite living room, Floyd walked back onto the balcony and approached Dr. Morana. "We have one condition: you need to tell us everything you know. We need to be a team and be able to trust each other if we're going to do this."

Dr. Morana smiled. "First, from now on, call me Alex. Second, I agree—I'll share everything I know. It's been a long time, so I'll need to refresh myself on some of the details, and I also need to conduct further research in Ireland to confirm my theory. I recommend we go to Dublin first."

"Okay," said Floyd. "We can go there first, but I'd like to take a couple of days to retrace their steps as well. So after Dublin, we'll rent a car and track their route through southern Ireland, and we can take the ship to Le Havre as well. I know it's been forty years, but maybe we'll figure something out, or maybe it will jog a memory for you, Alex."

"Good deal. Sounds like a plan."

"Okay. Welcome to the team, Alex. We're leaving tomorrow. I'll handle the flights. See you at LAX early."

Chapter 14

The Bluesbreakers

1983

WEDNESDAY, JUNE 8, 1983

I don't want to miss a day, so briefly: Bull and I went to Paris all day yesterday. Spent all of our money. Came back to Reims—saw John Mayall and the Bluesbreakers featuring Mick Taylor (of the Rolling Stones)—really good. Met two Irish college students—talked till 3 a.m. in the only all-night restaurant in town and returned to a wreck. To-morrow, hopefully, I'll b (new pen, the other one ran out) e able to expand on this very busy, funny, happy, slow, hot, sweaty, bluesy, shocking, and puzzling day.

Dylan and Bull were told the roadies were setting up the stage. Apparently, they were in no hurry. Dylan's concert ticket stated that the show was to start at 9 p.m., so they arrived at the Grand Théâtre at 8:30. They were shocked to find a crowd of what appeared to be hip-pies apparently transplanted from Haight-Ashbury in 1969 standing in a line outside the venue. *Where did all these characters come from?* Dylan thought. He hadn't seen anyone who looked like this in the three days they had been in Reims.

"Hey, man," a Charles Manson lookalike turned around and spoke to them in a British accent. "Have you ever seen these guys before?"

"No. We saw about a hundred posters on walls and telephone poles and decided to come to the show. We were in Paris all day, but took the train back and got here in time," Bull responded as he shook Manson's hand.

"Man. They're awesome. I saw them play at a small club in London in 1968—it was a great show. Then I saw Mick Taylor playing with the Stones at Hyde Park the next year. He was incredible. I think he was only twenty, but he brought something special. You're gonna love it."

The line started moving, and "Manson" turned around without another word and headed into the venue. Dylan and Bull found their seats. Second row! Dylan gazed around at the space, which looked like an elaborate movie theater with four balconies. It was warm, crowded, and sticky, and there was no sense of urgency from anyone.

Dylan and Bull settled into their seats and watched the roadies continue their work. It was as if they were in slow motion. Dylan looked at his watch. 10:20 p.m. "If they don't come onstage soon, maybe we should just leave."

Bull looked at him in disbelief. "This is how it always is. Don't worry, they'll be on pretty soon."

Sure enough, at around 10:30, the band hit the stage. Surprise—the bass player was John McVie, from Fleetwood Mac. The band charged through a tight set of blues brilliance, jump-started with the funky "Rock It in the Pocket" and concluding with an extended version of "Ridin' on the Santa Fe," featuring Mick Taylor on lead guitar, playing like his left hand was on fire. Dylan studied him the entire show, trying to memorize the chord patterns and solos, thinking he could try to emulate them on his own guitar later. Eventually, he gave up and just enjoyed the show. He wasn't meant to play like Mick Taylor. No one was.

As they were leaving the theater after the concert, Bull looked at Dylan and said, "Let's wait around and see if we can get an autograph."

Dylan thought it was unlikely and was ready to head back to their seedy hotel room, which had only one bed and one chair. It was after midnight, after all. But Bull insisted. Thirty minutes later, out walked John Mayall and Mick Taylor, carrying guitar cases and heading to a waiting van across the street.

"Great show!" Bull exclaimed as he walked straight toward them.

Dylan followed behind, a little embarrassed to be interrupting their evening.

"Thanks, man," John Mayall said in a voice that sounded like it came from a baritone saxophone. He and Bull began an animated conversation about the differences between touring in Europe and the States.

Meanwhile, Mick Taylor walked up to Dylan and offered his hand. "Hello, I'm Mick."

"I'm D...Dylan."

"Nice name. Is it related to *The Dylan*?" he said jokingly.

"Actually, it is. It turns out that my dad and Bob Dylan were friends in the '60s, and my dad named my brother and me Robert and Dylan. I didn't know this until maybe five years ago. But one day, he was driving with a friend, and from the backseat I overheard him talking—and he told stories about hanging out with Bob Dylan. I was thrilled to learn the story of my name. I'm gonna do something similar whenever I have kids," Dylan rambled. He was amazed that he was having a conversation with the guy who played the stunningly haunting guitar solo on "Can't You Hear Me Knocking."

"Your dad sounds mint."

"He's pretty cool. He loves music. It would be his dream to be here right now talking to you." Dylan looked over and saw that Bull and John Mayall were both laughing and talking loudly. He looked back at Mick. "So, are there any up-and-coming guitarists that you like?"

"I just saw this young Texan blues player the other day who was marvelous," Mick said after a few seconds. "He worked on Bowie's latest album."

"Stevie Ray Vaughan?!"

"Yeah. That's him." He looked at Dylan, surprised.

"I saw him in a small club in Houston last year. He lives in Austin, you know—my hometown. It was probably the best show I've ever seen. He played with his band, Double Trouble, and then did an encore with another band called the Ravens, playing only Hendrix covers. It was extraordinary," Dylan said with animation.

"He's very talented. I think he has a bright future," Mick said in his British accent. Just then, John and Bull joined them, and after introductions and handshakes, Mick turned to Dylan and said, "It was nice to meet you, Dylan. Take care of yourself." He shook Dylan's hand, and then he and John walked across the street, stepped into a nondescript white van, and disappeared.

"John Mayall is a really cool guy. He told me to mention my name to the roadies when he comes to Austin next year, and he'll get us backstage," Bull said as he hugged Dylan and lifted him off his feet with excitement.

"Did you just talk to John Mayall and Mick Taylor?" asked a woman with an Irish accent, wonder in her voice.

Bull placed Dylan back on the ground, and they turned around to see two twenty-something women staring at them in awe. The one who'd caught their attention wore ripped jeans, a Yes concert T-shirt, had fiery red hair and freckles, and seemed pretty drunk. Her friend was a contrast in every way, dressed in a formal, mid-thigh skirt that accentuated her legs, a tasteful blouse, and dark auburn hair; she was strikingly pretty, sober, and serious.

After a quick chat, they found themselves sitting in an all-night café, enjoying crêpes and coffee. The place looked like a British pub, even though it was situated on an old French street near Notre-Dame de Reims, a cathedral whose construction began in the 1200s. It had dark wood tables surrounding a large bar with yellow glass chandeliers hanging from a high ceiling. After discussing the concert and replaying every word John Mayall had told Bull, the conversation shifted.

"So, where are you all from?" asked Nessa, the flaming redhead.

"The States. Texas," said Bull.

"I've always wanted to visit Texas. Someday, I'll go there. I've always dreamed of going to Dallas," said Cara, the serious one.

"Forget Dallas," Bull interjected. "Austin is the place to visit if you come to Texas. We have lakes and hills, and it's a great college town. Dallas is sort of stuck up. If you come to Texas, call me and I'll show you around. You'll love it."

"Thanks, I may take you up on that. So...where have you been so far on your trip to Europe?" Cara said as she crossed her legs. Dylan had to force himself to look her in the eyes.

"We just started," he said. "We spent about four days in Ireland and since then we've stayed in Rouen, Chartres, and here, with a couple of day trips to Paris. We're heading south next. Not sure where at this point." He took a bite of his crêpe.

"As you can probably tell," said Cara, "we're from Ireland—Cork, actually. We're studying in Dublin. We took a semester off and have been traveling throughout the continent. We're headed back home now. What was your favorite part of Ireland?"

Dylan responded, "Bunratty Castle was fun. I also enjoyed spending the evening at a pub in New Ross with an older couple; they were so friendly and welcoming."

"I'm glad you enjoyed it. Ireland is special. Of course, there are the ancient churches, the castles, and the history. But as you mentioned, it's the people who make Ireland special. You can't really appreciate that unless you spend some time there. You must go back. If you ever get to Dublin, look us up, we'll show you around," Cara said, staring intently at him. "You have interesting eyes, Dylan."

"Thanks. Usually, people are freaked out by them," he said shyly. Cara smiled.

"Are there any places that we just must go on our trip through Europe?" Bull jumped in.

Nessa, still slurring her speech despite the coffee, exclaimed, "Pelekas Beach! So fun. I'm still sunburned in places that have never seen the sun before," she added with a sly smile.

Cara interrupted. "She's referring to a beach on Corfu, an island off Greece. We did have a great time there. It's a little decadent, but so beautiful. We stayed for an entire week—longer than we stayed anywhere on our trip. I recommend it as well. You should also visit Cassis. Simply beautiful. There's an older Irish couple there that run a B&B, the Kellys. Lots of Irish locals stay there. They have for decades. Mention my name, and they'll give you a good deal."

"Noted," said Dylan. "Corfu and the Kelly's B&B in Cassis are now on the itinerary."

Bull nodded, and Dylan wrote it down on a napkin and then placed it in his pocket.

Cara looked at Nessa and said, "Remember that intense guy we ran into a couple of days ago? He asked us if we'd seen two American travelers. I wonder if he meant them." She nodded towards Dylan and Bull. "Do either of you carry a guitar?"

Dylan's head swiveled towards her abruptly. "I do. Why?"

Cara looked at Dylan and continued, "We ran into an American guy on the train from Paris to Reims a couple of days ago and struck up a conversation. At first, we thought he was European, but we later found out he'd attended boarding school in Switzerland, so his accent was just unusual. He kept talking about museums and Renaissance art. He spent thirty minutes talking about the cathedral in Rouen after we told him we were visiting it the next day. It was like taking a class from a young, interesting professor."

"Yeah," Nessa jumped in. "And right before we departed the train, he got serious and asked us if we'd seen two college-age Americans traveling together recently. He described them as one really big guy and the other guy carrying a guitar. He said they were his friends, and they'd got separated on the trip. We told him we hadn't. He seemed a little disappointed. Anyway, I didn't think about it again until a few minutes ago, and it struck me that the 'big guy' might be Bull. Did you lose a friend along the way?"

Dylan looked at Bull. "I wonder—"

Bull cut him off. "I think it's a coincidence. Nothing to worry about." Then he turned to the girls and said, "There are so many college-age Americans traveling in Europe this summer, he must be talking about someone else. We haven't been separated from anyone; it's just the two of us."

After saying their goodbyes while standing in front of the café, Dylan and Bull were caught off guard when the girls both leaned in and gave them farewell cheek-to-cheek kisses.

Dylan said, "That's a custom I could get used to," and Bull laughed.

They then began walking, trying to find their way back to their hotel. There were very few lights on the ancient stone streets, so they walked blindly in the middle of the road with their hands outstretched, trying to avoid running into a wall or a sign. Whenever they found a streetlamp, they would stop to study their local map, then charge forward into the darkness towards the next streetlamp in the foggy distance.

Dylan said, "I think that guy they met on the train was the same one that was on the ship, and maybe even in Rouen cathedral."

"I'm not worried," Bull said. "We can take care of ourselves. Besides, we're leaving tomorrow. Let's leave early and make sure he isn't on our train. If he's following us, we'll lose him. Europe is a big place."

"I've been thinking about the envelope and key. Walking Death talked about the stolen Irish jewels. Maybe she was on to something," Dylan said as they turned a corner. "Man, these streets are dark. I can't even see my hands. I'd hate to trip and fall onto these cobblestones."

"Tell you what," Bull said. "When we can find a bookstore or library with English books, let's see what we can learn about it."

"That's a good idea," Dylan said as they approached the hotel. A drunk man lay asleep, blocking the doorway. They stepped over him and went inside.

They walked up three flights of stairs. Dangling light bulbs eerily illuminated the hallway as they made their way to their room. It was hot, and bugs scattered as they walked down the hall. It was definitely the worst room they had stayed in so far. Since they had splurged to attend the concert, they'd found the cheapest hotel in town, and it showed. They were going to have to share a bed, too. It was too risky for one of them to sleep on the floor due to the presence of bugs and rats.

"We are never staying in a place like this again," Dylan said.

"For sure. We'll skip dinner if we must. This sucks." Bull opened the door, turned on the light, and shouted, "What the hell?"

Dylan ran into the room from behind Bull. Their backpacks had been violently ripped open and the contents strewn throughout the room. Dylan raced to the window. It was open, the curtain swaying in the breeze. He looked out and saw a person running, who quickly darted around a corner and disappeared. Dylan heard a loud thud, and then rapid footsteps that gradually faded into silence.

"Bull, look!" Dylan exclaimed.

Bull turned around and stared at where Dylan was pointing. There, on the floor by the window, was Dylan's journal.

Chapter 15

Dublin

2025

Floyd looked around the lobby of the Trinity City Hotel, the renovated former headquarters of the Dublin Fire Brigade. Lanterns reminiscent of those in an old Renaissance painting hung from the ancient brick wall decorated with paintings of the Irish countryside. Across a narrow hallway, more lanterns hung beside window walls, adorned with red corduroy curtains pulled aside with gold sashes to showcase the view of College Street. Small wooden tables lined each side of the corridor, with three wicker chairs at each table. Only one table was occupied.

"Thanks for meeting this afternoon. I know it's been a long day," Floyd said to Lisa and Alex. He looked around the room to make sure they were alone. "Before we jump in, I'd like to hear everyone's thoughts about what we're trying to accomplish here and how we're going to go about it."

"That sounds like a good plan. Why don't you start, Floyd, and then Alex and I can chime in," Lisa said with a yawn. They had flown all night and arrived this morning. They were tired but excited to get moving.

"Okay. Here's what I know. Dylan and Bull traveled for one month, from Ireland to Corfu, and Dylan disappeared there. I've never heard any details of what happened or how. I figure Bull may have known, but I'm not sure if he told anyone. However, we do know that Dylan ran into Alex on a ship and received an envelope, and she was worried someone was following her. From his journal, it does appear that was the case. Whether it had anything to do with Dylan's disappearance, we don't know."

Floyd picked up his backpack off the floor next to him, placed it in his lap, and unzipped it.

"Alex, all of this came from my dad's safe deposit box."

He pulled out an old journal with a bumper sticker on the front. "This is Dylan's journal. There may be some clues in here. We all need to read it and see what we can find."

He pulled out an envelope and handed it to her.

Alex gasped. "That's the envelope I gave Dylan all those years ago! I thought for sure it was gone forever." She took it carefully, treating it as if it were a fragile piece of lace that would disintegrate if held incorrectly, looking at the front and back. She saw the familiar, strange poetic verse and noticed that it was unsealed.

"Was it empty when you found it?" she asked. Floyd noticed worry lines appear in her face.

"No." He unzipped a hidden pocket in his sports coat and pulled out the skeleton key.

Alex stared at the key in his hand, mouth agape.

"Tell me what's happening," Lisa interrupted.

Without a word, Alex clutched the key and studied it carefully. Then, as if awakening from a spell, she took a deep breath and said to Lisa, "I have a lot to tell you. Let's let Floyd finish, and then I'll tell you what I know."

While they were talking, Floyd placed an aged, water-stained money belt on the table. He tried to open it, but the zipper was stuck. "I haven't been able to crack this, and I'm scared to damage it." He dropped it on the table in frustration.

Lisa grabbed it and pulled the zipper firmly. It opened cleanly. She smiled at Floyd and then looked inside. "There's stuff in here. It's all stained from water, but pretty well-preserved." Within thirty seconds, the table was covered with a half-used American Express Traveler's checkbook and register, an unused airplane ticket from Amsterdam to Houston, via JFK, an assortment of Greek drachmas, Italian lira, and Spanish pesetas, and a business card. Lisa picked it up and handed it to Alex.

Alex stared at it, still in shock. "That's my business card from UCLA. The one I gave Dylan."

Lisa closed her eyes and put her finger in the money belt and felt around to see if there was anything else buried in there. Deep in the crease were two small pieces of paper, which she placed on the table. The first contained a drawing of a throne with the word Kaiser in front of it, and below that was a sketch of a trunk. It wasn't Dylan's handwriting.

Alex studied it and said, "I think I recognize the handwriting... I wonder how Dylan ended up with this."

Lisa carefully unrolled an old napkin with handwriting on both sides. "The note says Kelly's B&B in Cassis on one side and Corfu on the other, and it looks like it was written by Dylan." They looked at each other. "Cassis?" said Lisa.

Floyd responded, "It's one of the places that Dylan and Bull visited on their trip—it's on the French Riviera. I recognize the name of the

B&B from the journal. It must have been important. We'll see if it still exists when we go there."

Alex chimed in, "Okay, my turn." She took a deep breath. "I was a young college professor and had done my college thesis on important women in Irish history. I became interested in the women who were the first to be admitted to Trinity College. They were courageous and had fascinating stories. I won't go into all the details now, but before that trip in 1983, I had published a paper on this topic and hinted that there was a connection between one of these women and the missing Crown Jewels of Ireland."

Lisa asked, "Which are...what, exactly? Is that a big deal?"

"Picture this: they're a heavily jeweled badge and star created in 1831. Not only were the jewels beautiful and valuable, but they also had significant symbolic meaning for the country. They were stolen in 1907, just before a visit from the King of England, which was humiliating for the country. You see, the jewels had been temporarily moved to a library at Dublin Castle overseen by Sir Arthur Vicars, the Ulster King of Arms, until a special strongroom could be built. He wasn't the most reliable guy. He was known to get drunk on overnight duty and once awoke with the jewels around his neck."

"Sounds like they needed to improve their security," Lisa said with a smile.

Alex continued, "On July 6, 1907, they were found to be missing. Vicars blamed it on his second-in-command, Frank Shackleton. It was speculated that Shackleton got Vicars drunk, removed the key from his pocket, and stole the jewels. Supposedly, Shackleton later sold them in Europe. Shackleton was never charged, and many people believe it was because he was going to expose several high-ranking officials who were involved in inappropriate activities. The theft was covered up to avoid national embarrassment."

"Interesting. So, what did you discover? I'm sure people have been trying to figure this out for more than a hundred years now," Floyd said.

"I backed into my theory through my research into the first women students at Trinity College, which started in 1904. As a part of my research, I found every possible diary of each of these amazing women. One of them was a restless and perhaps promiscuous woman named Molly O'Leary. She's the one who I think wrote the note you just found, Lisa," she said, gesturing to the paper.

"Anyway, I also found references to Molly in other women's diaries. Typically, they were worried about her getting in trouble or concerned that her behavior would reflect poorly on them. I then noticed that there were several references to her disappearing at night and meeting a man named Arthur. After comparing diary entries and dates, I found that Molly was with a 'Sir Arthur' on the night just before the jewels were found missing. And then she disappeared."

"Fascinating. That could be more than just a coincidence," Lisa said.

"Yeah," Alex said. "It all changed when I visited the library on that trip to Ireland in 1983 and found a diary I had never seen before. It belonged to Cillian Donnelly, a young, wealthy merchant. He was the brother of a young female student, Sinead Donnelly, whom I was researching. I found the diary by accident, because it was misplaced. It turns out that Cillian and Molly were lovers, and he corresponded about it with his sister. Some of the letters were found in each diary."

"Molly seemed to be an adventurous girl," Lisa said.

"Cillian was in love with Molly for a long time, according to what I read, but Molly did not appear to want to be tied down to any one person. She did correspond with Cillian for several years, and she seemed to care for him. In subsequent letters to his sister, he made cryptic references to Molly, jewels, cliffs, and thrones. That reinforced my suspicion that Molly had taken the Crown Jewels, and these letters appeared to have clues about the treasure's location somewhere in Europe. Unfortunately, I didn't have time to review the entire journal and all the loose letters, though I did see a diary entry in 1909 that referenced 'Arthur's jewels' and a key in an envelope. I initially thought the word 'key' was symbolic, but then I found a hidden pocket at the back of the diary. And sure enough, there was an envelope and a real key."

"You took the envelope?" Lisa asked.

"I wasn't planning on it, but there was no documentation of this envelope or the key, and I was young and ambitious, so I took it. I'm not proud of it. It was wrong, and I regret doing it. My justification was that no one knew it existed anyway. I wasn't stealing anything that the library was aware of."

"So, what happened next?" Lisa urged.

"I left the library but quickly felt like I was being followed. I did everything I could to be evasive. I didn't take the normal train or plane out of Dublin. I hitchhiked, took buses, and eventually hopped on the ship to Le Havre at the last minute. I was exhausted and paranoid. That's why I gave the envelope to Dylan. I was feeling desperate, and perhaps a little guilty as well for taking the key in the first place. My naïve hope was that whoever was following me wouldn't see the exchange, Dylan and I would connect a few months later, and then I could continue my quest."

"Any idea who was following you?" Floyd asked.

"I kept seeing a young man with long blond hair. At one point on the ship, he approached me and got close enough to try to intimidate me into giving him the key. I was terrified. And that's when I ran into Dylan. He saved me, even if he didn't know it."

"What happened after your interaction with Dylan and Bull?" Lisa asked.

"When I got off the ship, I was hoping to tag along with them until I could catch a plane home. They made me feel safe. However, I couldn't find them after we disembarked. Interestingly, I didn't see the blond-haired man again either. Then I was back in Los Angeles within a couple of days. Like I said, I tried to look up Dylan several times over the years, but I didn't get his last name and couldn't ever track him down. I was disappointed in myself for how I handled the entire situation. I was sad to give up the key, and worried that I'd put Dylan in danger. It's weighed on my mind for forty-two years. I feel so fortunate to be with you both on this journey. Maybe I can, in some small way, fix a big mistake that I made as a young woman."

Lisa took a deep breath and said, "Wow. That's a lot to digest. Okay, we have all of these items in front of us and your expertise, Alex. I'm not sure what I can contribute, other than I'll do whatever I can to help us solve the mystery of what happened to Dylan, and to a certain extent, my father as well."

Alex said, "I want to go to the Trinity College library tomorrow morning and review several diaries. I still have credentials due to my tenure as a UCLA professor. My goal is to see if I can find any more clues that may have eluded me in 1983. Once I found the key and envelope, I stopped searching further and simply left. There may be more to uncover."

Floyd said, "Okay, while you're doing that, Lisa and I will go to Dublin Castle. We'll join a group and learn more about the lost Irish Crown Jewels—at least the tourist version. We'll also review the journal and develop an initial itinerary for our trip once we leave Dublin."

Chapter 16

Adriana

1983

JULIAN LIFTED AN ESPRESSO to his lips and gazed out at the countryside from a private estate outside Reims, France, deep in thought. It was dawn, and the sun was peering over the horizon, spilling orange and yellow rays across the green hills.

"What's on your mind, my handsome?" asked the soft-voiced woman sitting in the chair beside him.

"Just thinking. Those boys are tough to track down, and I came so close last night. They have that envelope somewhere," he snarled, referring to his break-in at the seedy hotel earlier that morning. He'd searched through the two backpacks but found nothing. Just as he'd started reading a journal he'd found in the room, the boys had unexpectedly returned, so Julian had leapt out of the ground-floor window and ran off. He must have dropped the journal on the way out. On top of everything, he had a sore shoulder from running into a wall on the pitch-black street. Still, he'd learned their names, Dylan Stone and Bull Eastland, and he read that they planned to visit Cassis and

Corfu at some point. He was pretty sure they had no idea what they had stumbled upon.

"Don't worry, those boys don't know what they're up against. You'll be successful." Adriana Valdon slowly stood up and faced him, blocking his view of the sun rising over the fields. From Julian's perspective, the view had just improved tremendously. Statuesque, with flowing chestnut hair, green eyes, and naturally golden-brown skin, she was Spanish perfection. He surely didn't deserve her. She was beautiful and brilliant. And, he thought with a smile, an unexpected benefit had been her ability to draw attention wherever she went, which turned out to be great cover for him when he was slipping an artifact into his jacket or conducting surveillance.

She sat back down in the chair next to him, stretching her toned legs out onto a small stool. Julian turned to her.

"You know," he said, "art theft requires extreme skills in observation and patience, as well as an ability to blend in with the crowd. When I was young, I was reckless and spontaneous. I would find a room in a museum or church that was unoccupied and slip whatever I wanted into my pocket or jacket." He looked at her. She was staring at the sunset, her skin so soft and tan. Who was he fooling? She was the work of art. "I'll never forget my first close call," he said, reminiscing.

"What happened?" She turned to look at him.

He had to avert his gaze so that he could focus. "I was in a small medieval church in southern France. I had just placed a 500-year-old cross into my pocket, and as I turned to leave, there stood a monk. I froze. I was just about to turn myself in and blame it on youthful indiscretion when he spoke to me. I'll never forget it. In French, he said, 'Hello, young man. Are you enjoying your visit?' I told him it was a beautiful church, and he smiled and said, 'I've been told that' and pointed at his eyes, smiling. He was blind! I was so lucky. As I walked out of that church, I committed to myself that I would be more careful and methodical from that point forward."

She leaned to her side and looked straight into his dark blue eyes and asked, "So, what did you do differently?"

For a second, he almost felt hypnotized by her, so once again he averted his glance and stared at the small cottage far in the distance, with white whisps of smoke billowing from its stone chimney.

"As I grew older and more experienced, I learned the art of surveillance. I would select a target, typically a museum or church, and then observe for several days. I would watch the security team. When did their shift change? When did they take smoke breaks? When did they take meal breaks? Did they work at night? I would tour the target, identifying cameras and security guard stations. In some churches, there were none. I would study how paintings and other artifacts were displayed. Were they secured or not? What would be the best way to remove them? It became a game. And I mastered it. I could walk out of a museum with a poster-sized painting inside my jacket, and joke with the guard as I left."

"Fascinating. That must have been exciting."

"Yeah, and scary. But over time, I became obsessed with finding missing art, treasures, and artifacts. I still enjoy an occasional targeted theft from a museum or church, mind you, but I needed a new challenge."

Adriana walked to the outdoor kitchen, poured herself a cup of coffee, and turned back to Julian. "So, what's so different about finding missing art?"

Julian stood and rested his arms on the balcony overlooking the rolling hills. "It's a completely different animal. Some of the most famous 'missing' paintings," he said, making air quotes, "and cultural artifacts are in private collections. The 'owner' might be a reclusive millionaire, the leader of a South American drug cartel, or even a dictator of a small African nation. Their security is state-of-the-art. Some are absolutely foolproof. I discovered an exclusive black market. I have limited access due to my dad's connections, but it isn't easy to play in this arena. Not impossible, but difficult—and dangerous."

"Yeah, and it's not your wish to buy on the black market, right?" she asked.

"Correct. I have no intention of buying their art. I hate that they even acquire it. They don't collect art because it's beautiful or historical but because it gives them a feeling of power. That's not right. Over time, I will figure out ways to extract art from these poseurs because the art belongs in a place where it's appreciated. So, in the meantime, I focus on trying to locate artifacts that are lost or misplaced."

"That sounds challenging," she said.

Julian rarely spoke this openly. He could tell she was engaged. "It is. For instance, a famous Renaissance painting was stolen and hidden in a barn in the French countryside. The thief died without telling anyone. It was finally found forty years later when the barn was being repaired. There are many examples like this."

"So, how do you find these lost or stolen items?" Her voice rose in curiosity.

"The best way to track down these works is through intensive research. There are always clues if one looks hard enough. I study police reports. I read contemporary newspaper articles and try to identify potential suspects. Then I learn about them, their families, and their habits. Eventually, people slip up, and my goal is to be there when it happens."

Adriana walked to the balcony and stood so close that her shoulder pressed against him. He clenched his muscles, as if shocked by an electric current, then he relaxed and smiled at her. "And then I ran into you. It turned out to be the best thing that ever happened to me," he said, looking forward again.

She looked up at him and smiled. "Tell me why."

"You get me," he said earnestly. "No one else ever has. You understand what I do. You understand that for me, it's all about the art. I appreciate it, value it, and take care of it like no one else can." Then he looked down at her and said, "And you're smart, interesting, and really good-looking." He winked. Then he smiled and said, "We make a good team. Do you feel like going on a vacation to the French Riviera?"

Chapter 17

Free and Clear

1983

DYLAN LOOKED UP AT the arched ceiling of the magnificent Gare de Reims, which had been in operation since 1858, and it was stunning. *A lot of work was put into the architecture of this train station*, he thought with wonder. *It's still beautiful, and it works so well.*

It was 4:45 a.m., and he and Bull were standing in a cavernous area surrounded by a handful of other travelers, all gazing upwards at the train station board, entranced, as if they were all watching the same movie in an enormous cinema. The incoming and outgoing train numbers updated by the minute, emitting loud clicking sounds as the numbers changed. They were waiting for the next one due south, their Eurail passes in hand. After the hotel break-in, they had quickly repacked all their belongings, left money on the bed to pay for the room, and walked straight to the train station in the dark.

"Whoever did that will never find us," Bull said. "Once we get on board, we'll pick a random stop and switch trains. We'll decide on our destination later today. We'll make quick moves and make sure no one is following us. Europe is a big place. If we do this right, we'll lose whoever is following us, and we can get on with our trip."

Dylan was relieved. Unfortunately, it had taken a break-in for Bull to believe him, but now he was fully engaged. Dylan was sure that they would be free and clear from this point on.

They took three different trains, randomly selecting each at the last minute before entering just as the doors were closing. They ended up spending one night in Bordeaux, where they had "the second-best French meal of the trip" (Bull had exclaimed this after a late-night meal of escargot, steak, and fries). Then, after taking an overnight train to Barcelona, Spain, followed by two standing-room-only metro buses, they arrived in the small coastal resort town of Blanes. The spot had come highly recommended by an older Spanish gentleman they'd met while waiting for a train in one of the four stations they'd passed through over the last couple of days. He told them it was beautiful and under the radar. "You might be the only Americans there," he said. That sounded perfect.

No sightings of the mysterious blond-haired man. Life was good.

Friday, June 10, 1983; Toulouse Train Station, 3 a.m.

Right now, we're in a train station with a bunch of old people, guys like us, amputees, and an assortment of yucky people waiting for the 5:10 a.m. train to Barcelona, and that's not even our final destination. It will take all day to get to Blanes. We got here at 1:20 a.m. (actually we slept too long on the last train and Bull fortunately woke up and noticed we were at our stop, so we hurriedly jumped off the train—packs, guitar and all—onto another set of tracks, which was stupid! What if another train had been coming?) and then we went into this waiting room.

It was too depressing to sit there for long, so Bull and I walked around town and found an all-night café that served some great omelets. Then we came back to the station, and I played my guitar by the train tracks (so I wouldn't disturb anyone's sleep). It was a little frustrating because I now only have five strings. I played for an hour or so and got my fix for the day. I guess I'll now re-read my Time *magazine.*

On their first night in Blanes, Dylan and Bull found a seaside café and sat at an outdoor table overlooking the Mediterranean. Blanes had the charm of an old Catalan coastal village. They helped themselves to wine from a well-worn wicker-covered carafe, tapped their glasses together, and happily settled in. A young couple strolled along the seafront promenade hand in hand, her head on his shoulder. A group of teenage girls sat on large white towels, like bedsheets, giggling and watching boys kick a soccer ball on the beach. The boys tried their best to play like their heroes, failing miserably, their shoes making sucking sounds as they approached the water.

"This is the life," Bull said as he sipped on the glass of rosé and looked at the menu. "For 500 pesetas, we can get a four-course meal and this bottle of table wine—that's $4!"

"Plus, we have a clean room with two beds, a bathroom, and a window for practically nothing. We'll be able to save money here. I love it," Dylan chimed in.

"And the girls are tan and pretty," Bull said, smiling as their waitress approached the table. Petite and athletic, with mahogany hair and dark, expressive eyes that twinkled when she spoke, she introduced herself in Spanish as Rosa. Dylan attempted to answer in his best high school Español, when she interrupted him in heavily accented English, saying, "I can understand you, if you speak slowly." She studied Dylan's unusual eyes for a moment, then asked, "Where are you from? Most of our guests are from the Continente."

"We're from the States," Bull responded, "as you could probably tell from our accents."

"Bienvenido a Blanes!" she said enthusiastically.

"We're happy to be here. We haven't eaten all day. What do you recommend?" Dylan asked.

"Don't worry, I take care of you. Trust me." She smiled.

Then Bull asked, "Do you have any suggestions on what we should do while we're here in Blanes?"

Rosa pulled up a chair, put her hand on Bull's arm, and said to them, "Come back at midnight when I finish work, and I'll show you around." She then stood up, winked at them, and strode back into the restaurant. *Like a runway model*, Dylan thought. They watched her every movement until she disappeared.

"I like southern Europe," said Bull. "It seems the further south we get, the friendlier everyone is."

"Yeah, and the meals get longer and later as well. We may not be done with dinner until eleven anyway. It will be easy to be here at twelve," Dylan said as he observed a man working on his sailboat at the nearby marina.

"As long as we're sitting here watching the sun set, with a glass of wine, and several dinner courses ahead of us, it's a good time to relax and actually talk," Bull said, unusually serious. Dylan was surprised. "I know that whole episode in Reims was upsetting," Bull continued. "I'm glad it's behind us, but I keep thinking about it. Tell me again what the weird professor lady told you."

Bull then placed his wine glass on the table and watched a girl in a bikini traipse by.

Dylan waited a beat for Bull to refocus on the conversation. "I've been thinking about that a lot too, racking my brain to remember as much as I can. She told me she just knew she could trust me. She was scared. I didn't take it that seriously at the time, but I understand it now, after what happened to us. Anyway, she told me she'd been studying Irish history. Based on her research she believed that these lost Irish Crown Jewels were hidden in a trunk in Europe. Then she gave me the envelope with the key. She thinks the note on the envelope is a clue to its location and the key opens the trunk. She wants me to return it to her when we get back home. She gave me her business card. Oh yeah, she also said we ought to try to figure it out ourselves if we can."

He looked around to make sure that no one was watching, then pulled up his shirt, unzipped his money belt, and placed the business card on the table in front of Bull.

Bull studied it. "Man, I guess she was the real deal. Maybe I underestimated her. As for the jewels, we know so little about this legend, other than what Liam O'Malley told us at the bar in New Ross. I've been looking for a bookstore or library to learn more, but haven't found one with books in English. Let's keep an eye out for that."

"Definitely," Dylan said. "Hey, when do you want to head to our next destination? Remember that Irish girl, Cara? She recommended Cassis. I checked the train schedules, and it's about seven hours from here, and it's on the way to Italy. And we know we want to spend time in Florence, for sure..."

"Let's talk more about that tomorrow. I can't think too much past midnight," Bull said with a laugh and a nod as Rosa appeared. She placed a large black pan filled with sizzling yellow rice, shrimp, fish, and clams on the table.

"Have you ever had paella?" she asked. "*Esta es nuestra especialidad*—our specialty. You will not find better."

Dylan and Bull both shook their heads as they marveled at the huge pan, which covered most of the table. Rosa had to move the carafe and a basket of bread to the next table to make room. It was unlike anything they'd seen before. Dylan took the first bite and looked at Bull, speechless. His eyes expressed pure pleasure—well, his right eye did—and he pointed at the plate, directing Bull to grab his fork as he dug in again.

Two hours later, as they sat back in their chairs with their hands on their bellies, they were pretty sure they would never be able to find anything better. Strawberries and cream followed the paella and, interestingly, a dessert of cheeses.

As the bells of the fifteen-hundred-year-old Iglesia de Santa Maria chimed twelve times, and then echoed for several seconds afterwards, Dylan and Bull stood outside the café, wondering if Rosa had been serious about meeting them. Suddenly, the door flew open, and she bounced through, wearing a pink halter top, white shorts, and sandals with straps around her tan ankles, and proceeded to hug them both. Before they could catch their breath, two more young women joined them. They introduced themselves in Spanish as Anna and Maria, and smothered Dylan and Bull in further hugs and cheek kisses. Anna was a petite girl with black hair and dark eyes, wearing a white sundress that contrasted with her dark skin. She spoke in rapid-fire Spanish and couldn't take her eyes off Bull. Maria was a little more reserved. Dylan hadn't heard her say one word. She was the tallest of the three, with golden hair, brown eyes, and long dark eyelashes, and was wearing a light blue blouse and knee-length white shorts.

"We are going to show you the real Blanes," Rosa said with a smile. "Follow me." And she took off at a trot, Anna and Maria immediately stepping in behind her, like a mother duck followed by her ducklings.

She led them through the Old Town, with its colorful storefronts, and then down a dark side street. Dylan could feel the vibration of a heavy bass from somewhere. Rosa stopped, and they all followed suit, almost running into her. She then walked up to an ordinary-looking building, knocked twice on a random door, and waited. A sliding window cracked open, some words were exchanged, and then the door creaked open slowly, like in a scary movie, and they all walked in.

It was a large two-story *edificio* with many small rooms. A full bar stretched across the entire back wall of the main room, lined with bottles of all shapes, sizes, and colors. Dylan opened the door to a room to the left of the bar and was struck by loud, pulsating music. He saw what appeared to be a hundred gyrating bodies, as bolts of light bounced off a large disco ball suspended from the ceiling. *Well, that's where the bass sound came from*, he thought. Across a wall in the disco, the word CLEOPATRA glowed and seemed to turn off and on as the fiery ball rotated above. Dylan looked to his right, and two young men came out of another room, laughing and smoking. *Those aren't cigarettes*, Dylan thought, a pungent aroma hitting his nostrils. Anna grabbed Bull and led him into the disco room.

Dylan felt claustrophobic. It was loud, sweaty, and smoky. He surveyed the entire room and didn't recognize anyone around him. He decided this wasn't his scene, so he quietly left the house through the door he had entered. Walking outside felt like that scene in the *Wizard of Oz* movie when it suddenly went from black and white to color, except in reverse, Dylan thought. But once the fresh air hit him, he could breathe again. Looking around to get his bearings, he realized he was on the edge of a neighborhood, with the lights of Blanes Old Town in the near distance. He wasn't lost. Though he didn't know the area, he could hear waves striking the beach every few seconds like clockwork, so he headed in that direction.

As he strolled to the water's edge, he saw the striking Sa Palomera rock jutting out of the ocean. He had never seen anything like it before—so stunning and beautiful—rising out of the waves and staring back at the shoreline. He decided to cross the narrow rock pathway out onto Sa Palomera. Once there, he found a place to sit and looked back at the lights of Blanes' Old Town shimmering in the darkness.

A few minutes later, he heard a soft voice. "Dylan, why are you here?"

It was Rosa.

"I hope I didn't offend you, but I had to get out of there; it was a bit much for me," Dylan said. "Please go and enjoy yourself. Besides, I'm sure Bull is having a great time."

"Nonsense. You are my guest. I stay with you," she said as she sat down next to him. She smelled like suntan lotion. Her arm touched his. They both looked at the twinkling lights across the water. After a pause, she said, "Tell me about yourself."

"Not much to say, really. I'm going to university in the Fall. Bull and I are traveling through Europe this summer—"

She interrupted him firmly but in a friendly tone. "No, tell me something special. I may never see you again. I want to learn about you, Dylan."

Dylan thought about this for a moment. He had never been asked a question like this. Here he was in the most romantic place he'd ever experienced, with Rosa, a girl who wouldn't have looked twice at him in high school, and she seemed sincerely interested in him.

"You ever think you're supposed to know what you're going to do with your life?" he said. "I'm getting ready to go to college, and I don't even know what I should study, much less what I should do for the rest of my life."

Rosa smiled faintly. "I think about it sometimes. Life is unpredictable. I figure I will pretend I know what I am doing until I figure it out."

He laughed. "Yeah. I guess I'm not even good at pretending. Look at Bull. He has it all figured out. He's going to play football and go to law school. My dad knew what he wanted to do when he was sixteen years old. I just have no idea, and it drives me crazy."

Dylan watched a canoe silently pass by, its paddler completely shrouded by darkness. Rosa placed his hand in hers.

He continued, "I love to read and write and play guitar, and...I have this unusual ability to remember things, like song lyrics, quotes, or just about anything I've read or heard. Sometimes I wish I could forget more easily."

She tilted her head and looked at him. "Why do you want to forget?"

"Because everything sticks. Even the things I don't want to remember. I'll wake up in the middle of the night, and it's still there. I feel like my head is full of all these pieces of other people's stories. But I can't even figure out mine."

Rosa turned and studied him. "Maybe *esa es tu historia.*"

"What do you mean?"

"You notice things most people don't. You listen. You carry things for other people. Maybe that's not confusion—maybe it's your gift."

Dylan looked at Rosa, the light reflecting off her skin. "A gift that won't make me a living."

She paused, then said, "I think the world has plenty of people chasing money. It needs people who listen, remember, feel things."

"Sometimes I wish I could just live like I am this summer, forever—traveling, meeting people like you, filling up notebooks with my observations. But that's not a realistic life aspiration, is it?"

She shrugged. "Maybe it is. Maybe you are collecting something, and one day all of this will add up to who you are. Maybe your life is about noticing things others miss. You know, Dylan, I think it's okay not to have everything figured out. We only live once, and we have no idea how long that will be. You are doing the right thing. You are experiencing life. Take it all in. Find someone to love—but make sure she loves you as well. Learn from your experiences. I am sure you will make the best of this life. I see it in your eyes and hear it in your voice."

"You are very wise. Tell me about you. I want to learn the story of Rosa." He looked straight into her eyes.

She smiled. "See, there you go, asking about others, listening, adding to your *biblioteca* of life stories. Let's see." Her tone became serious. "Though I am young, I have experienced great highs and *bajas devastadores*. My childhood was *muy dificil*. I have learned many things the hard way."

Dylan's eyes narrowed. "Tell me more. What happened to—"

"Hey! They told me you might be here," Bull exclaimed as he walked up, Maria under one arm, Anna the other.

"Come. Sit with us," Rosa said as she motioned for them to sit next to her. She looked at Dylan, squeezed his hand, and let go. Bull began to animatedly rehash his adventures in Club Cleopatra as Maria and Anna laughed and attempted to get a few words in. Though happy to see Bull, Dylan was disappointed he didn't have more time to talk with Rosa. It turned out he would never hear the rest of her story.

Chapter 18

Flashback

2025

Floyd raised his glass of Guinness, looked at Lisa and Alex, and said, "It's been a quick trip so far, but I feel like we're on the right track."

After spending a full day in Dublin the day before, they had left early this morning and fast-tracked their retracing of Dylan and Bull's journey so that they could catch the ferry leaving Ireland at 5:45 p.m. tomorrow. It left only once per week, so they could not afford to miss it. They rented a car in Dublin, and Floyd was designated as the driver. The trip from Dublin to Shannon was a thrill ride as Floyd fumbled with operating a stick shift with his left hand while driving on the opposite side of the car and the opposite side of the road. On top of that, the road widths often didn't accommodate two vehicles simultaneously, and there were occasional stops so that cows or sheep could cross in front of them.

After reaching Shannon, they cruised straight through Limerick, and had a late lunch in Cork, where Floyd tried to settle his nerves from the hair-raising driving experience. Then, after a two-hour trip through constant drizzle, they arrived in the town of New Ross.

"Mrs. Kavanaugh's B&B is nowhere to be found, but I'm so glad we've discovered the Theatre Tavern, where Dylan and Bull visited with the O'Malleys and first learned about the lost Irish Crown Jewels." Floyd looked around the place, abuzz with locals talking and laughing. "Hey Alex," he shouted over the din. Then he lowered his voice and asked, "Now that you've had a little time to think, tell us what you learned in Dublin."

Alex stirred her tea for a few moments, then said, "I read through Cillian Donnelly's records judiciously—his journal and all the letters I could find. I then read everything I could from his sister, Sinead, and, of course, Molly O'Leary. At first, I didn't think I'd found anything new. But as I started triangulating what I was reading, I came to believe that Molly had had a baby. A new name suddenly appeared in letters dated after 1910: Cormac. At first, it didn't make sense. I'd never seen the name before. But in one letter to Cillian, Molly cryptically wrote 'little Cormac, looks like his father.' I started to put two and two together."

"Cormac! Well, that's a twist. Could you find any more information about him? That could be an important clue. Did the letters confirm his last name?" Lisa asked.

"I'd assumed it was Cillian's baby, but now that I think about it, I can't guarantee that."

"I wonder where he grew up?" Lisa mused.

"There are references to Figline Valdarno, Velletri, both in Italy, and Corfu, Greece, in the later letters. We keep seeing these names. Everything is complicated due to World War I. Italy joined the war in 1915, and the island of Corfu was occupied by the French and the

Serbs in 1916. Somewhere in the middle of all that were Molly and Cormac."

Floyd chimed in, "It sounds like we need to focus on those places, plus Cassis, France. The boys visited all of them, which now makes sense. They were following clues. Can you recall anything else that seemed significant?"

"Yes!" Alex exclaimed. "I just remembered, there was a reference to a Giovanni Rossi from Figline Valdarno in one letter."

"Dylan talks about visiting Rossi's restaurant in his journal," Lisa said excitedly. "I re-read the entire journal last night."

Floyd felt more alive than he had in years. "This is fascinating! We have a lot to think about. So... here are the next steps, unless I'm missing something. We're going to take the ferry tomorrow. Then it gets really fun. We'll retrace their steps through northern and central France. I must admit, I've always wanted to visit these places. We'll tour the cathedrals and do our best to follow the path laid out in Dylan's journal. After that, we'll take a train to Bordeaux and down to Blanes. After Blanes, we'll go to Cassis. That's where I think things may get really interesting. I looked in my Rick Steves' *Europe* book and saw there's a Kelly's B&B in Cassis. Could it be the same family? I guess we'll find out when we get there."

Lisa chimed in, "Sounds like a good plan, but...we aren't going to sleep on the deck of the ferry, are we?"

Floyd laughed, "No. I booked rooms for all three of us. I figure we can get a feel for what they experienced without sleeping in deck chairs." He glanced at Lisa. "There's even a small gym. I know you like to work out. I may even see you there."

She looked at him and smiled.

Alex added, "I'm looking forward to the adventure. I never ventured beyond Ireland during my previous trips, so it will be great to visit other historic places."

Lisa interjected, "I'm curious to see Blanes. I was fascinated by the story in Dylan's journal about his interaction with Rosa. She seemed very wise."

Floyd drained his Guinness, looked around the bar, then at both of them, and said with a yawn, "I'm gonna crash. Look forward to tomorrow."

***

The ferry crawled towards France on its twenty-hour journey. Floyd and Lisa walked around the ship for an hour. Not much to see. They watched a movie in the TV lounge. Not very comfortable. Had dinner in a self-serve restaurant. The worst meal of the trip. After about four hours, they decided to go to their rooms and meet the next morning. Floyd thought to himself, *This is a pretty dull way to travel. I hope it wasn't a waste of time. I guess when you're eighteen, have a tight budget and a Eurail pass, you do what you have to do.*

Alex asked to be left alone. She walked around the entire ship. It was different from the one she'd traveled on over forty years ago, but it was close enough. She found an area with a railing overlooking the sea, which was similar to her experience in 1983. Looking over the railing, she watched the waves, then closed her eyes. The man was to her left. He was wearing a tan bomber jacket and a blue cap. He had long blond hair and dark eyes. He was patient, just watching her. She opened her eyes for a moment and then closed them again. This time, the man was almost upon her. Same long blond hair, but the hat was backwards...and he wasn't wearing a bomber jacket. He had something shiny in his hand. He spoke to her. She was scared. Then she saw Dylan...

She opened her eyes again. Her heart was racing. The memory was painful. She was sweating, even though the ship's movement created a breeze. What was her memory telling her? What was the deal with this guy? Why did the blond man's appearance change?

Later, as they headed towards the Rouen Cathedral, walking along stone streets constructed in the Middle Ages, she shared her strange memory with Floyd and Lisa.

"What do you think it means?" Floyd asked.

"I don't know. I always remembered the guy with long blond hair. It was just weird that he seemed different the second time I saw him. There could be a perfectly reasonable explanation. Maybe he turned his hat around due to the wind. I do that sometimes. He could have taken off his jacket for a multitude of reasons. I'm probably making a big deal out of nothing," Alex said with a sigh.

"I think there's a reason for everything," said Lisa. "As we retrace Dylan and my dad's steps, let's just note everything that seems like it could be important. You never know," she said, as she looked down to make sure she didn't trip on the cobblestones. "Some little thing could turn out to be critical to solving the mystery."

At that moment, they turned a corner and were immediately dwarfed by the massive cathedral towering over them.

"Now we're getting somewhere," Alex said.

Chapter 19

Kelly's B&B

1983

DYLAN AND BULL WALKED through the town of Cassis, a fishing village on the French Riviera known for its cliffs and sheltered inlets called *calanques*. They felt as if they had stepped into an impressionist painting, with pastel-painted buildings lining stone streets. It was late, after ten at night.

The pair had left Blanes on the 7:10 a.m. train and taken a circuitous four-train route to get to Cassis. At one point, they'd almost missed their stop and jumped off the train after it had started, landing on the opposite railroad tracks, packs and guitar in hand. Again, thankfully, there had been no train on that track. They were tempting fate. Racing up the stairs, they found the next train with three minutes to spare. Otherwise, they wouldn't have arrived until the next day.

Now they were looking for a bed-and-breakfast owned by the Kellys, which Cara had recommended after the John Mayall concert. Stopping under an awning, Dylan pulled out his *Let's Go Europe* book to find the address to the B&B.

"*Bonsoir*," a melodic and surprisingly Spanish accent caught their attention.

They turned and were stunned to see a woman looking at them. She had shoulder-length brown hair and striking green eyes.

"May I help you?" she asked in accented English.

They both looked behind them to see if she was talking to someone else and then turned back to her. Dylan said, "Uh. Um. Yes. We just arrived—we're looking for Kelly's B&B."

She took a step towards them, her short skirt highlighting her athletic legs as she edged closer. She was older than they were, but not by much. She smiled and said, "I know exactly where that is." She gave them directions, said "*Au revoir*," and then slowly turned around and walked away. They watched, mouths agape, until she disappeared into an alley. They looked at each other again.

"Well, that's a good start for Cassis," Bull said.

Kelly's B&B was a converted commercial building on Rue Elzeard Prévost, a side street. From its appearance, the place couldn't have more than two or three rooms. Dylan knocked on the unusual square wooden door. Nothing. Bull leaned forward and rapped a little harder. From inside, they heard, "Wait, I'm coming," spoken in French with an Irish accent. A pale, portly man opened the door, looked at Dylan and Bull, and observing that they were likely English-speaking, said sternly, "We are closed. Come back tomorrow."

Bull held up his hand. "Please excuse us," he said. And before the man could answer, Bull added, "but Cara from Ireland told us to come see you. You're Mr. Kelly, right?"

He nodded but was silent. Then his face lit up, his eyes sparkled, and he smiled broadly. He said, in English, "Cara, the college girl from Dublin? She was a bright girl." He looked both ways and then leaned in and said, "Isn't she the one with the nice legs?"

Bull laughed. "Yes. She was very nice to us and said you might be able to give us a room."

Mr. Kelly put out his hand and said, "Welcome. My name is Dan. I own this place with my wife, Kayleigh. Who, may I ask, are you?"

After introductions, Dylan said, "Mr. Kelly—"

"Dan, please call me Dan." He smiled and patted Dylan on the back.

"We came from Spain and have no French currency."

"No worries. We can settle later. I bet you are hungry." He yelled, "Kayleigh! Can you pull something together for my two guests, Dylan and...Bull?"

Bull laughed, "Yep, it's Bull."

***

The café only had four tables. It was on a narrow street that they would never have found on their own. Squeezed between a laundromat and a tobacco store, it had no name other than Bistro. The proprietor, a diminutive bald man with a neatly trimmed goatee, beret, and dour face, made an elderly man move tables and insisted Dylan and Bull sit at the one by the window. The best seat in the house. They asked for menus, and the owner shook his head violently and disappeared behind a small curtain in the back. A minute later, he returned and placed a bottle of wine and a carafe of water on the table, along with a baguette. Then he disappeared again.

"The Kellys are so nice," Bull said as he broke the bread and handed a piece to Dylan.

"Yeah, can you believe they put us in the extra bedroom in their actual house? That B&B is very popular, there's no way we could have gotten a room on such short notice," Dylan said.

"It's incredible, other than I bumped into Mrs. Kelly when I came out of the bathroom this morning," Bull said with a laugh. "Glad I was wearing clothes."

"And then he insisted we come to this restaurant. He knows the owner," Dylan said.

Mr. Beret brought them a large bowl of *moules marinière*, which they discovered was a bowl of mussels in their shells, served in a cream sauce with garlic, butter, shallots, and other herbs. He also placed a plate of French fries with mayonnaise between them, then disappeared.

Bull cracked open a shell and tried his first mussel. He looked at Dylan and said excitedly, "The sauce is amazing. Wow. Dan is the man!"

And that was the first of four dishes, each as good as the last. After lunch, Dylan and Bull pulled out their wallets to pay, and Mr. Serious Face shook his head sternly and said, "Dan, Dan."

Bull said, "Thank you very much, it was delicious," in French, and as they left, he loosened the top button of his pants.

After a ten-minute walk, they found the bookstore Dan had told them about the night before. From the front, it looked small; however, when they walked through the heavy metal front door, they realized that it was a labyrinth of rooms, each with a different category of books. They wandered through in amazement.

The first room was entitled Histoire, with the word stenciled on a stained-glass door. To its left was Biographie. After passing signs for Voyage, Fiction, Classiques, and La Science-Fiction, they found a hallway that led to even more rooms. To their happy surprise they found an Albums de Discs room, filled with record albums and posters of rock stars covering the walls. Then next to it, Livres de Anglais, with a picture of William Shakespeare on the door.

Dylan gasped, "I don't think I'll leave this place today."

Bull laughed, "Just remember we have dinner with Dan and Kayleigh and their granddaughter tonight at eight."

Dylan smiled. "Okay, I can always come back tomorrow."

They walked into the Livres de Anglais room, packed wall to wall and floor to ceiling with books published in English. *A beautiful sight*, Dylan thought.

Bull looked at Dylan and said, "Let's divide and conquer. Yell if you find something," and they separated to search for books on Irish history.

Dylan walked by an entire wall of Kurt Vonnegut's books. He was in heaven.

Bull glanced over and noticed Dylan leaning against a chair, immersed in *Slaughterhouse Five*, and smacked him on the shoulder. "There'll be time for that later, let's find the Irish book."

"Okay, okay. Couldn't help it," Dylan said.

Five minutes later, Bull motioned Dylan over. "Here we go."

They each started pulling Irish history books from a bookshelf next to a large window. Dylan glanced outside and observed an alley filled with young people reading while sitting on metal chairs and sipping coffee or tea. *We aren't the only ones that love this place*, he thought. He flipped open a book and read the table of contents. "I found one!" he exclaimed. He handed Bull the book, *The Twentieth Century History of Ireland*. "Look at Chapter 13." Sure enough, it was dedicated to the Irish Crown Jewel theft. There was also a chapter on the first women at Trinity College in Dublin. "I kinda wish we'd visited Dublin," Dylan said.

Bull nodded. "Yeah. I think we'll find there are many places we'd like to visit, but we won't be able to fit them all in. We'll have to plan a second trip—maybe after we graduate from college."

Dylan's face lit up. "That sounds great. I'll start noting these places in my journal." After a thorough search, they found another book with copies of contemporary news articles about the theft of the Irish Crown Jewels, then headed to the record album section.

"I've been wanting to check out the new David Bowie album, *Let's Dance*, the one Stevie Ray Vaughan played on," Dylan said. "It seems like every magazine we've seen in the train stations has had Bowie's face on it. Maybe they'll have a cassette I can buy, if it's not too expensive, so I can listen to it on my Walkman."

Bull found a section of albums by the Rolling Stones, and said, "Look, here's a bootleg live album with our friend Mick Taylor playing guitar with Keith Richards."

"This place is great," Dylan said as he thumbed through the sleeves of Neil Young albums he'd never seen before.

Two hours later, they left the store with a little extra bounce in their step. They were two new books, two cassettes, a set of guitar strings, and a *Rolling Stone* magazine richer, and 84 francs poorer.

***

"So, what did you do all day?" Dan asked Dylan and Bull after they sat down at a corner table in a small restaurant in an alley two blocks from the B&B. Dan, short and stout, with wispy brown hair and a pale complexion—despite the beach location—sat at the head of the table. His wife, Kayleigh, sat to his right. She was petite with short brown hair, blue eyes, and slightly tanned skin. She said she rode five to ten miles per day on her bicycle, and it showed. Across the table from Dan, and in between Dylan and Bull, was their granddaughter, Shannon. Dylan guessed she was in her early twenties. She was maybe five feet tall if she was lucky, he thought. She had short red hair and green eyes and was wearing a long tan dress, which looked out of place among the other patrons dressed in light fabrics and bright colors.

"Lunch today was incredible. Thanks for the recommendation," Bull said enthusiastically.

"Pierre is an amazing chef," said Dan. "I'm glad you enjoyed it. It's very difficult to get a table there. He doesn't advertise, but he's always full, with a waiting list. People come from Marseille all the time to eat there."

"We also spent a good part of the day at the bookstore you recommended," Dylan added. "It was by far the best bookstore we've seen in Europe—and it also had records, which was a pleasant surprise."

"What were you looking for in the bookstore?" asked Shannon quietly.

"It's an interesting story—" Dylan started to say, only to be interrupted by a waiter arriving at the table. Dan spoke to him sternly in French, and he quickly left.

"Please go on, Dylan," Dan said, as a young waitress in a short black skirt and white blouse appeared and placed carafes of wine and bowls of bread on the table.

"Okay. We were on the ferry from Ireland to France, and I ran into a woman who's a professor from UCLA in California," said Dylan. "She was exhausted and anxious, and she latched on to me. She thought she was being followed. Anyway, she told me a story about research she was doing on the lost Irish Crown Jewels and a young college girl in the early 1900s who she thinks was somehow involved. It's possible that she traveled through Europe. Bull and I are interested to learn more about this legend." He didn't mention the key or the blond man.

"Do you recall the name of the college girl?" Kayleigh interjected.

"I do. The name has stuck with me: Molly O'Leary. Apparently, after the jewels went missing, so did she."

Kayleigh gasped. She and Dan exchanged glances. "Go ahead and tell them," Dan said.

"You're not going to believe this," she said, "but Molly O'Leary was my nanny when I was a child. She arrived on our doorstep and asked for work. She knew we were Irish. I was six years old. She lived with us for about two years. I remember this time clearly. I loved her. She was so nice to me. Interestingly, you mention missing jewels and a trunk. I have a story about Molly that I've thought about many times over the years. It made a huge impression on me. I shared it with Dan once, but I haven't told anyone else, other than my mother—and she told me I was imagining things."

"Please, tell us the story!" Bull said.

Shannon, drawn into the conversation, said, "Yes, I've never heard it either. Tell us."

Kayleigh continued, "I was playing dress up with Molly. She was fun like that. She was more of a playmate than a caregiver, from my perspective. We were putting on old clothes and modeling them for each other, and she told me to follow her into her room. She pulled an old trunk out from beneath her bed, inserted a long key into its lock, and opened it. Then she reached underneath a white blanket, removed the most beautiful necklace, and put it on me. I was only a child, but I could tell that it was made of real gems and so many diamonds. I remember she called me the Queen of Ireland, and we each wore the jewels and laughed. Suddenly, we heard my mother walking down the hall. Molly put her finger to her lips, then quickly took the jewelry, placed it in the trunk, and pushed it under her bed. I never saw the trunk or the jewelry again. But I have remembered this for my entire life."

Dylan pulled the *Twentieth Century History of Ireland* out of his backpack, opened it to Chapter 13, then handed it to Kayleigh. It was a picture of the missing jewels.

"Oh *mon Dieu*. That's it! I'll never forget them."

Bull looked at Kayleigh and Dan and said, "What are the chances? This is incredible."

"What happened to Molly?" Dylan asked, his expression serious.

Kayleigh's face turned pale. "It was a sad ending. Not long after our dress-up game, Molly started to get skittish. She told me privately that she thought she was being followed. She had hoped that Cassis was far enough off the beaten path that she could live here forever but, alas, it wasn't meant to be. One day, I came home from school, and she was gone. I was devastated. She hadn't even said goodbye. I remember that night, as I got ready to go to sleep, I found a letter from her under my pillow."

"What did it say?" Dylan asked breathlessly.

At that moment, the waiter appeared and began placing bowls of onion soup on the table. Dan asked him to hurry and leave them to talk.

All eyes at the table were directed at Kayleigh, except for Bull's. He was tasting the soup. Just as Keyleigh was about to speak, he gasped and said, "This soup is amazing." Dylan looked at Bull, frustration flashing in his eyes. Bull said, "Sorry, please go on," as he took another sip and winked at Dylan.

"I don't remember all the details, and the letter is lost to time. I do remember it mentioned Figline Valdarno, which is a town in Italy, and

Corfu, a Greek island. And Molly told me not to tell anyone. I guess it's okay now, since it's seventy years later..."

"How on earth did you remember the names?" Dylan asked gently.

"I had never heard of either place, but they stuck with me. I've since visited both spots, hoping I would somehow run into her again. Both places are worth visiting, by the way. I hadn't thought of Molly in years until this conversation. I missed her for a long time after she left."

Bull looked up from the map in his *Let's Go Europe* book. "Figline Valdarno is just outside of Florence, which we've been planning to go to all along. And, of course, Corfu is on our itinerary. Even Cara and her friend, Nessa, recommended Corfu. Pelekas Beach."

"Everything points to Pelekas Beach," Dylan said with a smile, as he wondered about the significance of these two places to Molly and possibly the lost Irish jewels.

They finished another incredible French meal and walked outside, headed back to the B&B. Dan asked, "So, what's your plan tomorrow?"

Bull looked at him and said, "First, thanks for being such a great host. We've had a wonderful experience in Cassis—all because of you and your family. As for tomorrow, Dylan and I want to explore more on foot. He's a runner, and I want to climb to the top of the cliffs."

Dan said, "That sounds like a good day. Please be careful. The cliffs are some of the highest in all of Europe and the trails can be dangerous. It's a 1,300-foot drop to the ocean. It would be a sad way to end your trip."

Shannon spoke up, "If you'd like, I could meet you tomorrow morning and give you some suggestions for your Cassis adventure."

"That would be great," Dylan said. "How about 9 a.m.?"

***

Julian sat across from Adriana at the streetside café table, glancing through a newspaper while slyly watching the building across the street. To anyone walking by, they looked like two serious hikers having a coffee before heading into the mountains.

"So, tell me what you've observed so far," he said in a serious tone.

Adriana said, "Two nights ago, I saw the Americans get off the train, and I followed them. They appeared lost, so I asked them if they needed help. They were looking for Kelly's B&B. I pointed the boys in the right direction. I later visited the establishment and met the owners. The Kelly family has had a B&B in Cassis for a long time, decades. And...they're Irish."

"Well, I saw the note in the journal about a B&B in Cassis, so that makes sense. I don't know if there is any significance to the Kellys or if it was just a recommendation from a fellow traveler," Julian commented.

"Yesterday, I tailed them again. They spent several hours in a bookstore. After waiting for a long time, I went in and found them both thumbing through record albums. I didn't notice anything special. Then they had dinner with the Kellys last night—and their granddaughter. After dinner, I overheard one of them saying that they were going to separate and go on adventures today. They were planning to meet the granddaughter at 9 a.m."

Just as she finished the sentence, Julian saw the three of them exit the B&B and begin walking towards the trail to the cliffs. The young woman looked at the big guy and spoke animatedly, as if she were drawing a map in the air for him. Then she turned to the slim one and pointed in a different direction. They talked for a couple of minutes, and then the two men headed away from town, towards the trail system.

Julian threw some francs on the table, and he and Adriana followed them at a distance.

"I'm pretty sure the big guy is Bull, and the other is Dylan. I'll follow Bull," Julian said.

At the trailhead, the boys separated, and so did Julian and Adriana. Several other people were heading into the mountains, so it was easy to join them and blend in.

Geez, this guy is in good shape, Julian thought as he struggled to keep up with Bull. At first, the trail was relatively flat. But after about five minutes of walking, it quickly turned into a strenuous hike on rocky trails that meandered up the mountain. Julian tucked in behind an older couple hiking with ski poles and backpacks. There were two or three other people in the vicinity as well. He was well hidden, and he could see Bull effortlessly pushing his way up the mountainside.

Bull was relentless; he never slowed down. Finally, he reached the peak of the highest mountain, which overlooked a narrow, white limestone-walled inlet, highlighted with a cliff-framed beach. A beach that could only be reached on foot. Bull headed straight for the edge of the cliff, with its thousand-foot drop-off. Julian could see Bull standing on the rim, looking down at the shore for a moment, and then he did a little celebration dance. A moment later, Julian saw another hiker heading directly towards Bull. Before Julian could react, the man had casually bumped into Bull and walked away. Julian tried to see where the man went, but lost him on one of the nearby steep trails. He quickly looked back to check on Bull, but he was gone.

Julian rushed to where he had last seen Bull and quickly spotted the big guy. He'd fallen over the side of the cliff onto a ledge, and he was grasping for purchase, his large body swaying as he held on for his life. Julian lowered his hand and yelled. Bull grabbed it and was able to pull himself back onto the top of the cliff edge. He lay there momentarily, catching his breath. His clothes were torn and bloody, but he seemed okay. Julian, not wanting to be recognized, quickly left the scene. As he hiked down the mountain, he thought, *Who would want to hurt Bull, and why?* He searched for the mysterious man on the trails, but he was gone.

***

Adriana hadn't realized she'd have to run today. As soon as the boys separated, Dylan took off at a brisk trot. Fortunately, she was a skilled runner, so she followed him, trying to keep enough distance so that he didn't notice her. He headed up a steep trail and kept a strong pace. *This is going to be tough,* she thought. Within a few minutes, she'd lost him. She decided to continue following the trail, hoping to catch up with him again.

Thirty minutes later, she reached the top of a cliff. She looked around as she caught her breath. Nothing. She thought she'd lost him for good and was going to head back down when she noticed a movement by the cliff edge. It was the American runner! He was lying on his stomach, with his head over the edge, looking down. After a few moments, he pulled himself up and started walking along the edge. He occasionally stopped, looked down, stared, and started walking again. Then he leaned over, stretched his hamstrings, bounced a couple times, raced toward the trail, and started sprinting down, almost recklessly, due to the angle of the descent. She attempted to follow, but he quickly lost her.

***

Remy's Bar, with a view of Cassis harbor, was a popular spot for the locals. It was constructed on an overlook with views of the ocean from every table. Colorful umbrellas blocked the sun as needed. Shannon sat at a table with two empty chairs, sipping on a cold drink as she waited for Dylan and Bull. She fumbled with the bag she'd brought, placing it beneath her chair. She was almost unrecognizable compared to the night before, wearing a white crochet cover-up, the bright green bikini underneath showing through. Her skin glowed after spending the day at the beach with friends, in striking contrast to her pale green eyes.

Dylan arrived first, wearing cargo shorts, running shoes, and a white T-shirt with 1980 Dallas White Rock Marathon stenciled in small print across the back. After a double-take to make sure it was the same woman he'd met the night before, he sat down next to her and said, "Good evening, Shannon, it's nice to see you."

"How was your adventure?" she asked.

"I had a great run up the mountain, and the view from the cliffs was incredible. The trip back down did a number on me, but it was worth it. Now, Bull had a slightly different experience."

"What happened?" she asked, suddenly serious.

"I'm not sure. Bull told me to meet you and that he'd follow shortly after taking a shower and changing. He looked pretty beat up."

"I hope he's okay. Would you like a drink?"

"A beer would be great. I'm parched," Dylan said as he looked around the bar. There were six other tables, all fully occupied. The ambience was casual, shorts and bathing suits being the standard attire. Dylan heard French, Spanish, and English being spoken. The average age was probably twenty. "Interesting place," he said.

"Yeah. It's our version of a speakeasy; it doesn't show up on any maps. My friends and I come here to avoid the tourists. It's a combination of locals and expats," she said as she studied Dylan's eyes.

At that moment, they spotted Bull in the distance, limping like a bear who had been shot. As he got closer, they could see scratches across his face and on his arms. He was wearing khaki shorts and a loose, sleeveless shirt. He finally reached the table and sat with a thud.

A bikini-clad waitress arrived with Dylan's beer. Bull grabbed it and drank it down in one gulp.

"Sorry," he said to Dylan. Then he turned to the waitress and held up two fingers. She chuckled and headed back to the bar.

"Okay, Bull, I'm dying to know what happened to you. Spill the beans," Dylan said.

"Well...it started off great. I hiked for a long time. Then it got really steep, so I had to use my hands to climb the last few yards to the top of the mountain. When I got to the top, I walked over to the edge of the cliff. A few other people were doing the same climb. I didn't think much of it. Anyway, as I was enjoying the view, someone bumped me, hard enough to push me over the edge. Fortunately, I didn't fall 1,300 feet into the ocean. I slid down the rocky surface, trying to grasp anything I could along the way, and finally landed about ten feet below, on a ledge, barely holding on. I'm not gonna lie. I was scared. There was no way to pull myself back up, and I started losing my grip. I thought it was the end—"

"What happened next?" Shannon and Dylan said simultaneously.

"I heard someone yell to get my attention, and then a hand appeared from above. I grabbed it and, with his assistance, was able to get back to the top of the cliff. I lay there for a minute, catching my breath. Then I stood up and looked around so that I could thank the guy...and he was gone. Never saw his face."

"Wow! I'm so glad you're okay," Shannon said, concern in her eyes.

"I'll be fine. Just got a bunch of scratches. It could have been disastrous. I think I'm done with cliffs."

"Do you think you were pushed?" Dylan asked.

"I sure hope not. I want to think it was simply an accident and someone just bumped into me. But I'm not sure..."

Dylan worried that their mysterious stalker might have found them. If so, his behavior was escalating.

The bikini girl showed up again, smiling, with four beers. "I thought you might want another round," she said in broken English with an alluring French accent. She looked at Bull's scratches and said, "Are you okay?"

"I'm fine. It's nothing compared to football practice," he joked.

Shannon changed the subject. "I was intrigued by my grandmother's story last night. She and I spent most of this morning going through her old scrapbooks and boxes of things from her youth." She grabbed the bag from beneath her chair, opened it, and placed a letter on the table.

"What's this?" Dylan asked.

"This is a letter to Molly from a person named Cillian. Molly had left it behind. My mom remembered that a man named Cillian had visited a couple of times and stayed at the B&B. He was Irish."

"What does it say?"

"Read it for yourself." She handed Dylan the letter.

He placed it on the table so Bull could read it too.

"It was received not long before Molly left here. It's dated January 3, 1909," she added.

Dylan read the letter out loud.

Dearest Molly,

I was glad to hear of your comfort in Cassis—a fine place, as you well know. I hold fond memories of my own time there. The sun, the air, the sea—all better than the grey and damp climate of Dublin this time of year. But the finest thing there is you, and the truth is, my heart grows sore missing you.

First, let me thank you for the key. You've shown great courage, Molly, and trust in sending it. I swear to you now, by the Blessed Virgin and all the saints, I shall guard it with my life. The plan is nearly in place. I shall write again with the particulars of our meeting, and once we are together, we'll be free of this cursed bounty and begin our life as we always dreamed—somewhere warm, and far from all this noise.

But you mustn't delay, Molly. You must leave Cassis at once. Word has reached me that your hiding place is no longer your own. It is no longer safe. I fear eyes are upon you. You must go swiftly and with care.

My father's friend, Giovanni Rossi, will receive you. He has a modest stone house outside Figline Valdarno, southeast of Florence. Quiet and out of the way. He knows nothing of the chest, but he knows to expect you. Pack only what you need. Place the chest among your things—as if it were nothing—and travel light. Do not tarry.

I shall try to write to you again in Figline Valdarno. Until then, my prayers and my heart are with you always.

Yours, in love and haste,

Cillian

Dylan looked up. "Figline Valdarno—that's the place your grandmother mentioned in the letter Molly left her."

Bull finished his beer and slammed it on the table, then said, "I'd say it's time we head to Italy and see if we can learn anything about Giovanni Rossi, and if we're lucky, more about Molly...and maybe even the jewels."

"I think you should," Shannon said. "I hope you find what you're looking for. But, hey, you can't leave now, so let's enjoy Cassis for one last night together." She raised her glass.

***

At a table on the other side of the bar, Julian and Adriana casually sat and observed Dylan, Bull, and the Kellys' granddaughter.

"It's good to see that Bull is okay. A little scraped up, I think. I'm glad I was there. I don't think he'd have made it otherwise," Julian said, as he observed Bull talking and gesturing, while Dylan and the girl listened intently. He tried unsuccessfully to hear what Bull was saying.

"Yes. I still can't figure out who would have tried to push Bull," Adriana said as she adjusted her bikini top.

"Someone else is on their trail. This surprises me. I thought I was the only person who had observed the professor in Dublin. Then, when we were on the ferry, I got a bad feeling about someone else on the ship, but I didn't put two and two together at the time. Unfortunately, whoever it is has a very different intention from mine. He seems to want the treasure at any cost. I simply want the Irish Crown Jewels. I don't want anyone hurt," said Julian.

Adriana nodded. "I believe the boys are starting to figure some things out. We need to stay close to them—not just to try to find the jewels, but also to protect them."

"Look, the girl pulled out something, and they're reading it. They seem very excited." Julian squinted to see what they were studying at their table.

Adriana stood up and headed toward them. She sauntered by. They were distracted and didn't notice her as she stood at a nearby table, pretending to look at her watch. She heard them mention the name Figline Valdarno. *That must be where they're heading next*, she thought.

Chapter 20

Figline Valdarno

1983

JUNE 21, 1983; FIGLINE Valdarno, Italy

This morning, I ran through the hilly area of Figline, then came back and put on my last clean clothes. We were out late last night at this strange commune in the mountains outside of town. I played guitar for a few hippies who seemed impressed. Fun. It was raining and cool this morning, which felt good. Yesterday, we took the 7:24 a.m. train to Florence and met Melinda, an American college student studying here. She gave us a free tour! Besides being smart and knowledgeable, she was beautiful. I had a hard time deciding whether to stare at the incredible Renaissance art or her. Florence is astonishing—maybe my favorite place we've visited so far from a cultural perspective. Of course, getting a college-level history lesson in real life didn't hurt. It was a great day. We're meeting her again today for lunch at a place called Rossi's—maybe it will lead to a clue. By the way, Italian money is even more fun than Spanish. It's 1,700 lira to the dollar. We're practically millionaires! Listened to "Who's Next" this morning. Interesting reference to the bad man behind blue eyes...

Dylan hopped off the train at the Figline Valdarno station, backpack in one hand, guitar in the other. The doors closed behind him, and the train headed south, away from Florence. He could see Bull banging on the doors from inside the train as it sped away. Bull had missed the stop. *Those doors close so quickly.* Dylan and Bull had prepared for this type of event. The plan was for Bull to get off at the next stop and catch the first possible return train. Since Dylan didn't know how long that would take, it was his job to find a room. Then he'd return for Bull.

It was a half-mile walk to the city center, relatively short compared to many of their hikes from train stations to their lodging. It was a quiet place at this time of day. Dylan had trouble finding information on Figline Valdarno. It was barely covered in *Let's Go Europe*, so it became an adventure. Though it was an ancient city with a rich history and impressive architecture, there were very few tourists. They all flocked to Florence, about twenty miles north. The city center was an immense plaza surrounded by yellow two- and three-story buildings, an ancient church, and other impressive historic buildings. He saw a sign for a *pensione* in one of the buildings overlooking the plaza and entered through a wooden door that was older than the entire United States of America. The innkeeper had one apartment left. An apartment! It had two bedrooms and a living room. And it was affordable. Dylan immediately decided that this would be a good home base for visiting Florence, exploring Tuscany, and doing their research on Giovanni Rossi and Molly.

The innkeeper spoke in broken English. She reminded Dylan of Cruella de Vil from the *101 Dalmatians* movie he'd seen as a kid.

She was gaunt and wrinkled, with short black-and-white hair and a crooked nose. However, she had a warm smile and was excited to brag about the commune.

"Figline Valdarno...is a small town, but very old, very proud. You know Dante? He wrote about this place in his book, *La Divina Commedia*, a long time ago... Early 1300s, I think. We are happy for that. This is big thing for us."

She pointed behind Dylan's head, "There, across the piazza—you see?—That is the Church, Santa Maria. Very old. The name comes from Pope...Pope Alessandro Borgia, in the year 1493. Inside, so many beautiful things. Painting, sculpture, all very old, *molto classico*. Next to the church, we have the museum... Museo d'Arte Sacra, yes? It has many old works, from the fifteenth to sixteenth centuries. Real treasures. And here also, we have an old monastery—*Santa Croce delle Agostiniane*. A very peaceful place. From year...1542, I believe. Very quiet, very spiritual. You feel it. Figline Valdarno is a great place to stay."

Dylan noted the attractions they should visit, then lugged his backpack and guitar up three flights of narrow wooden stairs. After walking through a long, dimly lit hallway, he placed the slender bronze key in the well-worn lock on the door to the apartment. He wondered what to expect. He pushed the heavy door open and entered a spacious sitting room, with a picture window overlooking the plaza—and a couch! He dropped his gear by the front door and checked out the two bedrooms. Each had a good-sized bed, a desk, and a closet. This was the nicest and largest place they had stayed in on the entire trip. The communal bathroom was down the hall, but that was to be expected. He gazed out the window at the plaza. Restaurants had placed tables with umbrellas in front of their shops. Locals were eating and drinking while enjoying the music of a harpist in the center of the square. A small child licked an ice cream cone as he walked beside his mother, who was window shopping. *I think we'll like it here*, Dylan thought.

Minutes later, he was sitting alone on a long wooden bench, gazing into the distance as the next train approached. It was a peaceful railway station, with a small light-yellow ticket office and two uncovered tracks. At that moment, he was the only person there. "Every Breath You Take" by the Police played on his Walkman radio as he finished reading the most recent issue of *Time* magazine, emblazoned with a close-up of British Prime Minister Margaret Thatcher, and the headline, '*Maggie By A Mile*'. He was fascinated that most of the songs on the local radio station came from English-speaking artists, and he chortled when the DJ spoke rapid-fire Italian between songs.

The doors opened abruptly, and Bull barreled onto the platform, holding his heavy backpack as if it were a toy. He was laughing and waved at someone in the window of the departing train. Dylan rose, rolled up the magazine, put it in his back pocket, and walked towards Bull.

"Hey, how was your train ride? And what was all that about?" Dylan asked when Bull turned around.

"Sorry about missing the stop earlier. Those doors closed so quickly. Anyway, the ride turned out great. I met this American college girl, Melinda. Believe it or not, she's from Texas. She's doing a semester abroad at a college campus just outside Figline, studying art history. We agreed to meet in Florence tomorrow, and she'll show us around. She's heading there now and staying with a friend tonight," Bull rambled before quickly changing gears. "Hey; any luck finding a place?"

"I found a *great* place," Dylan said. "This looks like a cool town—lots of history. No tourists. Great home base for a few days. A trip to Florence tomorrow sounds great. Let's grab some pizza and ice cream on the way to town. I saw a place. I'm starved."

***

Melinda extended her hand and introduced herself to Dylan. As he took her hand, Dylan thought, *How does Bull do it? She's beautiful.* Brunette hair, brown eyes shimmering beneath dark lashes, and a smile that made his heart skip a beat. Dylan had to stop himself from staring. He got it together and responded, "Great to meet you, Melinda. I'm Dylan. I hear you're our tour guide today."

She grinned. "It will be my pleasure. I've been here since January, so I'm sort of an expert now. I can also show you around Rome, Venice, and Milan, if you'd like," she said with a laugh. "Ever since running into Bull yesterday, I've been thinking about this. I'm excited to show you Florence, which is my favorite place in the world. I have a completely free day—so let's enjoy it together!"

Dylan looked at Bull, then back at Melinda, and said, "Sounds like a great day. Can't wait."

She continued, "First, we're going to the Accademia Gallery to see the *David*. There's not a lot more to see there, so we'll get that out of the way before the tourists show up. Then we'll head to the Uffizi Galleries, which contain Renaissance art from Michelangelo, Leonardo da Vinci, Botticelli, and more. We'll spend a lot of time there. After that, we'll go to the Duomo, which is Florence's amazing cathedral. It was completed in 1436. Think about that! I hope you're in shape, because we're going to climb to the top—all 463 steps. It's so worth it. The view is like no other. After that, I'll take you to a small ristorante; it's my favorite hole-in-the-wall restaurant in Italy. I think the proprietor likes me. He always gives me special desserts and drinks. You'll never taste better pasta. Finally, we'll visit the Ponte Vecchio, which is a medieval bridge lined with shops. That should be plenty for one day in Florence."

"Melinda, that sounds incredible," Dylan said. He was so distracted that he'd only heard half of what she'd said.

"It's my pleasure. I've been here for a long time. I love it, and it's so nice to meet people from home now and then—especially from my home state. I hadn't heard a 'y'all' in months until I ran into Bull on the train. Oh, and after our busy day, we'll take the train back to Figline Valdarno, and I'll show you the college campus. It's unique. You'll see what I mean when we get there. Oh, and I brought a camera."

"That's great!" said Bull. "We don't have one picture from this trip. It would be nice to be able to send some pictures home to the family."

***

Dylan sat on a deep leather couch in the back of a large parlor in an ancient estate located several miles outside Figline Valdarno. An old guy in a tie-dyed shirt walked by and clapped in Dylan's direc-tion—apparently in response to Dylan playing some guitar earlier in the evening. The three of them had hitched a ride here after returning from Florence. Melinda said she did it all the time since the bus service didn't stop nearby. According to her, there were always people going back and forth, and it was common practice to accept rides from anyone commuting to or from Figline Valdarno. "Little Wing," the Derek & the Dominoes version, blared from speakers placed in each corner of the room.

Next to Dylan was a cowboy. Yes, a cowboy. Wearing pointed boots, jeans, a western shirt, and a ten-gallon hat. He was fast asleep and snoring. At a table to his right was an intense poker game between two college-age American girls and two middle-aged hippies, one with long gray hair pulled back in a ponytail and the other with no hair on his head but a bushy beard that reached his belt. To his left, a half dozen Italian locals were screaming at a soccer match on a small TV, while drinking beers. One woman sat at the bar, reading a paperback novel. Dylan could see her profile. She kinda looked like the woman they had seen in Cassis—the one who'd given them directions; she was certainly memorable. He looked around and found Bull, surrounded by three college girls, giggling and laughing. *He's going to love college*, Dylan thought. He looked back at the bar, and the woman was gone. *Was his mind playing tricks on him?*

Then Dylan spotted Melinda across the room. She motioned for him to join her. He jumped up, forced himself to slow down, and then walked her way, as cool as he could.

She led him out of the craziness and into a small, unoccupied study room down the hall. "I told you this place is unique," she said with a laugh. "It's a tiny campus, and it's right next to an old American commune. And I mean 'commune,' like a socialist society where everyone shares everything. A bunch of these folks are real '60s holdovers. They're harmless. Actually, they protect the girls from the Italian guys."

"Unique is a good word," Dylan said. "So, when do you go home?"

"I head back to Houston at the end of the summer. I took a semester of Italian and several art history classes. Then I was able to convince my parents to let me stay for the summer. I'm teaching Italian to English ex-pats in Florence. It pays really well, and it's a lot of fun." She looked closely at Dylan's eyes.

"I know, my eyes are weird," he said, self-consciously.

"No. Sorry, I didn't mean to stare. I think they're cool. You're different. That's a good thing. Reminds me of Bowie."

Dylan was caught by surprise. *She's familiar with David Bowie? And knows he has unusual eyes? What a cool girl*, he thought.

They walked outside, found a bench, and continued talking. He learned that she was the oldest of four, that she had been in the marching band in high school, and that she had broken up with a long-term boyfriend ("the best thing that ever happened to me," she said) just before leaving for Italy. He surprised himself as he shared his thoughts and dreams with her. There was a special connection, he thought. They talked about meeting up when he returned to Texas in a month.

Then he changed the subject. "Hey. Since you've been in Figline Valdarno for several months, I have a random question for you. Have you ever heard of anyone named Giovanni Rossi or Molly O'Leary? It's a long shot. They would have lived here seventy years ago or so."

"Neither of those names rings a bell." Melinda thought hard. "Wait, there is a restaurant in town called Rossi's. Who knows, maybe there's a connection. Let's go tomorrow. I can help with the translation. Why do you ask?"

"It's a long story," Dylan said just as Bull entered the room and joined them. "Hey, Bull, I was just asking Melinda if she'd ever heard of Giovanni Rossi or Molly."

"Good idea! It's a small town. Maybe someone will know something," Bull said.

"We're going to visit a restaurant called Rossi's tomorrow—worth a try," Melinda said. "So, what's the story? That's an unusual question."

"Tell you what," Dylan said. "We'll explain it over lunch tomorrow. It's getting late. How can we get back to town?"

"There's always a way back," Melinda said. She walked into the party room and yelled, "Anyone returning to Figline?!"

The cowboy woke up, raised his hand, and said in a slurred southern accent, "I am. Someone need a ride?"

She walked over to Dylan, kissed him on the lips, and said, "Cowboy will take you. I'll see you tomorrow."

And she was gone. Dylan stood frozen in place, trying to make sense of what had just happened, until Cowboy tapped him on the shoulder and said, "Let's go."

****

Rossi's was on a side street about two hundred yards from the plaza. It had six tables inside and four on the sidewalk. A sign on the wall stated, Fondato del 1900. "That means it was established in 1900," Melinda told Dylan. "Sounds old, but that's not that old here."

Luigi, who introduced himself as the owner, noticed Melinda and offered her the best table in the house. He made a point of placing his hand on her back, and as he directed her to the table, his hand slowly crept lower. Bull gave Luigi a stare. The owner looked up at him, then lowered his head like a child caught doing something naughty, and his hand fell to his side.

Melinda ordered drinks and appetizers and turned to Bull as they settled into their seats. "Don't worry about Luigi," she said. "Italian guys are handsy. I'm used to it. They're harmless." Then she changed the subject, "Okay, I thought about it all night. Tell me what y'all are up to?"

Bull said, "It's a long story. It's going to sound really strange. We're looking for a lost treasure...maybe."

"You know, you do sound kinda crazy right now," Melinda said, grinning.

"I'm sure we do," Bull continued. "Look, we came to Europe to travel and experience the culture. But Dylan ran into a professor who'd been researching this particular missing treasure. She believed she'd found some important clues and passed this information on to him. So, we've been following leads while trying to enjoy our trip, and the latest one brings us to a Giovanni Rossi who lived in Figline Valdarno in the 1910s. An Irish woman named Molly O'Leary may have lived with him at some point. Crazy, huh."

While Bull was talking, Dylan looked at the pictures covering the restaurant's walls. There were the typical touristy shots of the Duomo and the *David*, as well as Michelangelo's *Pietà*, but there were also pictures of the Rossi family over the years. Slightly hidden behind the cash register was an old photo that was difficult to see. Dylan stood up and walked over. He studied the image. It was a black-and-white picture of a middle-aged Italian man and a young, striking fair-haired woman who definitely wasn't Italian. And she was pregnant.

Chapter 21

Shannon Kelly

2025

As the train approached Cassis, Floyd remarked, "The last few days have been really fun, but I'm ready to get to the village and see if we can make any progress on our real objective. According to my research, there's a Kelly's B&B. Let's go there first and see where it takes us."

"This has been fun," said Lisa. "I enjoyed mirroring some of the boys' activities and imagining myself with them back in 1983. It's fun to read about my dad through Dylan's eyes. I'm learning so much about him."

"Yeah, do you remember that journal entry when they went to the Louvre in Paris and got kicked out because they had their backpacks and guitar?"

"And then they placed all of their gear in a park across the street, in broad daylight, figuring anyone who would see it would assume they were close by, because of course no one would just leave two backpacks and a guitar out in the open. That was pretty daring," Alex chimed in.

"I can't imagine doing that. I guess they had to make tough judgment calls. Just think what would have happened if someone had taken their stuff. They would have had nothing."

"I must say I agree with what Dylan wrote in his journal," said Lisa. "The Sa Palomera rock formation jutting out in Blanes Bay is one of the most romantic places I've ever seen. When I sat in that same spot, I imagined what Dylan felt all those years ago," she said, wistfully, glancing at Floyd and immediately looking away when she saw him looking at her.

"We've seen our share of cathedrals too. They're all incredible in their own way. I like the smaller churches as well. I agree with the boys, though; Rouen's Notre-Dame is my favorite," Alex said.

They took a cab from the train station to the city center on the oceanfront. While they were riding, Alex commented, "Those boys walked into town from the train station with their packs and guitar every time. This particular trip is more than three miles. They never complained. Oh, to be young."

The car dropped them off in front of Kelly's B&B. Beneath a tasteful banner displaying its name was an unusual square wooden door, clearly an antique. The inn was sandwiched between a laundromat and a tourist shop, and across the street from a charming café with tables on the sidewalk, full of people enjoying the summer evening. At the front desk, Floyd asked the attendant, "*Pardonnez-moi*, can we speak to the owner?"

The woman behind the desk was small and round, with short gray hair and glasses. She smiled broadly and said, "You are speaking to the owner, but I'm afraid we have no rooms available."

"May I ask your name?" Alex asked.

"Ms. Kelly, Shannon, that is," she responded.

Floyd looked at Lisa and Alex and then back at Shannon Kelly. "Would you have a moment to talk on a personal matter? We won't take too much of your time."

"Of course. We're fully booked for the next few weeks, and I don't have much to do behind the desk right now. Please, put your bags down and follow me. Let's have a cup of tea." She turned to them and grinned. "I'm Irish, you know."

They entered a small office, highlighted by an antique round wooden table that looked like it belonged in one of the ancient cathedrals they had visited. After Shannon served tea and sat down, Floyd asked, "Do you happen to remember two boys who visited this establishment in 1983—"

Shannon cut him off, "I've probably checked in several thousand people over the last forty-plus years."

Floyd persisted, "Their names were Dylan Stone and Bull Eastland."

Shannon gasped, "Dylan and Bull? How could I forget them? And Bull is such an unusual name, hard to forget. I wasn't much older than they were when they visited. They stayed several days, and we were together constantly. They made an impression on me. Dylan was so sincere and thoughtful, and Bull was quite the charmer. I'll never forget that my grandfather invited them to stay in our home. And they were such gracious young men."

"I'm Dylan's nephew," Floyd blurted.

"And I'm Bull's daughter," Lisa added.

"And I'm not related," Alex said with a chuckle, "but I met the boys in 1983, and they made an impression on me as well."

"It's so great to meet all of you. What brings you here some forty years later?" Shannon asked.

Alex jumped in and gave a quick summary of the Irish diaries, the lost jewels, and how Dylan and Bull had got mixed up in it, because of her. "There was a note found in Dylan's money belt that simply referenced Kelly's B&B in Cassis. It seemed important. Plus, there are several references to you and your grandparents in his journal, including a comment about a letter they read here that was significant to him."

Shannon was quiet for several moments. She stood up, walked across the room, and looked out the window towards the café across the street.

"I recall having breakfast with Bull and Dylan and helping them plan hikes to the top of the cliffs one day." She turned around and looked at them. "I remember Bull coming back covered in cuts and bruises. Dylan later told me he was concerned someone was following them and may even have tried to push Bull off the cliff. It scared me. Things like that didn't happen in Cassis. Why would someone want to do that?"

"My theory is that someone wanted Bull out of the way; he was sort of Dylan's protector," Floyd responded.

Shannon nodded, "Yes. Bull was big and could be intimidating, I suppose, though I never saw that side of him. I could see why someone would want him out of the picture if they wanted to get to Dylan.

"That evening after Bull was hurt, we had drinks at a beachfront speakeasy that no longer exists—only the locals knew where it was. I'll remember it forever. We had a real connection. We had a great last night together, talking and laughing. At one point, though, the conversation got serious, and Bull told us he was done with mountain climbing and hoped never to be anywhere near a cliff again. He'd thought he was going to die that day."

She was silent again, then walked back to the table and looked down at them, "It's been a long time. I need to reflect and refresh my memory before we talk further. I put some documents away a long time ago, and I need to find them. They will be helpful for our conversation. I do have a lot to tell you." Her expression changed to one of concern. "Do you have a place to stay in Cassis?"

"Actually, no. We were so focused on finding you, we assumed we would figure that out after we met with you," Floyd said.

"Nonsense. You will stay at my home. It's just down the street. It only seems right, since Dylan and Bull also stayed there so long ago. I have three extra bedrooms. It will be perfect. Please follow me. Once you get settled, I'll take you to dinner, and then we'll continue this conversation."

Chapter 22

Rossi's

1983

LUIGI RETURNED TO THE table with a bottle of wine and a basket of bread. Per Dylan's prompting, Melinda looked at Luigi and asked in Italian, "Who is in the picture behind the cash register—the man and the pregnant woman?"

Luigi looked at the photo, then turned to them and spoke in Italian, "That is my grandfather, Giovanni Rossi, rest in peace. He was the founder of this restaurant."

"Who is the woman?" Melinda asked in Italian.

"That is Signorina Molly. She lived with the family for a while. She was somehow related, I think, though I don't know how. Everyone loved her. She was in this restaurant every day for a couple of years. People would come to the restaurant to see her."

Melinda quickly translated for the table, as she would throughout the conversation.

"Do you know what happened to her?" she asked.

Luigi pulled up a chair, sat down at the table, and poured himself a glass of wine.

"You must understand, it is a family legend. I am not sure how much of it is true. What I understand is that she became pregnant and, for some reason, she decided that she needed to leave Figline. It was a difficult time. World War I was on the horizon, and things were changing fast. I think she wanted to go somewhere where she felt the baby would be safe. From what I have heard in the family stories, she was here one day and gone the next—and never seen again."

"Do you have any idea where she went?" Melinda asked.

"I do not know, but my father might. He is in the back. I will get him." Luigi trudged through a door behind the cash register and disappeared.

Not long after, he returned with an elfin figure, a silver-haired skeleton of a man who limped towards their table. He sat in the chair Luigi had left and said in Italian, "My name is Carlo. I hear that you are asking about Signorina Molly. She has a special place in my heart." He then lit a cigarette and sat back.

"What can you tell us about her?" Melinda asked.

"I loved her. I was a young boy, and she was like a big sister to me. She was so different than the Italian women in my life. I loved her red hair and blue eyes. She was also funny, affectionate, and could barely speak Italian. But she always could figure out a way to communicate with me and make me feel special."

"What happened to her?"

"My parents told me that she became with child and had to leave, since she was not married. But I heard from my older brother that she left because someone was following her and she was scared. This made me sad and frightened for her."

"Do you know where she went?" Melinda asked.

"Yes."

"Can you tell me?"

Luigi hesitated. He looked around the table at Dylan, Bull, and Melinda, brow furrowed and eyes flickering. "Why do you ask?"

"We are trying to understand what happened to her," Dylan said, and Melinda quickly translated. "She was a courageous young woman and we would like to learn more about her."

He seemed satisfied. "First, she went to Velletri with my mother. My mother cared deeply for Molly, and she wanted to make sure that the baby was born in a safe place. Her family, the Martinellis, lived in Velletri, outside of Rome. I went there to visit my grandparents when I was a child. Their place was out in the country, a long walk. They had a vineyard. Very beautiful."

"What was your mother's name?" Bull asked, and Melinda translated.

"Sofia, may she rest in peace," he answered.

"Does her family still live there?" Dylan asked.

"I assume so. The Martinelli Vineyard is famous. They have been there for many generations. Unfortunately, our families do not talk to each other. So, I don't know anything about them at this time."

After Melinda finished the translation, Bull looked at Dylan, and they were both thinking the same thing—it was time to visit Velletri.

Bull said, "You said Molly first went to Velletri. Does that mean she went somewhere else afterwards?"

"She then went to Corfu. She thought she would be safe there, with her young child. She sent letters to my parents for a year or so, but then we never heard from her again."

"Can you tell us anything about the letters?" Melinda asked.

"She talked of her baby son, Cormac. She was so happy. She also mentioned she was still scared of people following her."

"Did you ever hear of a man named Cillian?" Bull interjected.

"Yes. I met Cillian. I could never forget him—he was so pale, and his Italian was terrible. He visited us a couple of times while Molly stayed with us. I liked him. He was nice. He brought me candies. I always figured he was Cormac's father."

Dylan chimed in, "Did you ever hear why she was being followed?"

Carlo nodded. "Years later, my brother told me that he heard she stole something very valuable. I find that hard to believe. She did not seem like a thief. I will go to my grave believing that she was a saint."

Dylan stood and offered his hand. Carlo slowly pulled himself to a standing position and shook Dylan's hand. Bull and Melinda also rose. Carlo shook each of their hands, then he turned and limped back behind the cash register.

After finishing what may have been the best pizza they had ever eaten, they stood up to leave and noticed Carlo shuffling over to the table with his hands extended. "Lunch is on me," he said as he kissed Melinda on the cheek and patted Dylan and Bull on their backs. "I hope you find what you are looking for."

***

Sitting, sipping an espresso at a table on the sidewalk across the street, Julian watched the interaction through the window of Rossi's ristorante.

Chapter 23

The Letter

2025

FLOYD LOOKED UP FROM his plate of steak au poivre with red wine pan sauce and took a breath. The entrée followed escargot and a delicious soup, not to mention the bottomless wine bottle. Shannon smiled, seeing they were enjoying the meal in her favorite seafront restaurant in Cassis, where they sat outside at candlelit tables draped in white tablecloths and sheltered by umbrella pines.

After dinner, she led them to a balcony overlooking the water and provided them with their choice of espresso drinks. Then she pulled a folder out of her purse, laid two letters on the table in front of her, and told them the story her grandmother, Kayleigh, had relayed to Dylan and Bull at that dinner forty-two years ago. Then she pointed to a letter from Cillian to Molly, dated January 3, 1909, telling her to leave Cassis because she was being followed and to meet his uncle, Giovanni Rossi, in Figline Valdarno.

"I also saw a reference to Giovanni Rossi in a letter from Molly to Cillian during my research," said Alex. "It's starting to fit together."

"She shared this letter with the boys," Shannon said.

"That explains why they went to Figline Valdarno," Floyd said. He read the letter carefully and handed it to Lisa, who then passed it to Alex.

After all three had read the letter, Shannon picked up the second letter and held it against her chest. "I found this after my grandmother died. There is no date. She had kept it in an old scrapbook and apparently forgotten about it; as a result, she didn't share this with the boys. Molly sent this letter to my grandmother from Greece during the war. She was still a young girl at the time. I couldn't throw the scrapbook away. Maybe it will be helpful for you. You can have it."

She handed the yellowed parchment to Floyd, who read it out loud.

My Dear Kayleigh,

I hope this letter finds you safe and well, and that you're still singing those sweet songs you used to hum when I tucked you in. I often think of you—those long summer evenings chasing fireflies in the back garden, or how you'd curl up on my lap after story time, fast asleep before the second page.

Oh, how I loved the cliffs and our walks along the Cape, hiding in caves, running and shouting from the highest point. I look forward to doing the same here in Corfu.

There's no easy way to say this, love, but I want you to know the truth, or as much of it as I can give. I had to leave quickly and without saying goodbye—because some very bad men were following me. They were looking for something I took...something that wasn't mine to begin with. I never meant harm, Kayleigh. I swear that on my mother's grave. At the time, it seemed like the right thing to do. Or maybe I didn't understand how dangerous it really was.

I thought I could give it back, make it right. But then it was too late. Doors closed, people vanished, and the danger didn't. And so, I ran.

It was in Velletri that I had a little one of my own. Giovanni's wife took care of me, a saint she is. The baby boy has bright eyes and soft fingers that curl around mine like he never wants to let go. He is my whole world now. Everything I do is to protect him. That means I can't come back, not now or ever.

So, I've hidden what they're after—the thing I took, with the Kaiser's help. Every treasure deserves its throne, or does it? And I don't even have the key. If luck's on my side, they'll find it. Or maybe in time, they'll forget. All I want now, Kayleigh, is to be left in peace, to raise my child, and to put the past behind me.

The war is here, and with it, so many people; it is quite Drastic. Please be safe.

I don't expect you to understand all of this. You're still young. But someday you will. And when you do, remember me not for what I ran from—but for how much I loved.

With all my love,

Molly

Floyd handed the letter to Lisa. "This is incredible! A letter from Molly! Do either of you think it's trying to tell you something? There are some unusual references in here."

"I think so," said Lisa, matching his excitement. "Every treasure deserves its throne? That sounds like a clue."

Alex carefully held the letter and reread it. "And what about the random reference to Kaiser?"

Shannon had a serious look on her face. "I thought this letter was strange too. My grandmother told me that she never went to the cliffs here in Cassis. Cape Canaille, which is the highest sea cliff in Europe, was definitely off-limits to her—she was scared of heights. I think you're right. She was trying to say something with the words."

"The comment about the treasure seems obvious. I think that's the Irish Crown Jewels," Floyd said.

"It makes sense. And I think she's hinting at where it's hidden," Alex said.

"This reminds me of something. There are many caves along the cliffs here," Shannon said. "Over the years, people have constructed walkways for some of them. They are dangerous but popular among adventurers. Molly would have been very familiar with them, though she avoided them herself. Are there cliffs in Corfu?"

"I don't know," Floyd said. He pulled out his phone and searched the internet.

He read the first sentence, "Corfu is an island in the Ionian Sea known for its old town, spectacular beaches and striking cliffs—"

"Home run!" Alex interrupted. "*Ionian* is the word written on the envelope I gave Dylan."

Floyd pulled the envelope out of his backpack. He read the handwritten lyric, "Where sun dies soft in Ionian blue, / The crowned heart waits beneath the view." He looked at Lisa and Alex.

"Wait! You have the key?!" Shannon exclaimed with surprise.

"Yes. I got the journal and Dylan's belongings, including the key, from my father's estate. Alex found it in 1983 and gave it to Dylan. He had it when he was here with you way back then. I don't think he knew what to do with it at that point. And...someone else wanted this key. That's why he was being followed," Floyd said.

Shannon stared at the envelope—everything was coming together for her.

Alex continued, "Okay—the Ionian Sea reference ties to Corfu. I've always thought the 'crowned heart' referred to the jewels. I still think it does, but maybe the word 'crown' has additional meaning—especially when Shannon's letter includes the words 'throne,' 'Kaiser,' and 'treasure.'"

Lisa said, "So, what I'm hearing is we believe the clues point towards the treasure being hidden in a cave on Corfu, either in or near a cliff."

"Wow," Floyd exclaimed. "This is a huge breakthrough."

"However," Lisa said, "there must be a lot of cliffs and caves on Corfu. How can we narrow it down?"

Alex looked up from the letter. "Maybe these other strange references will eventually make sense. The reference to the Cape, the cliffs, the weird capitalization of Drastic...but the most obvious seems to be the line: 'every treasure deserves its throne.'"

"Yeah, it does," Lisa said. "We need to learn more about Corfu, and we need to research these keywords and see if we can learn anything that would help us pinpoint the hiding place."

"In the letter," Floyd commented, "Molly says that she had the baby in Velletri. I just looked it up. Velletri is a town about twenty-five miles south of Rome. It's a place where Dylan and Bull spent one night, according to their journal. Now that makes sense. I always wondered why they went there when Rome was so close. I'd thought we'd skip that stop, but now I think we should go. If Giovanni's wife took Molly there, maybe they had a place there? Maybe the boys learned something there?"

Alex agreed. "Let's not get ahead of ourselves," she said. "Let's go to Florence and Figline Valdarno. We can't go to Italy without spending time in Florence. Plus, we can see if the commune is still in Figline and see the apartment where they stayed. That plaza sounds fascinating, and maybe Rossi's restaurant is still there. Wouldn't that be amazing?"

Floyd was ready to go. "If I could catch a train tonight, I would," he said, then turned to Shannon. "Thanks so much for everything.

You've given us so much to think about. We'll need to leave in the morning."

"It's been my pleasure. I'll have a car waiting to take you to the train station, along with a light breakfast to go. Please keep in touch. I'd love to hear how everything turns out."

Chapter 24

Velletri

1983

June 23, Velletri, Italy

Last night, the Socialist Party brought in a TV celebrity rock group to play in Figline. The whole town showed up. We had a great view from our living room window. The plaza was filled with thousands of people—parents, grandparents, kids, teenagers. Bull even saw a monk in the crowd. They were all there, but they weren't that enthusiastic. They never clapped, they just stood and watched. Maybe that's how concerts are here. Maybe it's because it's a political deal. The band was okay. They had a pretty girl singer—typical—she sang mostly in Italian, but she also sang "Stand by Me," "Honky Tonk Woman," and for an encore, "Cocaine." I couldn't believe it. It was a terrible version, but nice to hear anyway.

The sound system, lighting, and stage were excellent. I was really surprised that such a top-notch concert would be held in little Figline Valdarno. After the show, the lead singer came into our apartment building to change. Apparently, she was staying in our place. Hundreds of people crowded the entrance to get a glimpse of her. Bull and I hap-pened to be coming down the stairs at that time, and we passed her and her entourage, followed by a bunch of socialist political candidates dressed like love gods with gold chains and unbuttoned shirts, as they were going up. Bull joked that they looked like Steve Martin and Dan Aykroyd from the "Wild and Crazy Guy" skit on Saturday Night Live.

We left the crowded plaza and hitched a ride to the commune for our last night. Due to their small cars, we had to split up and get rides with two different Italian guys. The commune was hopping. Like before, there were a bunch of leftover '60s throwbacks in the audience. A man and a woman were playing guitar and singing. They sang old Bob Dylan, Beatles, Neil Young, Joan Baez—all '60s stuff, it was great! The guy was really good on the guitar, too. Someone told him that I played, so he got me up on stage and we performed "Wish You Were Here" together. What fun.

After the show, I talked to one of the hippies. He told me that a whole bunch of Americans live on a farm and work together in a little socialist society—a '60s dream world in the boonies of Italy. When Bull and I finally left around 2 a.m., I kissed Melinda, and she kissed me back and held me tight. I think she's special. We talked about meeting again. I hope we do. She may even try to meet us in Corfu, if she can get away.

The next morning we packed, checked out, grabbed some patisserie food, and caught the 9:54 train to Florence, then the 10:37 train to Rome. Got to Rome at 3:30 and took another train out to Velletri. Once again, the town was too small to be detailed in our Let's Go Europe *book, so we had no idea where any* albergos *or* ristorantes *were. We found a* pizzeria *after walking for fifteen minutes and stopped there. The pizza was amazing, and we were starving. The waitress gave us directions to the only* albergo *near the Martinelli Vineyard. She said it was a long walk. She wasn't kidding! It was nine kilometers—more than five miles—mostly uphill. Thank goodness it wasn't raining. Finally, we got to this really nice hotel and found it to be pretty expensive. We had no other choice, so we took it. We're going to walk to the vineyard tomorrow and see if anyone knows anything about Molly O'Leary or Sofia Rossi.*

The bellhop at the hotel gave Dylan and Bull directions to the vineyard. After a thirty-minute walk along the side of a two-lane motorway, they saw a sign for Martinelli Vineyards with an arrow pointing them down a dirt road. They opened a gate, let themselves through, and began heading into the vineyard. At first, all they could see were lines of grape-bearing vines. After fifteen minutes, which Dylan figured to be about a mile, they could see an enormous estate at the end of the path.

"That must be the place," Bull said as he picked up his pace.

"Yeah. It's enormous. Quite the operation." There were rows of grapevines as far as they could see.

An old Jeep appeared and headed toward them, kicking up dust as it picked up speed. As it got closer, they could hear a man yelling in Italian. Then they saw a fist appear and disappear, like a piston.

Dylan and Bull stopped in their tracks and waited. They didn't want to appear aggressive. The Jeep skidded to a stop a few inches from them, and an old Italian man jumped out, screaming and waving his hands at them, pointing behind them. He wanted them to leave.

Dylan pulled out his *Let's Go Europe* book. There was a brief English–Italian dictionary in the back. He said in Italian, "Pardon, sir. We are here to meet with the owner of the vineyard."

The man stopped. He was short, maybe five feet tall. His skin was tanned and rough. He wore a wide-brimmed hat, a work shirt, loose denim pants, and boots. He couldn't speak English, and they could tell that he was caught off guard when they said they wanted to talk to his boss.

Though it was clear he was unhappy about it, he pointed at the back seat of the Jeep. Dylan and Bull jumped in. It had no doors or windows, other than a windshield. As soon as they were in, the vehicle accelerated violently. Dylan and Bull had to hold on to the seat in front of them to avoid being bucked off.

They arrived at an all-glass building on a hill. As they were led inside, Dylan was struck by the view. There were vineyards for what seemed like miles in all directions, like an elaborate maze that went on forever. The old man led them down a hall and into a conference room. He pointed at a large table, surrounded by chairs, in the center of the room, and said, *"Per favore, siediti!"* Then he left, slamming the door behind him.

Bull looked at Dylan and smiled, "I think he just told us to sit down."

"Yeah, this is gonna be an adventure," Dylan said as he toured the room, observing pictures of the wine-making process on the walls and the incredible view out the window.

They were startled when the door opened and a middle-aged man walked in. He was tall and athletic-looking, dressed neatly in khaki pants, suede shoes, and a light blue button-down shirt. Long, full gray hair framed his light-complexioned face, high-lighted by piercing blue eyes and a neat grayish-red beard.

"How may I help you?" he asked in perfect English. Dylan thought it sounded like he had a combination of a British and Italian accent.

Bull began, *"Ciao.* My name is Bull Eastland, and this is my friend, Dylan Stone. We were sent here by Carlo Rossi from Figline Valdarno. We've been researching a woman named Molly O'Leary, who supposedly lived here around 1910."

The man was caught by surprise. "Molly O'Leary, you ask?"

"Yes," Dylan said. "We've come across information about her and are trying to validate it."

"What type of information?"

"With all due respect, sir, can I ask your name?"

"Cormac Martinelli. I'm the president of this vineyard, which my family owns."

Bull and Dylan exchanged glances, and Bull blurted, "Cormac? Would you happen to be the son of Molly O'Leary?"

Cormac pointed to the conference table. Bull and Dylan took seats next to each other, and Cormac sat at the head of the table. A young woman entered the room, poured each of them a cup of tea, then disappeared as quickly as she'd entered.

"Believe it or not, I don't drink alcohol," he said, with a half-smile. "Yes, Molly O'Leary was my mother. You are correct. Please tell me why you're asking about my mother—and me, for that matter."

Dylan told Cormac about meeting the professor on the ferry from Ireland, though he didn't mention anything about the key or the envelope. He focused on the professor's speculation about Molly. He then briefly talked about meeting the Kellys in Cassis and Carlo Rossi in Figline, and how each had such positive things to say about his mother. He was purposefully evasive on the details because he didn't know what to think of Cormac yet.

Cormac listened, his face rapt with fascination. When Dylan finished, he took a deep breath and began, "I was born here. I consider the Martinellis to be my family. I was given their last name, as I never knew my father. When I was young, we moved to Corfu. We lived in the Old Town, but my mother loved visiting the beaches and the mountains. Corfu is a beautiful place."

He looked out the window, apparently lost in thought for a moment, and then he continued, "I only knew my mother for a few years. We moved to Corfu when I was a baby. My actual memories are hit-or-miss due to my age at the time. However, I've filled in the holes over the years through conversations with locals, as I vacation there almost every year."

He stopped, looked at Dylan and Bull, and said, "I'm sure you're hungry. Come, we have a dining room, and I'll feed you as I tell you my stories. You've brought back memories I haven't thought about in a long time. It is nice to have someone who wants to listen." He smiled, stood up, and motioned for them to follow him.

Cormac walked quickly. Dylan was surprised by how nimble he was for his age as they strode down a long hallway. One side was glass, offering a view of the vineyards, while the other was decorated with paintings and photos of the vineyard through the years. Dylan was looking out the window when he ran into the back of Cormac, who had stopped abruptly. Cormac was focused on an ancient black-and-white photograph of a white-haired man standing beside a pale-haired woman, both holding a baby, gazing out over the vineyards. He turned around and said, "Pardon me, Dylan." He looked at the picture and said, "That's me and my mother. She wasn't here long, but my mother made a lasting impression on the family during her time there."

Dylan took in the room around him. It resembled one of those fancy boardrooms he had seen in the movies, with a beautiful marble table in the center, surrounded by a dozen plush chairs, and a dark wooden floor that shone, even though it was probably a hundred years old. Several dishes were placed in front of them, including what looked like salami, tomatoes, and several cheeses.

"Please, help yourself. This is just the beginning, so don't overeat. It only gets better," Cormac said as he placed a slice of tomato and some cheese on his plate. "Are you ready for a short history lesson?" he said in an exaggeratedly serious voice.

Dylan and Bull nodded as they filled their plates.

"I was born here in 1910. My mother had come here to live when she was pregnant. It was a safe place for an unmarried woman, away from prying eyes in the city. She was loved here, especially by 'my grandmother' and her sisters. They enjoyed taking care of her and me, as well. We lived here for a year or so, and then we moved to Corfu. I later learned that she thought she would be safer on the island, though it turned out not to be the case."

Cormac put his napkin in his lap, neatly organized his silverware, and continued, "We lived in Corfu Old Town. You must visit this place. It's a beautiful tangle of narrow streets, yellow neoclassical buildings with painted shutters and wrought iron balconies. It has an incredible history dating back to the eighth century BCE. It is still, to this day, populated mainly by locals, not tourists. I have good memories of that time. We lived a simple life.

"Here's an interesting and true story. She used to love to explore the island. Her favorite place was this steep rocky spot above Pelekas village. It was a spot where you could see the entire island in every direction. My mother loved to watch the sunsets there. When we would visit, an older man would often be there, enjoying the same view. He loved it so much that he had an elaborate observatory built at the peak, with stone stairs and railings. We watched it being constructed. I remember him clearly, because he had a very unusual mustache—the ends of it pointed up. Anyway, my mother and this man would often talk, and he would bring me little toys, coins, or snacks. Much later, I found out that he was a very famous and powerful man: Kaiser Wilhelm II, the last German emperor. He visited Corfu each spring for several years. During that time, the locals liked to call this spot the

Kaiser's Throne. The name stuck, and you can visit it today, if you like."

"Kaiser's Throne?" Dylan asked as he looked at Bull.

"Yes. I thought you'd be interested in that story. The Kaiser was very nice to my mother and me. However, I do remember that many men were nice to my mother and me. She especially enjoyed spending time with outdoorsmen—mountain climbers, divers, and spelunkers. She was quite beautiful and looked very different from the typical Greek woman, with her long red hair and blue eyes. Looking back, I think she had a difficult time handling the attention, which ultimately led to her demise."

Steaming bowls were placed on the table: *ribollita* (white bean soup), *pappa al pomodoro* (another soup with garlic, tomatoes, bread), and *penne strascicate* (traditional pasta with meat sauce). Dylan and Bull tried each dish and then grabbed seconds.

Cormac smiled as he watched the boys eat. "I'm glad you like your lunch."

Bull looked up with a spoon almost to his mouth, "This is the best food I've ever had...in my life."

"Just wait," Cormac said, "the best is yet to come." He sat back in his chair and began speaking, as if he were a college professor. "Corfu actually had a significant role in World War I. Not many people know this."

"Really?" Dylan asked. "I don't know that much about World War I. Please tell us. Bull and I both love history."

"In 1914, Serbia was invaded by the Austrians and the Germans, who blamed Serbia for the assassination of Archduke Ferdinand—the event that started the war. The Serbian army defied the Austrians and Germans for more than a year, but eventually, their country was overrun. By December 1915, the Serbian military and government were forced to flee their homeland. Initially, they retreated into Albania and various ports on the Adriatic Coast. The Western allies were determined to help them and sent an armada to rescue them. A massive rescue operation took place in early 1916, involving more than two hundred ships from the Italian, French, and British navies. They did an incredible job, saving the entire Serbian Army and government. However, the three hundred thousand men, women, and children were all taken to Corfu, and the island became their home base. The island's population grew from 100,000 to 400,000 overnight. Imagine the chaos. My mother and I were in the middle of this madness. People were sleeping in the streets. There wasn't enough food. There were concerns that the island would be attacked.

"I was about six years old when all of this happened. My mother did an amazing job of keeping me safe and protecting me from the bedlam of Corfu at that time. I remember being scared. And then it just becomes a blur."

"Fascinating," Dylan said.

The soups and pasta were removed, and a steak was laid on the table in front of them. It covered an entire plate.

Cormac explained, "This is the *bistecca alla Fiorentina*, which comes from an ancient breed of local cattle, known for its flavorful meat. In America, they would call this a porterhouse steak. It includes both a strip and a tenderloin filet, connected by the T-bone. But this is special. You will never have a better steak."

They all ate in silence. Finally Bull said, "Mr. Martinelli, this truly is the best steak I've ever eaten, and I'm from Texas, where we take special pride in our steaks. I don't know how I can ever return to America. The food here is just too good."

"You are welcome. By the way, please call me Cormac. It's nice to have guests from America. That's very rare for us. I actually spent time in California years ago, studying their winemaking techniques and working on my English. I don't get to use it often," Cormac said in his best American accent.

He then became serious, "You expressed interest in my mother. That was unexpected—and it means a lot to me. As a result, I have been very open with you about my life. It has been nice to remember those days from so long ago, even though it is also sad. Is there anything else I can tell you?"

Dylan thought about this for a moment. "Cormac, can I be frank with you?"

"Please do," Cormac said seriously. "That is how I do business, and that is how I handle my personal relationships as well."

"Okay," Dylan said, leaning forward in his chair. "As we've been researching your mother, it's come to our attention that she may have been involved in a theft of jewels...from Ireland. We've heard that she was being followed, and that's why she kept moving—from Cassis to Figline to here and then to Corfu. Do you have any knowledge of this?"

Cormac looked Dylan in the eyes, then he studied Bull. There was an uncomfortable silence for more than a minute. Finally, he spoke. "Years later, I heard the legend of the lost Irish Crown Jewels, and the speculation that my mother was involved. It was only then that I recalled she had a trunk she kept hidden away. I saw it many times and I remember it clearly. She was cautious with it. It was an old Victorian-era dome-top steamer trunk. It had a leather and oak frame with geometric diamond-pattern metal trim. It was smaller than a typical traveling trunk and, therefore, easier for her to carry. I never saw what was inside. She told me that she didn't have the key. We used to make trips to different places on the island because she wanted to find a safe place to hide it. So, I believe the legend could be true."

"What happened to the trunk?" Bull asked the obvious question.

"I don't know. When the island was overrun during the war, I assume she hid it to keep it safe. But I don't know where. It's a big island, and it could be anywhere. You know," he said, "her apartment is still there. In an old building in Corfu Town. The last time I looked, it was for rent. I'll give you the address. If you are so interested in her, this will give you a feel for how she lived, and maybe it will spark a clue for you."

"One last question," Dylan said. "What happened to your mom?"

Cormac looked at Dylan closely, studying his eyes for several moments, then he said with a sigh, "I don't know. You have to remember I was a young boy. It was so hectic. There were so many people. Everywhere. I have tried to remember what happened, but all I can recall is that one day, I was living with my mother in an apartment, and the next, I was on a ship back to Italy with my nonna. I never saw my mother again. I have always missed her. It has been a hole in my heart for all these years."

Chapter 25

Lost

1983

JUNE 24, ROME

Well, we hiked the five miles to the train station and hopped on the first train to Rome. When we got there, we checked our packs (and guitar) in the baggage place and then headed out to see the city. We had some fantastic pizza, then we trudged to the Colosseum. We explored all around inside it. It's pretty weird to think of all the things that have happened there over the last 2,000 years or so—the gladiators, wild animal exhibitions and hunts, executions...even sea battles. After a visit to St. Peter's Cathedral, the Vatican, and the Sistine Chapel, we walked through the Piazza del Campidoglio and saw many old churches and sculptures everywhere. Finally, we found the Pantheon, which was built in 24 BCE, and we sat at a sidewalk café, had dinner and wine, and watched the people. This spot is a social hub in Rome and young people filled the piazza—holding hands, sipping drinks, smoking cigarettes, and kissing in the shadows. It was very interesting, and there were lots of beautiful girls. Tomorrow we are taking an early train to Napoli, so that we can see Pompeii before racing across Italy to catch the nightly ferry to Corfu. I hope we can get some answers in Corfu so we can enjoy the next month of our trip with that behind us.

"Pompeii was fascinating—those plaster casts of people that were caught in their tracks by lava were unforgettable," Dylan said as he and Bull hopped on a train headed back to Naples after a morning visit to the ruins from the Vesuvius volcanic eruption in 79 BCE.

"Yeah, I wish we had more time there," said Bull. "But we need to catch the 2:22 train to Brindisi so that we can catch the ferry to Corfu. It only leaves once each evening. I don't want to miss it and get stuck in Brindisi for a whole day."

"I know. Okay, let's go over the plan. When we get to Corfu, we are going to find Molly's apartment in the Old Town and see if it gives us any clues. Then we'll head to Pelekas Beach, find the hotel, and check in. At some point, we know we want to visit Kaiser's Throne. Otherwise, we need some R&R. We haven't gotten more than five hours of sleep for the last several days. Also, if we don't figure out anything further about Molly and the jewels in Corfu, let's try to put that behind us and enjoy our next month in Europe. I'm looking forward to Venice, Zermatt, and Munich—and all the other places we'll explore along the way," Dylan said with exhaustion in his voice. Then he perked up. "Plus, Melinda said she'd try to go to Corfu—so we may run into her there."

"I thought she had a thing for you," Bull said with a grin. "I hope we run into her. She's a good one. I'll take my chances with the girls on the beach."

After a quick lunch of spaghetti at a small *pastaria* across from the train station, Dylan glanced at his watch and noticed they had an hour until the train was to leave. "I'd like to do some souvenir shopping," he said to Bull. "I'll meet you on the train."

"Sounds good. I saw a couple of places I wanted to check out as well. Let's plan to meet in car three. If that doesn't work for some reason, we'll find each other—it's a five-hour train ride."

Dylan got distracted looking at funny postcards and realized he only had five minutes until the train was to leave. He raced out of the store, backpack in one hand and guitar in the other, and ran awkwardly into the train station. He located the track number from the big board and then jumped on the train just as it was leaving. He noticed a commotion just outside, but when he turned to see what was happening, he just saw a crowd of people entering the train as the doors closed. He found a place to stow his backpack and guitar and set out to find Bull.

It didn't take long for Dylan to realize that not only did the train not have a car three, but also that the journey wasn't covered by his Eurail pass, so he would have to pay a fine. *Great.* He spent thirty minutes walking through each car, searching for Bull. He went all the way to the final carriage. No Bull. Maybe he missed him somehow, or maybe Bull was walking the other way. Dylan turned around and slowly started backtracking through all the cars a second time. He was about halfway through the trek when he thought he saw a young man with long blond hair staring at him from a packed compartment. Dylan turned to look more closely. The man suddenly appeared to be sleeping with his head in his hands.

People were piling up behind Dylan, and gesturing and yelling in Italian for him to move or get out of the way, so he pushed forward in his search for Bull. He finally reached the front car, and still no Bull. *Maybe he missed the train.* There wasn't anything Dylan could do about it now. He would have to re-evaluate his options when he got to Brindisi. He turned around and began looking for a seat. The train was packed, almost claustrophobic. He finally found a compartment that was holding seven people. Of course, it only held four comfortably, but it was the best he could find. He squeezed in, placed his Walkman headphones over his ears, pulled out his brand-new *Rolling Stone* magazine with the Australian band Men at Work on the cover, and read it as slowly as possible, hoping it would make the train ride go by a little faster. He had a hard time concentrating, thinking about how or if he would find Bull again, while also wondering whether the blond-haired guy was the mysterious follower. *Didn't we lose him a long time ago?* he wondered.

Five hours later, he gathered his gear and jumped off the train. He looked around, hoping Bull would somehow be there waiting for him. Still no Bull. He only had thirty minutes to get across town to the ferry, or he would miss the nightly sailing. No cabs were in sight; he'd have to run. It was about two miles, which was a challenge with a full backpack and guitar. Dylan sprinted through side streets as sweat ran into his eyes and down his back. He could hear footsteps behind him but didn't have time to look back. He figured he wasn't the only one racing to the ferry.

As he turned the last corner, he could see dock workers preparing to raise the gangway. He had at least a hundred yards to go. He then noticed that locals were sitting in outdoor cafés on both sides of the street, jeering at the stragglers racing to catch the ship before it left. He quickly figured out that this was a nightly event, and he could see people were betting on whether he would make the ship or not. He jumped on the gangway as it was being raised, and he heard a loud groan from the crowd, and then a handful of happy cheers thrown in from the winning bettors. *I hope someone made a lot of money betting on me*, he thought, *because I wasn't going to miss the ship. I knew all that training for cross country would come in handy someday.*

After a thorough tour of the ferry, it was clear to Dylan that Bull was not on the ship. *Oh well*, he thought. *I guess I'm on my own for a while.* Then he thought with concern, *I wonder what happened to Bull. He never misses deadlines.* He knew that once he departed the ship, he would have twenty-four hours until the next boat arrived, so he planned to make the best of that time. Hopefully, Bull would walk off the next day's ferry, and Dylan would be there to greet him.

After a thirty-minute walk from the ferry terminal into the historical neighborhood of Spilia in Corfu Old Town, Dylan turned a corner and saw the five-story, pale yellow Anesis Studio apartments. It was in a great location near the Old Courthouse and Cathedral of St. Theodora, and across the street from a park overlooking the ocean. *This was the building that Molly lived in seventy years ago*, he thought. *I wonder how much it's changed. It looks like it's been here for a couple of hundred years.* He looked up at the narrow Venetian manor with five floor-to-ceiling shuttered windows lined horizontally across each level. Most rooms had balconies, some of which had clothes lines weighed down with laundry, he noted as he walked through the arched doorway into the foyer.

The attendant spoke enough English to communicate with Dylan, which was a relief.

"I'm interested in seeing Apartment 13," Dylan pleaded.

"You'll have to rent it to see it," the attendant said without emotion.

Dylan figured he'd stay in town tonight and head to the beach with Bull after he arrived, so he paid about three times what he would normally pay for lodging and booked Molly's room for the night.

The apartment was located upstairs on the first floor. It was a nice flat. Though it had been seven decades since Molly had lived here, it didn't look like much had been done structurally during that time. There were two bedrooms, a combined living room/kitchen, a small bathroom, and a closet. Surely the bathroom was different now, but other than that, Dylan felt like he had walked back in time. Glass doorknobs, ancient, well-worn furniture, and black and white photos of the old town on the walls. Dylan turned the brass handle on a glass door and walked out onto the balcony. He had a great view of the park across the street and the Straits of Corfu beyond. He stood for a moment and watched a large passenger ship pass by. Then Dylan turned to his right and looked down at a stone alleyway that appeared as if it hadn't changed in five hundred years. A biker emerged from the darkness and pedaled towards the park across the street. Dylan could see others in the shadows between the buildings, walking and biking along the stone pathway.

Back inside, when he opened the closet to stow his backpack and guitar, he noticed some pencil etchings near the bottom of the door. Dylan got on his knees and looked closely. He saw the name Cormac written in minute block letters next to a series of penciled-in lines with numbers beside them. It was Molly's tracking of Cormac's growth! Dylan was amazed to see this actual link to mother and son. This gave him hope that there might be others.

He looked throughout the closet. Nothing there. He went through the smaller bedroom and searched under the bed. Then he examined each drawer of the dresser, studied each wall, and explored the crown molding. Nothing. He then surveyed the master bedroom—Molly's room. He inspected the bed, the dresser, and the walls. Nothing. There was one more piece of furniture. An antique mini roll-top desk. He opened the drawer and studied it closely, seeing nothing. The roll-top was stuck in the up position. It was clear that it had not been closed in years. Dylan tried to pull it down but was unsuccessful. He got a Swiss Army knife out of his pack and tried several of its tools. Suddenly the roll-top rammed down, almost smashing Dylan's fingers. He looked at it closely. Something was stuck at the base of the roll-top. Using his knife, he dug out a rolled-up piece of paper, like cigarette paper. As he unfurled it, his heart beat faster. It was clearly a drawing of a throne, with the word Kaiser in front of it. Below that was a sketch of a trunk. It looked like a pirate's treasure chest from books that Dylan read when he was a boy. Despite his excitement, the discovery seemed too easy and too obvious, but there was no way he was going to wait for Bull. Dylan grabbed his room key and headed down the stairs. It was time to visit Kaiser's Throne.

***

A blond-haired man stood in the shadow of the alley outside the apartment building and waited. His ball cap was turned backwards, and he wore sunglasses. *What's the significance of this place?* he was thinking. *Dylan seemed determined to come here. Why?* After about twenty minutes, Dylan raced down the front steps, turned left, and jogged to a motorbike rental shop four doors down. Five minutes later, he emerged with the shop's proprietor, who showed him how to operate the bike. He threw Dylan the keys and disappeared back into the shop. Dylan slowly mounted the motorbike, inserted the key in the ignition, entered the street with a series of jerks and stops, and headed west. The man casually put on his helmet, started his motorbike, and pursued Dylan at a distance.

***

Having never ridden a motorbike before, Dylan cautiously drove up the switchback road towards Kaiser's Throne, parking near the top.

Still feeling shaky, he slowly climbed the winding stone stairway to the observatory at the peak of the outcropping, searching for any clues in the crevices of the rock walls and along the well-worn stairs. Nothing. He reached the top. Cormac hadn't been kidding; the panoramic view was breathtaking. Dylan looked down at what must be Pelekas Beach, then at Corfu Old Town, with its ancient urban beauty contrasting with the trees, green hills, and sandy beaches of the rest of the island. An old, faded plaque on a stone near the top of the structure caught his attention. It appeared that it had been there as long as the observatory itself. His heart began to race as he read the words:

"Where sun dies soft in Ionian blue, The crowned heart waits beneath the view. Where once a throne watched empire's flame, A shadow points to the jewel's new home. Beneath the cliffs where the lion's silence leans, The sunken crown guards secret queens."

He took out his journal and wrote it down word for word, then sat down to try to decipher its meaning.

Based on what we've learned from Shannon and Cormac, we know the first verse tells us the jewels are here in Corfu, he thought. *Corfu is on the Ionian Sea. Then there's the reference to the throne, Kaiser's Throne, where I am now, but then it refers to the jewel's apparent new home—beneath the cliffs where silence leans. What is the sunken crown? It appears that it's been moved. How do "cliffs" and "sunken" tie together?* He carefully scanned the entire 360-degree view. *What is this telling me?* He studied the words again and then looked back out over the island. He shook his head, knowing the answer was eluding him, and decided to ride back to town before dark. Tonight, he would think about it, and maybe Bull could help him solve the puzzle tomorrow.

***

The man watched from the shadows as Dylan slowly rode down the switchbacks towards the highway, and then he leisurely walked up the stone staircase. He had seen Dylan studying something at the top. *Is this the place where the jewels are buried?* he thought with excitement. As he walked up, he looked for a keyhole or a false stone compartment but didn't see anything. Reaching the top, he walked to the place where he had seen Dylan studying something on the wall. He looked around and didn't see anything significant. Just as he was about to descend, he saw the small plaque. *This must be the clue*, he thought. He read the strange quote several times, but it didn't make any sense to him. As he walked down the stairs, he decided he needed to find a way to get closer to Dylan.

Chapter 26

The Uffizi

2025

FIGLINE VALDARNO TURNED OUT to be a dead end in their quest. Although they found the apartment on the plaza that the boys had rented, it told them nothing new. They couldn't find the old college in the country, and a souvenir shop had replaced Rossi's restaurant. Frustrated, they decided to visit Florence. After touring the Duomo and checking off their list of must-see city highlights, they went to the Uffizi Gallery for a formal tour.

Floyd, Lisa, and Alex followed their tour guide through the grand rooms, hallways, and courtyards of the gallery. They learned that it had been built in 1560 as an administrative office for the city, ordered by the Medici family, which had accumulated one of the most significant art collections in the world. Over the centuries, the building had evolved into Italy's most popular gallery, visited by more than two million people per year. They viewed Botticelli's famous goddess on a seashell, *The Birth of Venus*, as well as Caravaggio's *Medusa*, and Michelangelo's *Holy Family*, one of his few remaining paintings. Their guide, Aldo, spoke excellent English and shared fascinating trivia throughout their afternoon tour. After talking for two hours straight, he turned to their trio and asked, "Do you have any questions?"

Lisa looked at Aldo and asked shyly, "I know this has nothing to do with the Renaissance or the Uffizi, but do you know anything about the lost Irish Crown Jewels?"

Aldo's eyes widened. "The lost Irish Crown Jewels? Interestingly, our curator is fascinated by this topic. What is your interest?"

"This may sound crazy, but we're sort of looking for them."

"You must meet Dr. Marks, our curator," Aldo exclaimed. "He's an American. Can you believe it? The first American ever to be the curator of the Uffizi. He just arrived last year and has already brought many unexpected artworks to our museum. He came from the Art Institute of Chicago."

"Yes, we'd love to meet him!" Lisa said as Floyd and Alex nodded enthusiastically.

Aldo led them through a side door, down an ancient stone hallway, and finally to an enormous doorway with an arched entrance. Floyd felt like he'd walked back into the sixteenth century as they followed Aldo into a cavernous office that looked like a museum itself, neatly organized with priceless paintings on the wall, life-sized sculptures in each corner, and a vast, ornate olive-wood desk with gold trim along the back wall. There was a conference table to its left, and a video screen that could have been in a movie theater on the wall above it. Its screensaver was a picture of *The Birth of Venus*.

An elegant man, with slicked-back gray hair, and dressed sharply in an Italian suit, stood up behind the desk and then walked towards them.

"Welcome to the Uffizi," he said in English.

The accent sounds like a cross between American and British, thought Dylan.

"My name is Julian Marks. I'm the curator here at the Uffizi." He offered his hand to the group.

Among handshakes, Floyd, Lisa, and Alex briefly introduced themselves.

"I understand you have an interest in the lost Irish Crown Jewels," Julian noted.

"Yes, we do," said Alex. "I've been studying Irish history for more than forty years, and for most of that time, I've been fascinated by this mystery. I came close to finding them a long time ago, but it didn't work out."

Julian looked closely at Alex. "Please explain further."

"I found a clue in a diary in Dublin back in 1983, but I lost the trail."

Julian pointed at the conference table and said, "Please have a seat." He settled in at the head of the table, with Floyd to his right and Alex and Lisa to his left. Coffee was served by a young man in a suit.

"I've also been fascinated by this mystery since I was in boarding school," said Julian. "I haven't focused on it lately because I've been so busy running this gallery and trying to make it the best in the world." He studied Floyd and Lisa, then looked at Alex. "This is going to sound incredible, but I believe our paths have crossed. You're Dr. Alexandra Morana, the UCLA professor, correct?"

"Yes," she said, stunned. "Though I'm now a former professor; I'm retired."

"I'd read your paper on the lost jewels and actually followed you back in 1983. I was a college kid fascinated with lost treasure and artifacts at the time." He didn't mention that his focus at that time was primarily to steal art. "My life changed that summer. Something happened which completely upturned the direction of my life."

Alex's eyes narrowed. "You...you threatened me on the ferry!"

He calmly looked at her. "No. That wasn't me. I was on the ferry, yes, but it was someone else who attempted to intimidate you. I didn't realize until later."

Alex looked confused as she studied Julian carefully. "I remember a blond man threatening me."

"Yes, I was blond back then, but so was this other man. I know it's confusing," he said, changing the subject. "I have a lot more to tell you about 1983. But first, tell me about your current effort." He looked at Floyd and Lisa and asked, "And how are the two of you involved in this?"

"On that ferry, I gave something important to Floyd's uncle, Dylan Stone," Alex quickly interjected. "He disappeared later that summer. We've decided to retrace his steps and try to find out what happened to him and possibly find more information about the jewels as well," she said as she looked at Floyd and then back at Julian. Floyd nodded at her.

"The key," Julian said blankly.

"What?" she asked.

"You gave something important to Dylan. It was a key."

"Yes! The key. How did you know about that?"

"I'll explain," he said, then looked at Lisa. "And how do you fit into this?"

"My father was traveling with Dylan that summer, his name was Bull..."

"Eastland," Julian interrupted her. "Yes, I knew Bull. It's nice to meet you both. I liked Dylan and Bull. They found themselves involved in something that got completely out of hand. I did as well."

He continued, "We don't know each other well, and I'm sure you're trying to decide how much you want to share with me. Let me tell you a little about me."

Julian stood up like a professor before a lecture hall. "In 1983, I was a punk kid who thought he was the world's expert on art. I grew up in Europe and studied all the greats. I visited every museum, cathedral, and gallery you can imagine—from the Louvre with its masterpieces to St. Martin's Church in Aulendorf, Germany, with its bejeweled Gothic skeletons on either side of the altar. My goal at that time was to create my own museum because I didn't think anyone else cared about art as much as I did.

"After the events of 1983, I decided to dedicate myself to exposing art to the world and helping others appreciate it as much as I did. I left UVA and went back to Europe for my PhD. I studied at the Royal College of Art in London, with stints at Zurich University of the Arts and the University of Texas at Austin as well. I took a job as an assistant curator at the Musée de Cluny in Paris—the National Medieval Museum. Without boring you with the details, I worked at several museums in Europe before taking on the job in Chicago. I figured that would be the crowning achievement of my life. But then the Uffizi reached out to me. I couldn't turn down this opportunity. And I don't regret the move at all.

"Over the years, my specialty has been finding missing and stolen artifacts. The museums I've worked at have benefited from this passion. I've become a world expert on finding art that was stolen by the Nazis. You may have read that I was able to track down two of the lost Fabergé eggs, as well as the missing and dismantled Amber Room. I still have several items on my wish list, and at the top of that list is the Irish Crown Jewels. In 1983, I came very close to finding them. I learned then that some things are more important than art and missing treasures."

Floyd was in shock. He had come to the Uffizi today as a tourist. He'd seen the museum highlights on a tour that thousands of people took each week. Now, here he was in an office buried in the catacombs of the Uffizi, with one of the most respected art curators in the world—a man who happened to have run into Dylan, Bull, and even Alex during that fateful trip forty years ago!

Julian sat back down and said quietly, "I would love to discuss this further with you, but I have a meeting I must attend presently."

Floyd said, "Dr. Marks..."

"Please, call me Julian."

"Ah...Julian...we'd like to discuss this further as well. We really want to hear everything you can remember from 1983. Lisa, Alex, and I are desperate to learn whatever you can tell us about what happened to Dylan and Bull. Plus, we've gathered various clues that we feel are pointing us towards the lost Irish Crown Jewels being hidden somewhere in Corfu, but we haven't been able to put it all together yet."

Julian paused for a moment, deep in thought, then quickly stood up and reviewed a piece of paper that had been placed directly in the middle of his desk.

"I have a suggestion," he said. "Let's continue this conversation in Corfu. I'm curious to learn what you have discovered. I haven't been to the island since 1983. And I won't just tell you about what happened to Dylan and Bull, I'll show you."

Floyd looked at Lisa and Alex, who were both nodding at him. "We'd love that," Floyd said.

"I just checked my calendar. I can meet you there in two days. My assistant will provide you with the details."

Chapter 27

The Cliffs

1983

DYLAN LEFT THE APARTMENT building, walked across the street to the park, then strolled down an avenue looking for a place to eat. He observed fishermen unloading their catches and wealthy sailors working on their yachts in the marina, then came upon a small café with tables on the sidewalk. He sat down. Besides the excellent view of the marina, it was a great people-watching spot. He was fascinated by how people in different countries socialized and engaged with each other. The northern Europeans were more formal and withdrawn (until you entered a pub), whereas the further south he traveled, the more relaxed and convivial he found the people. Italy and Greece were very social places. People were laughing, holding hands, smoking, and talking everywhere.

He observed the slight waitress as she approached his table. Her curly brunette hair peered out from beneath a purple beret, and she was swallowed by a loose-fitting white blouse and knee-length, baggy shorts. She handed him a menu and said in broken English, "Here menu." Then she asked, "Drink?"

Dylan responded, "Coke." She pivoted and walked through the front door of the narrow restaurant.

"Are you American?" a voice erupted from behind him.

Dylan turned to put a face to the voice. The man sitting at the table directly behind him spoke English with a loud, thick Greek accent. He looked to be about thirty, with short, wavy black hair and a permanent five o'clock shadow. His eyes were dark and warm. He wore a white linen shirt, and his dark skin glowed in contrast.

"Yes," Dylan responded.

"We are both alone. Would you like to visit over dinner?" the man asked.

Dylan was a little uncomfortable with this, but what could go wrong? He hadn't talked to anyone all day. "Sure," he said, and the man stood, wine glass in hand and a cigarette dangling from his lips, and walked to his table. Dylan rose to shake his hand, and they both sat down. "My name is Dylan."

"I am Yiannis. I am from Corfu. My whole life," he said with a smile. "This is a great restaurant. You must have the *pastitsado*; it's a rooster stew served with pasta. Excellent! Also, they have the best stuffed tomatoes and eggplant."

"Well..." Dylan started.

Yiannis said, "I will order for us. Trust me. You will love it."

He snapped his fingers, and the waitress appeared. Yiannis spoke in Greek with great animation, his hands constantly in motion. The waitress left and promptly returned with a bottle of local wine and some pita bread, and what looked to Dylan like yogurt.

After two courses of incredible food, they moved on to a second bottle.

Yiannis asked, "So, why have you decided to visit the most beautiful Greek island, Corfu?"

Dylan was feeling a little woozy, so he slowly sipped a glass of water. He responded, "A couple of reasons. We've been told many times during our trip that we must visit Corfu, and specifically Pelekas Beach."

"Ah. Pelekas Beach is lovely. You will find many Americans there. I personally prefer other beaches on the island. What was the other reason?"

Dylan debated whether he should say anything about the missing jewels, but he figured, what could go wrong? And maybe Yiannis would know something useful, like an old myth or local story.

"Well, this might sound crazy, but we're searching for a missing treasure. And we've been pointed to Corfu."

"That sounds exciting!" Yiannis said. "Corfu has a notorious history with pirates. Could it be that? Maybe I could help."

"It's a long story with many twists and turns. One clue pointed towards Kaiser's Throne, but when I went there, I found another hint sending me in a different direction. I don't understand what it means."

"Kaiser's Throne! I love that place. It's been here for a very long time. I have been there many times. What is the new clue?"

Dylan opened his journal and read to Yiannis: "A shadow points to the jewel's new home. Beneath the cliffs where the lion's silence leans, the sunken crown guards secret queens."

Yiannis put his hand to his chin in thought. He took a sip of his wine and snapped his fingers. The waitress returned. Yiannis spoke loudly, laughed, and patted her on the back when she left. She returned with two tall, narrow glasses of clear liquid.

Yiannis handed a glass to Dylan and said, "This is a tradition. You must drink this. It's ouzo." He raised his glass, motioning for Dylan to follow his lead.

Dylan didn't want to drink any more alcohol, but he also didn't want to offend Yiannis. They both gulped down the liquid. Dylan immediately regretted it. The fiery licorice spirit burned on the way down and compounded the effect of the wine. "Thank you for your hospitality," he said with a bit of hesitation, "but this will be my last." He waved to the girl and ordered an espresso.

Yiannis looked at the sky for a moment and then looked at Dylan, "I think I may know where you should look next. Cape Drastis."

"What is that?"

"It's one of the most beautiful cliffs in all of Europe. The summit is a striking green with trees and vegetation, but the cliffs are chalky white, and they are filled with caves, both above and below the water. It is at the northwesternmost point of this island. You can hike to it from the village of Peroulades, or you can rent a boat and see it from the sea. It's not that famous, though it is easily as magnificent as the White Cliffs of Dover in England or the cliffs in Cassis."

"What made you think of Cape Drastis?" Dylan asked, gratefully sipping his espresso, its grounds coating his teeth in black specks.

"The reference to the cliffs is pretty obvious. And there are no others like it on the island. But also, when I was a boy, I heard a legend that something valuable was hidden there. Many, many years ago, it was common to explore the caves in search of treasure, but none has ever been found, and several people died while looking. I have a feeling you are hearing this same old story."

Yiannis studied his glass for a moment, deep in thought, then looked at Dylan and abruptly said, "Also, there is a place in the center of the largest cliff, a rock formation that is known as the lion's head.

Perhaps your clue refers to that location, or maybe a cave below it on the face of the cliff. Let me warn you: it will be very dangerous to explore that area. It's a sheer cliff, and a fall would likely be fatal." He looked at Dylan with concern etched on his face.

Dylan took out his journal and made some quick notes, then returned it to his backpack. When he looked up, a woman had appeared at Yiannis's side. Apparently, Dylan was the only one who hadn't noticed, as he saw heads turning from several of the nearby tables. She was tall and tan, with long brunette hair, dark eyes under long lashes. Wearing short shorts and a tight, low-cut blouse that she filled out perfectly, she pouted at Yannis.

"Yiannis! I have been searching for you all night," she said.

He spoke to her in Greek and then said, "This is Dylan from Texas." He pointed at Dylan. "This is Penelope, my wife. She is from Athens but now calls Corfu home."

Penelope studied Dylan and spoke in English with a slight accent, "I have lived here since I was a little girl. But the locals still consider me an outsider." She eyed Yiannis. He looked down. Then she turned back to Dylan, "It is nice to meet you, Dylan."

"I can relate. It is like that in Texas...if you aren't born there, you're not a Texan," he said with a slight slur and a smile.

"Poppy...I call her Poppy," Yannis said, "is an excellent mountain climber. She has experience scaling Cape Drastis."

"Please tell me about it." Dylan struggled to keep eye contact with Penelope, as her shirt was losing its battle to contain her.

Penelope adjusted her blouse and said with a smile, "You should visit a Greek beach." Dylan blushed.

"Anyway, back to your question. Technically, climbing the cliffs is not allowed. They are considered too dangerous. They are steep, and it is difficult to get a good grip." She looked to her left and then to her right before continuing, "However, yes, I have climbed there two times. What can I tell you?"

"Yiannis and I were discussing the caves and the phrase 'lion's head.' I believe that something may be hidden in a cave there. What can you tell me about it?" Dylan said as he attempted to focus on her eyes.

"Lion's Head is the local name for an outcropping in the center of the main cliff. There are a few caves that are very close to the top of the cliffs, and there may be one directly below the Lion's Head. I suppose someone could be helped down and then into a cave, but it would be dangerous. Only the most skilled climber should even consider it." She thought for a second as she leaned over and grabbed Yiannis's wine glass. "I highly recommend you forget about this. Many people have searched those caves. And many have been hurt or died trying. I think this is a, how do you say, crazy goose chase."

Yiannis smiled. "She means wild goose chase."

She glared at Yiannis and then abruptly added, "There are also some underwater caves. They are extremely difficult to get to. They are so narrow that you cannot wear scuba gear. The ocean is not friendly there. And you have to be careful about the tides."

Penelope turned to Yiannis, clearly impatient. "Let's go to the club. I'm ready for some fun."

Yiannis looked at Dylan. "Would you like to join us? We are going dancing."

Dylan, still feeling a little wobbly, responded, "Thanks for the offer, but I'm going back to my room. I have to get up early tomorrow."

They stood up. Yiannis hugged Dylan. "It has been nice to meet you, Dylan."

Penelope kissed Dylan on both cheeks and casually rubbed her body against his. She then stepped back slowly, while holding his hand in hers, and asked him, "Are you sure you don't want to join us? There will be a lot of pretty girls there. I promise you'll have a good time." Dylan's face turned crimson. He thought about her invitation but knew he wasn't up for it. He looked at each of them and said, "It's been nice to meet you both. I'll be on my way..." and he stumbled away from the table and into the dark.

Chapter 28

Positano

1983

Just as Bull was stepping onto the 2:22 train to Brindisi, he felt a yank on his backpack. He quickly turned around and saw it slipping into the crowd on the back of a shadowy figure with a ball cap turned around. In panic, he looked at the train. It was leaving in five minutes and only went to Brindisi once a day. Dylan would be on that train waiting for him, but Bull had no choice. He jumped off the train and chased after the man with his backpack.

Thirty minutes later, he found the backpack stuffed under a bush by a trash can just outside the entrance to the train station. Nothing appeared to be missing. Bull sat for a minute, thinking about what had happened. It didn't make sense. *Could this be related to the robbery in Reims? And the cliff push in Cassis? If so, why didn't they keep the backpack?* After a few moments, he regrouped and decided that if he had a day by himself in Italy, he was going to make the best of it. He'd studied this area and had always wanted to see the Amalfi Coast, a peninsula in southern Italy known for its picturesque landscapes and colorful villages built into the hills overlooking the ocean. It hadn't made the cut on Dylan and Bull's itinerary, but now he had a chance to experience it. He jumped on a packed bus from Naples to Sorrento, so crowded he wasn't able to sit down, then he took a "standing-room-only" ferry to the seaside town of Positano. As he arrived, he was stunned by the beauty of the white, pink, and yellow houses built into the mountains overlooking the water. The sweaty and cramped commute had been worth it.

Bull hiked up a hilly pedestrian walkway from the port, passing colorful local shops, cafés filled with laughter, bikini-clad girls heading to the beach, and tourists taking pictures of the buildings that stared down at them from the mountains above. He then turned onto the main street, Via Cristoforo Colombo, which was magnificent in its own right, with the ocean far below to his right and shops and hotels built into the mountain on his left. He had no hotel reservation, which was risky. It was relatively late, and he was tired after traveling all day. *I hope this wasn't a bad decision*, he thought. After passing several hotels with no vacancies, he was starting to feel demoralized. *Well, I do have a tent, just in case.* Then he noticed a beige building with an interesting name: Hotel California. It was a three-story structure highlighted with a series of rooms fronted by balconies and framed with brown wooden shutters overlooking the sea. Being a huge Eagles fan, he crossed his fingers and walked in, hoping he could get a room for the night.

He pulled out his *Let's Go Europe* book, flipped to the "English to Italian phrases" section, and asked the clerk, "*Parli Inglese?*"

The clerk nodded and replied, "I speak a little English."

Bull was in luck. He rented the cheapest room they had. Then, he just had to ask, "Is this hotel named after the song by the Eagles?"

The clerk, clearly tired of this question, responded sharply, "No. This hotel got its name in 1968 when the current owners bought it. It's a refurbished eighteenth-century palace that was once the residence of a Neapolitan nobleman. The new owner's father was from California. I like to think the Eagles named their song after us," he said with a slight smile.

Bull placed his backpack on the bed in his room. He hoped the mattress was long enough for him. He'd found that many of the European beds just weren't built for someone his height. He surveyed the tiny room. Besides the bed, it had one wooden chair, a small desk pushed up against the wall, and a print on the wall of a view of Positano as taken from the water. That was it. *The bathroom must be down the hall.* He opened the swaying curtains and stepped out onto a narrow terrace, where he sat down on a metal chair and took in the million-dollar view of the Amalfi Coast. *This is the life.*

After a late dinner alone at a nearby sidewalk café overlooking the ocean, he was about to leave when he heard a loud, slurring voice.

"Hey, big guy, are you American?"

Bull turned to see an inebriated guy pointing at him. He was accompanied by a college-age girl, who seemed embarrassed by her partner.

"Yes, I'm American," he said. "Name's Bull. I'm from Texas."

"Texas! I heard everything was big in Texas, but geez," the sloshed guy said, laughing, as he looked up at Bull.

The girl, petite, with short auburn hair, glasses, and a pink knee-length dress, said, "This is Tom. I'm Julie. We are traveling with some friends from our college."

Before Bull could respond, Tom pushed Julie aside and said, "Hey. Wanna go to a club with us? It's built into a cliff and overlooks one of the most famous beaches in Europe. It's only just down the road. It stays open until dawn!" He stumbled as he spoke.

Bull, unhappy with Tom's behavior, stared angrily at him. He was ready to put this drunk idiot in his place. Tom was oblivious.

Bull glanced at Julie. He could tell she was worried he would get violent. Her eyes implored him to stay calm. He decided to join them, if only to assure Julie was protected.

Bull responded sharply, "Sure. I just finished dinner. I'll join for a bit."

He stood between Julie and Tom as they entered a line of more than a hundred people.

Julie said, "Wait here." She went and spoke to the bouncer, and he immediately motioned Tom and Bull to enter.

The three passed in front of the entire line and entered the club. They heard several grumbles as the door closed behind them.

"How did you do that?" Bull asked Julie.

She looked at him shyly. "My father spends a lot of money here when he visits. They all know him."

Bull looked around in amazement. The club was built on a cliff edge with a terrace overlooking Spiaggia Grande beach, a quarter-mile-long stretch of dark volcanic sand renowned for its ideal location in the center of Positano, amid a multitude of restaurants and bars. The top level of the club overlooked the beach, a hundred feet below. The bottom level, built into the mountainside cave, could have been a nightclub in the middle of Rome or New York City. Yet to Bull's surprise, it wasn't busy. He pointed to the sparse attendance and looked at Julie.

She smiled and told him, "The real crowds don't get here until after one a.m. It's open until dawn. It's busy every night. People come from Naples and even Rome. It's the place to be seen."

They grabbed a table overlooking the beach and ordered drinks. Julie paid. Bull was relieved. When he saw the bill, he realized one drink would have cost more than his lodging for the night.

Julie started to say something, but Tom interrupted her and asked, "So, Bull, what's your story?"

Bull ignored him. "Julie, what were you going to say?"

Tom stood up shakily, pointed at Bull's face, and said, "What's your deal? I asked you a question."

Julie stood up, turned to Tom, and placed her arm on his shoulder, attempting to guide him back to his seat.

Tom pushed her back into her seat, and she fell to the floor.

Bull shot to his feet. His knees hit the table between them, causing it to tip and spill drinks on Tom, infuriating him. He swung wildly. Bull pulled Julie aside and blocked Tom's punch with his forearm. Tom lost his balance and fell face down next to the table, which tumbled onto its side. He didn't move.

Bull grabbed Julie's hand. "Let's get out of here," he said, glancing back with relief as Tom stirred slightly.

They walked silently, hand in hand, until they found a café that was still open. Slipping inside, they grabbed a table in the back.

Julie looked at Bull and said, "I'm sorry about all of that."

Bull was angry. "You deserve better."

"I know. We just started dating. My parents really like him. They don't see what I see."

"It's not worth it. Please tell me that you won't go back to him."

"No way. That was the worst I've ever seen him. We're done."

As a tired-looking waitress approached them, Julie looked at Bull and said, "Let me order. It's my treat." She then started a lively conversation with the waitress in Italian, which ended with laughter and a hug. Before she left, the waitress looked at Bull, then gave Julie a thumbs-up before heading to the kitchen. Moments later, she returned with a pot of tea, two espressos, and a plate of tiramisu.

"That was impressive," Bull said. "I had two years of high school French, but that's it for me."

"French is my favorite foreign language. Languages have always come easily for me. Hopefully, I'll figure out a way to use that in life."

"I'm sure you will." Bull looked at Julie closely for the first time as he took his first bite of the creamy dessert, the espresso perking him up. There was something special about her. She was nothing like the girls he usually dated. She was kind. She was genuine. As she took off her glasses to clean the lenses, Bull was struck by how her eyes radiated intelligence...and she had a great smile.

"This cake is great. Thanks. So, you said you were traveling with college friends. Where do you go to school?"

"LSU. I'll be a sophomore next year. Double major: accounting with a minor in German."

"No way! I'm attending LSU this fall. Pre-law. Curious—why are you studying German?"

"I already placed out of Italian and French, and I've always wanted to learn German. I might study Mandarin as well, if I can fit it in."

"Impressed again. You're a regular polyglot," Bull said, laughing. "I learned that word in my fourth-grade spelling bee—which I won, by the way—and this is the first time I've gotten to use it in a conversation. So, how do you like Baton Rouge?"

"I love it, other than the dumb guys," she said with a half-smile.

"As soon as I get home from this trip, I'm heading to LSU for football practice."

He then filled her in on his expected itinerary for the next month, which included potential stops in Venice, Switzerland, Germany, and Amsterdam. "We keep our travel schedule flexible, so I'm not sure how long we'll stay anywhere. However, we've planned to check into a place in Zermatt on July 7th, stay a few days, and fly out of Amsterdam on July 23rd. So, we'll work around those two dates."

"If I'm able to get away, maybe I could meet you in Zermatt?" Julie said. She averted her eyes and blushed. Then she quickly continued, "Whatever the case, I'll be there when you arrive in Baton Rouge. I tutor summer school students. I'd love to show you around."

He studied her for a moment. She stared at her hands and fumbled with her teacup. He then placed her hand in his and said, "If you can get to Zermatt, I'd love that. We'll be staying at the Salzeberger House. It's a four-hundred-year-old cabin that's now a hostel. We made a reservation in advance, but I'm sure they'll have room for you. Otherwise, I'll definitely see you at college in August."

They continued talking for more than an hour, unaware that the tea had grown cold and the café was about to close. The waitress stood by the bar in the distance, watching them. She smiled as she began to count the money from the cash register.

After finishing her tea, Julie asked Bull, "Do you happen to travel with a guy who carries a guitar?"

Bull's eyes opened wide. "I do. My buddy Dylan has a guitar. Why do you ask?"

"We ran into this guy at that cave bar who was asking everyone if they'd seen a big football player guy and his buddy with a guitar. Now that I know you're a football player, I thought—"

"Did he say anything more?"

"Yeah. He got pretty drunk, and he started talking a lot. He said that he was traveling with you and got lost. He was trying to find you."

"Interesting," Bull said. "What else did he say?"

"He said you all were looking for a lost treasure. I think he was trying to impress me. It bothered Tom, as you would guess."

"I bet. Did the guy say anything else?" Bull asked.

"Yeah. He said that he had tried to find you in Figline. Have you ever heard of Figline?"

"Yes. It's a great place, near Florence. Anything else?"

"He said he was heading to Corfu. He seemed to think that he would find you there."

"When did you have this conversation with him?" Bull asked.

"Hmm, the days tend to run together. Oh yeah, it was actually just last night. I remember because he said it was important for him to leave today. He said he'd calculated that would be the time his friends would arrive in Corfu."

Bull closed his eyes for a moment, deep in thought. *Dylan is in Corfu tonight by himself, and this guy is there looking for him. That can't be good. I need to get there as soon as I can.*

Bull then looked directly at Julie, his expression serious. "What did he look like?"

"He was a good-looking guy. Blond hair. Medium build. Wore his cap backwards most of the time. He had an accent—not sure what it was. Weird, but there was something about him that made me uneasy."

Bull knew he needed to get to Corfu as soon as possible, and he needed to get some rest. It would be a long travel day tomorrow. He put his napkin on the table and motioned to the waitress, who happened to be the last employee in the café. "Julia, will you be okay if I walk you back to your hotel now? Do I need to talk to Tom?" His eyes narrowed.

"Tom will leave me alone. There's nothing to worry about."

After making sure Julie had got to her hotel room, he turned to leave.

Julie said, "Wait!" She ran inside the room and immediately returned with a pen.

She grabbed Bull's hand and wrote a telephone number on his palm. She then stood on her toes, put her arms around Bull's shoulders, said, "This is my number in Baton Rouge. I hope to see you even sooner," and hugged him hard.

As Bull turned to leave, a door from a room across the hall opened. It was Tom. He had a black eye and was holding an ice pack. As soon as he saw Bull, his eyes opened wide and he shut his door.

Serves him right, Bull thought.

Chapter 29

The Reunion

1983

DYLAN OPENED HIS EYES slowly. The sun streaming through the crack in the curtain hit him like a hammer. His head throbbed, and he was so thirsty he was tempted to drink out of the flower vase on the bedside table. He looked around. He was in Molly's apartment. He had no recollection of anything that had happened after leaving Yiannis and Penelope at the restaurant. That ouzo had done a number on him. He looked at his watch. It was mid-afternoon! He never slept that late. The ship would be arriving soon. He needed to get to the dock so he could try to find Bull when he disembarked.

His journal was on the floor in the middle of the room and his backpack was leaning against the wall by the front door. He could have sworn he'd left them both in the closet. He checked his waist. His money belt was there. Quickly unzipping it, he fumbled around inside. All good. His guitar was under the bed, untouched.

He stood up sluggishly. Things didn't feel right, but he didn't have time to worry about it. He got dressed, collected his things, checked out of the apartment, and began the two-mile trek back to the ferry terminal.

He arrived an hour early. He grabbed a coffee and a seat on a bench by the ticket office. He pulled out his journal, reviewed what he'd written the previous night, and made some additional notes.

"Hello."

Dylan looked up. A smiling young man was looking at him, his hand extended.

"I'm Nels. Are you waiting for someone?"

Dylan stood, shook his hand, and responded, "Dylan. Yes, my buddy Bull will be arriving, hopefully, on the next ferry."

"I've been traveling by myself for a while. It's nice to talk to someone."

"Where are you from?"

"Norway. I travel every summer. It is my passion."

Nels was slender with tan skin, blond hair, and blue eyes. He noticed Dylan looking at the small bag he carried. "Over the years, I have learned to travel very light," he said with a smile.

Just then, a horn blared, and they could both see the ferry entering the harbor.

"Where are you going when your friend arrives?" Nels asked.

"Pelekas Beach. Everyone's told us we have to go there," Dylan said.

"I'm going there too. Would you mind if I tagged along?"

Dylan thought about this. Nels seemed like an okay guy. It might be nice to have him along for a while. They could learn about Norway and other places he'd traveled. "Sure. Join us."

The ferry began its disembarkation process. The first person off the boat was Bull. Dylan waved at him, and he rushed over.

"Dude," Bull said, "someone yanked off my backpack as I was getting on the train in Naples, and I got stuck there. Sorry about that."

"What? That's crazy," Dylan said. "I was sure glad to see you get off the ferry. If you hadn't, I wouldn't have known how we would ever find each other. Did you spend the day there? Naples wasn't my favorite place," he said.

"Actually, I went to Positano on the Amalfi Coast. It was great. If we have time, we need to go there. You'll love it."

Dylan remembered Nels, who was standing and watching this reunion. "Bull, this is Nels, from Norway. He's going to hang out with us for a bit."

"Nice to meet you! You're always welcome. I've wanted to learn about Norway," Bull said. Then he added, "Let's grab something to eat and then head for Pelekas Beach. I've been looking forward to this for a long time."

Nels interjected, "I know a great restaurant within walking distance. Then we can catch a bus to the other side of the island."

As the three were heading into Corfu Old Town, Dylan fell back and walked alongside Bull. "We need some private time so I can catch you up," he said. "I've learned a lot in the last day here in Corfu."

"Sounds good. I have a little to share as well."

"Hey, Nels," Bull shouted to get his attention. "Dylan and I need to discuss a few things. Give us directions to the restaurant, and we'll meet you there in an hour."

***

As Bull and Dylan walked towards a local bar to compare notes, Nels fell behind and thought to himself, *I pulled it off. They think I'm Nels from Norway. I need to gain their trust and then somehow get Dylan to Cape Drastis. From what I read in his journal last night, that may be where the jewels are hidden. I think he knows more than he wrote, and I need to get that out of him, at whatever cost. I may have to get rid of Bull once and for all. He's in the way. And after I have the jewels, I'll have no need for Dylan either...*

***

As they sat at the bar, Dylan recounted his experiences of the last twenty-four hours, including his trip to Kaiser's Throne, dinner with Yiannis and Penelope, and the theory that the lost treasure could be located at Cape Drastis in a cave near an outcropping called Lion's Head. He also mentioned that someone might have gone through his belongings in his room this morning.

Bull then summarized his trip to Positano, his chance meeting with Julie, and the warning he'd received about someone following them, then commented, "So, tell me again about Penelope. What was she wearing?"

Dylan looked at him. It was as though Bull had heard nothing Dylan had said other than his description of the voluptuous Greek woman from last night.

Bull continued, "Just kidding...kind of. Oh, let me finish. We need to remember someone is following us, and he's already here. I wouldn't be surprised if that's who was in your room this morning. We need to keep an eye out for him."

Dylan concluded, "At some point on this trip, let's go to Cape Drastis, and we'll figure it out from there." He pulled out his journal, made a few notes, then put it away quickly.

Bull finished his drink and stood up. "Sounds like a plan. Okay, let's meet Nels, grab some dinner, and head to Pelekas Beach."

Chapter 30

The Lost Journal Entry

2025

Lisa sat on her bed in the apartment they were renting in the heart of Florence. It was housed in an old building on Via della Vigna Nuova, two blocks from the Arno River and a short walk from Piazza di Santa Maria Novella, one of the most beautiful squares in Florence. The building had been there since the Renaissance. It had taken them a while to find it. From the street, there was simply an old stone door, among many others. No name. No address. They'd walked around the entire block twice before figuring out which door was theirs. After finding the hidden keypad mentioned in their landlord's cryptic instructions, they'd entered a code, pushed the heavy door inward, and found themselves in a dark, damp hallway. They then opened a rusty metal gate, which led them to the bottom of a gloomy spiral staircase made of stone. They lugged their suitcases up four flights of stairs before finding their flat, which turned out to be a spectacular three-story apartment with floor-to-ceiling windows, wooden floors, and Renaissance artwork decorating the walls.

Lisa was reading Dylan's journal for what seemed like the tenth time, focusing on his entries from Velletri and Rome, and a short instalment from Corfu on June 27th—the last entry. These last five pages were stained with some sort of liquid—she'd been cautious when reading them to avoid accidentally ripping the paper. She noticed some smudges on the last page and held the journal up to the light on her bedstand. It looked like there were words on the back of the previous entry, but when she turned the page, there were none. She then noticed that the last page seemed too thick. She carefully inserted her fingernail at the top of the page, and it started to split into two. The pages had been stuck together—there were more entries!

She abruptly sat up and then slowly peeled the pages apart. The first new entry was dated June 28th. The writing was smudged and difficult to read in some places, but she could make out most of it.

June 28, Corfu

A lot has happened over the last day, and I expect the next day or two will answer many questions. I stayed in Molly's apartment in Corfu Old Town last night. Bull got stuck in Italy, so I was on my own. I found pencil markings on the closet door in Molly's apartment with baby Cormac's height changes, so I knew I was in the right place. I also found a note from Molly stuck in an old desk. It pointed me to Kaiser's Throne. So, I went there. And I found a new clue:

"Where sun dies soft in Ionian blue, The crowned heart waits beneath the view. Where once a throne watched empire's flame, A shadow points to the jewel's new home. Beneath the cliffs where the lion's silence leans, the sunken crown guards secret queens."

Wow. The quote on the envelope was only part of the verse. *This is important*, she thought.

At this point, the journal became difficult to read. She could make out the names Yiannis and Penelope. The word "ouzo" was circled with a little picture of a frowning face next to it. There was a mention of Yiannis discussing a treasure and a lion's head at Cape Drastis, and Dylan planning a visit there. That seemed important. There was a note about Bull meeting a "Julie" in Positano. *Hmm.* She was able to make out the sentence, *"Bull and I are convinced someone is following us. He has blond hair. We think he may be European. He's here right now."* Then she read the next entry, which was fully intact.

June 29, morning, Corfu

Bull and I went down to the ocean this morning and walked through the sand right into the water. It's the first soft sand we've experienced in Europe so far. The water is practically waveless. It's like a lake. People were waterskiing on it while we were at the beach. Also, the water is as clear as drinking water. We went out where we couldn't touch the ocean floor, but we could look down through the water and see the sand ripples on the bottom easily. It's so different. As you look inland from out in the water, you see beautiful, high, green mountains covered with little trees. Also, you see cliffs to the right and left. It's spectacular.

The only bad thing is that a lot of people know about this pristine place. At the beach, there are lots of college-age kids, many American. Everyone's heard of Corfu. The people on the beach are very uninhibited. More than half of the girls are topless, and I saw one woman totally nude. Also, several of the guys were playing frisbee without any clothes on. They say this town lights up at night, mainly because there are so many college kids here. I guess we'll find out.

We're committed to staying here at least three more days. We plan to motorbike around the entire island, check out the beaches, and try some Greek food at small cafés off of the beaten path. Nels stayed with us last night. And we ran into another guy, Julian, from UVA this morning.

We're gonna hang out with them today and see how it goes. Both have been here for a bit and know their way around. I figure it's good to be in a group, especially if there's somebody here who's after us. Bull and I are determined not to let that get to us. We're finally here! We're going to enjoy it.

Lisa read the entries twice, trying to absorb everything. The note about her dad meeting a girl named Julie was fascinating, considering her mom was named Julie. *Could that be her? If so, I wonder why they never told me about meeting each other in Italy?*

She then texted Alex and Floyd, who were out for a walk along the Arno River, and asked them to meet her at the bar two doors down so she could share this information with them.

The bar was built into the side of a timeworn building, which opened onto a stone alley. It was empty except for two older men who were drinking beers and watching soccer on a small TV above the bar. After Alex and Floyd had read the surprise journal entries, they looked at Lisa in stunned silence. A bartender took their order and disappeared into the cavernous structure.

"Everything is now pointing towards Cape Drastis in Corfu," said Floyd. "The Lion's Head reference is interesting. Must be important—"

Alex interrupted, "What about the reference to Julian? That must be Julian Marks. It appears he was with them very close to the time Dylan went missing. Do you think we can trust him?"

The drinks were delivered. Bottled water for Lisa, as usual, a Sprite for Alex, and Floyd had a glass of Tuscan red wine. *We are in Tuscany*, Floyd thought. *Might as well.*

Floyd spoke. "I still think we should meet Julian in Corfu, and let's hear what he has to say. Based on how that goes, we can decide how open we want to be. We can go to Velletri and Rome on the way back through Europe after Corfu."

Alex nodded. "Yes, we need to be careful. Julian could be a good guy, but he also could be the mysterious blond man who was following the boys."

***

Julian sat down on a metal chair at a small conference table in the drab office of Konstantinos Papadopoulos, the lieutenant general of the Hellenic Police for the island of Corfu. The WWII-era building looked like it could have been a prison if it had not been the headquarters of the local police.

"I understand that you are the curator for the Uffizi Gallery in Florence," said Lieutenant Papadopoulos. It is our pleasure to welcome you to Corfu. How is it that I can help you, Dr. Marks?" he asked formally, though he made it clear from his tone that he would prefer to be anywhere other than talking with Julian at this moment.

"Thank you. I have an unusual request. I would like to see the file on the disappearance of Dylan Stone from June 1983," Julian responded.

Lt. Papadopoulos' eyes opened wide, just for a second. Julian could tell that he'd struck a nerve.

"That is a long time ago. It may take some time to research that," the lieutenant said, clearly stalling.

"It is imperative. I'll wait here," Julian said sternly.

The lieutenant barked out some words in Greek, and an assistant quickly left the room. "Why, may I ask, are you interested in an event that occurred more than forty years ago?"

"I'm hosting the nephew of Mr. Stone. We're going to visit the location of the incident," Julian said with no emotion, purposefully not mentioning the fact that he had been at the scene of the incident himself all those years ago.

"I strongly advise against this. We do not want to dredge up such negative memories. It is the tourist season."

At that moment, the assistant rushed back in with a small manila folder and handed it to the lieutenant, who reviewed it briefly and then gave it to Julian.

Julian opened it. It was a one-page typewritten report from June 29, 1983. After reading it, he asked, "Is this all that you have?"

"Yes. There is not much to it. I was a young officer at the time. I personally interviewed Mr. Eastland. He had very little to say, though I believe he was in shock. He left the country within a day or two."

"Dylan's body was never found?" Julian asked.

"No. And that is unusual. Normally, when a person falls off the cliff, we find the body on the rocks below or nearby. We did find his money belt and gave it to Mr. Eastland to return to Mr. Stone's family."

"Did you have any indication that this was anything other than an accidental fall?" Julian asked. He was suspicious.

"We had very little evidence to evaluate. We ruled out homicide quickly."

"What about the rope that was attached to the tree and hanging off the cliff?" Julian asked.

The lieutenant was caught by surprise "What? How...? I do not know what you are talking about." He stumbled through the words.

Julian stood. He had made his point.

"I'll excuse myself. Thank you." He quickly left the room, walked through the front door, and entered a waiting black limousine, which promptly accelerated and disappeared.

The lieutenant turned to his assistant and said with authority, "Keep an eye on him. We cannot afford to turn this into a public relations nightmare. I want them off this island as soon as possible."

***

Floyd, Alex, and Lisa sat at a small round wooden table in the courtyard of their quaint hotel across from the marina in Corfu Old Town. A carafe of water sat in the middle of the table, surrounded by three small glasses.

"Well, I'm looking forward to today," Lisa said. "I hope we'll finally learn what happened to Dylan and Bull."

At that moment, Julian walked in, hair slicked back, and sunglasses on. Next to him was a striking woman with short brown hair streaked with gray and piercing green eyes. All attention gravitated to her instead of the dapper Julian. It was evident that he was used to it.

Julian smiled and exclaimed, "Floyd, Alex, Lisa, please meet my wife, Adriana. Definitely my better half."

Adriana held out her hand. After brief introductions, Julian pulled up two chairs, and they sat down at the table.

"I hope you are enjoying your stay in Corfu," said Julian. "Before we start our adventure today, let me give you some more context. As I hinted earlier, I was a precocious child who attended a snooty private school in Switzerland and became obsessed with European history and artifacts. I thought I understood it and appreciated it more than anyone else. I went through a phase where I stole some valuable pieces and created my own illicit museum."

Alex gasped. Floyd and Lisa exchanged glances.

"Yes. I'm not proud of it. After the summer of 1983, I turned myself in and returned every piece to its rightful owner. Fortunately, I was not charged with a crime. Believe it or not, my notoriety in the art community resulted in opportunities for me, both educationally and commercially. Initially, I became a world expert in countering art theft and consulted at many museums, churches, and palaces. After I received my PhD, I took my first curator job, and that has been my passion ever since.

"That summer, my goal was to obtain the lost Irish Crown Jewels. Initially, I followed you, Alex. I was at the library in Dublin, observing you when you were studying the diaries. Based on your behavior, I knew you had found something important. I was hoping I would follow you to the jewels. I never intended to hurt you in any way. My plan was to stay in the background and eventually obtain the jewels."

Alex grumbled, "Between you following me and that person threatening me, I almost had a nervous breakdown."

Julian looked at her sincerely, "I'm sorry about that. I realize that now. But at the time, I was unable to think about things from your perspective."

He continued with his story, "I saw you meet with the young man by the railing on the ferry, who I later found to be Dylan. I saw you give him something in that restaurant. I was convinced it was related to the jewels, and at that moment, I focused all my attention on Dylan."

Julian turned his attention to Floyd. "I followed your uncle and Bull through France. I'm ashamed to admit it, but I broke into their room one night and went through their things. They almost caught me. I had to jump out of a window and run to avoid them. I was lucky. I bet both of them were faster than me."

"From what I heard, Dylan was fast, and Bull eventually became an NFL football player—no slouch there," Floyd said. "It's a good thing he didn't tackle you."

"You're right! After that night, it was hard to follow them. They got up early and left town. I had no idea where they'd gone. But I had read some of Dylan's journal and knew they would eventually go to Cassis, so I went there and waited. Adriana was with me at that point. They didn't show up for several days. I almost gave up on them. I was about to leave Cassis and head back to Virginia, but one day, they suddenly hopped off the train and ran right into Adriana."

Floyd looked at Adriana.

Adriana spoke. "They were standing on a street corner late in the evening with heavy backpacks weighing them down, and Dylan was also carrying a guitar. They were both studying a book and were apparently lost. I offered to help and gave them directions to a B&B in town. They were very polite...and cute."

Julian continued, "We kept an eye on them while they were in Cassis. They were clearly enjoying their time with the Kellys. The granddaughter seemed to have a thing for Dylan."

Adriana smiled as she recalled watching them together. "Dylan apparently had that effect on girls, though I don't think he knew it. Bull did as well, but in a different way. Bull was the athletic guy that girls were naturally attracted to. Dylan was the thoughtful, sincere one that girls fell in love with."

"It was in Cassis that I realized that the search for the jewels was dangerous," Julian said in a serious tone. "One day, Dylan and Bull decided to hike up to the cliffs over Cassis. I followed Bull, and Adriana tried to follow Dylan, not realizing that he was such a strong runner.

She did her best, but she lost him. However, I was able to keep up with Bull. When he got to the top of the cliff, he walked to the edge and did his impression of Rocky. You know the scene in the movie when he reaches the top of the steps at the Philadelphia Museum of Art and jumps up and down while raising his fists in triumph? It was quite entertaining, I must admit. Then, out of nowhere, another person appeared and pushed him off the cliff."

Lisa gasped.

Julian continued, "The guy just casually walked on. I ran over to the place where I'd last seen Bull and looked down. He was hanging on to a ledge. He was about to fall several hundred feet to his death. I reached down, and he grabbed my hand. I pulled him up. He flopped on the ground to catch his breath. He was covered in scratches and bruises. I slipped away before he got a glimpse of my face."

Pausing to take a sip of water, Julian became more animated as he recalled the events of that day. "I remember talking with Adriana that night. I was shaken. It was at that moment that I decided to protect Dylan and Bull. Someone was willing to kill them to get the jewels. I wanted the jewels, of course, but I couldn't just watch someone hurt them or even kill them. It's just not right."

"Why would they want to hurt Bull?" Lisa asked.

"I realized later it was because this person saw Bull as a threat. Dylan was the key, and Bull was his protector. He wanted to get rid of Bull to get to Dylan."

Floyd jumped in, "So, what happened after that?"

Julian responded, "I decided to follow them and keep an eye on them. I didn't want them to get hurt. Adriana and I would try to overhear conversations at restaurants, for example. We were pretty good at it."

"I watched them meet with the owner of Rossi's Restaurant in Figline. They learned something important there. I was at a café across the street. I heard them talking about the hotel on Pelekas Beach in Corfu as they walked by, so Adriana and I headed there.

"Once again, they disappeared for a few days. But then one morning, I was cooking some breakfast on a grill behind the hotel. I'll never forget. It was a beautiful day. The ocean was so clear that it was transparent. Very few people were awake. Pelekas Beach is famous for its late-night parties, so most people sleep in. A door opened, and Dylan appeared. He moved like a gazelle. And he had those unusual eyes. Anyway, we talked for a few minutes. I think he was a little suspicious of me, but that's understandable. I liked him right off."

Floyd looked at Julian and said, "It's nice to hear positive things about Dylan."

Julian smiled faintly, then got back to his story. "Just as Dylan and I started talking, Bull and another guy came out the same door. Bull was great. So friendly and...confident. He had a presence. But the other fellow..."

"What do you mean?" Lisa asked.

"I knew when I saw him that he was bad news."

Julian stood up. "That's enough background. I have a car waiting for us outside. It will take us to Kaiser's Throne and Cape Drastis. On the way, I'd like to hear whatever you're willing to share with me. Perhaps between what you've learned and my experience, we'll make some progress today."

Chapter 31

Cape Drastis

1983

AFTER RENTING FOUR MOTORBIKES, the guys headed towards Corfu Old Town so that Bull and Dylan could get some Greek drachmas. It took a while, but they finally found an open local bank, and Dylan and Bull entered. After waiting in line, they reached the teller, who didn't speak any English. They each unzipped their money belts and removed American Express traveler's checks, which they exchanged for local currency.

"We're getting the hang of this," Bull said as they left the bank.

"Yeah, it's a challenge managing the different currencies in each country. Kind of fun, though. Plus, their bills are way prettier than US dollars. I'll bring back my leftover currency and give it to my grandmother. She'll love it," Dylan said.

The group left Corfu Old Town and headed out to explore the island. They rode through Esplanade Square, overlooked by an old Venetian fortress from the seventeenth century, then headed about six miles south to Achilleion, a neoclassical palace that had been the summer residence of the Empress of Bavaria in the late 1800s. It had later become the home of Kaiser Wilhelm II, who constructed his namesake throne. After riding around the palace, they cruised on back roads until they arrived at the thirteenth-century Paleokastritsa Monastery, still managed by eight monks and covered in geraniums. After walking around the monastery, they rode until they came to a small restaurant buried in the hills of Corfu, where they dined on *sofrito*, a beef dish with lots of garlic. Lots.

"Where do you want to go next?" Nels asked sharply.

Dylan looked at him, surprised by his tone. This was a vacation, after all. "We're just enjoying the day," he answered casually.

"I'd like to see Kaiser's Throne," Bull said, trying to calm things down.

Dylan observed Nels. *He's acting strange; what's his deal?*

Julian cut in, "Kaiser's Throne sounds great. I've always wanted to go there. Let's do it."

Chapter 32

The Limo Ride

2025

ALL FIVE WERE COMFORTABLY seated in the back of the limousine, with Julian and Adriana facing Floyd, Alex, and Lisa.

"We're heading to Kaiser's Throne," said Julian. "It will take a while. I've shared a lot with you. You mentioned that you've been gathering some clues. Would you mind sharing them with me? I might be able to help you."

Floyd looked at Lisa and Alex, then turned to Julian. "First, how can we know that you're not just using us to try to find the lost jewels?"

"That's a great question. First, I've been very open with you. I hope it has built some trust. Additionally, I'll tell you everything I know about that day. Ultimately, though, all I can do is give you my word that I want to help you. For more than forty years, I've felt bad about what happened to Dylan and Bull. I'm hoping I can, in some small way, make it a little better."

Floyd thought about it for a moment and looked closely at Lisa and Alex. They both nodded at him. "Okay."

Alex began with a summary of her research in Dublin, including her theory that Molly O'Leary was involved in the theft of the Irish Crown Jewels.

Julian was fascinated. "That makes sense. Brilliant research," he said sincerely.

Then Floyd talked about their trip to Cassis and meeting Shannon Kelly, whose grandmother knew Molly, and the story of her playing with the jewels as a child. He pulled out Dylan's journal and unfolded the letters that they had been provided.

Julian studied the letters carefully. He was deep in thought when the limo driver announced, "We have arrived."

They vacated the limo and hiked up the steps to the top of the observatory. Once he reached the top, Floyd whistled and exclaimed, "They weren't kidding about the view. Wow." As the rest reached the peak, each stopped for a moment to take in the panorama.

Lisa found the plaque mentioned in Dylan's journal and exclaimed, "Here it is—the quote that Dylan found when he was by himself in Corfu."

They all studied it.

Lisa looked at Julian and said, "We just found a lost journal entry from Dylan where he learns that Cape Drastis may be the location of the jewels. There was a reference to 'Lion's Head'. It implied he was going to visit the cape and try to figure out where the Lion's Head was located on the cliff. However, there were no further entries, and we don't know what happened."

Julian looked at them somberly and said, "I'll take you to Cape Drastis and tell you what happened." He walked to the driver's side window and motioned for the driver to lower it. After whispering to him for a moment, Julian returned to the back of the limo, and they began their journey to the cliffs of Cape Drastis.

Chapter 33

The Switchbacks

1983

AFTER RIDING THEIR MOTORBIKES to the top of the switchbacks and touring Kaiser's Throne, Nels looked at the group and said, "I want to go to Cape Drastis."

Dylan exchanged glances with Bull. Nels's impatience made him a little suspicious. Plus, why was he focused on that area? There were so many other things to see on the island. Did he know something?

Julian chimed in, "That's a beautiful place. Let's go check it out. It's a pretty long ride from here, so let's stay close so no one gets lost."

As they walked down the stairs from the Kaiser's Throne observatory, Dylan pulled Bull aside and whispered, "Nels is acting strange. Let's be careful as we go to Cape Drastis."

"I'm on it," Bull said. "I'm not intimidated by him. I could crush him if he gets weird. Let me handle it."

"Okay. I really want to go there anyway. When we arrive, let's try to figure out where the Lion's Head is. Then we can return another day to check it out more closely, just the two of us," Dylan said in relief.

After thirty minutes of mainly highway riding, they saw a sign directing them up a dirt road to Cape Drastis. The four motorbikes headed onto the trail in single file. Dylan led the group, followed by Julian and Bull. Nels held the rear.

***

Finally, we're heading to Cape Drastis, "Nels" thought to himself. *I was beginning to think we'd never get here. I've been thinking about this day for a month.* He looked at the three motorcyclists ahead of him. He knew the road well. *At the first switchback, I'll take out Bull. At the second, Julian will go over the side. That will be a happy moment.* He had wanted to get back at Julian for years. Then it would be just him and Dylan. *The jewels will be in my possession by the end of the day.*

***

The road became exceedingly steep and evolved into a series of sharp switchbacks. Dylan slowed down to make the first turn safely. As he rounded the bend, he heard a loud thud from behind, but he couldn't place it. Then he came to the second switchback. Again, he slowed down significantly to avoid going over the side of the road, which had a steep drop-off. Once more, he heard an unusual sound, like a person getting punched in the gut. Then it stopped. He kept going. It wasn't far to the top. His bike was struggling to climb the slope, so he hit the accelerator, and it gained traction, eventually reaching the peak. He pulled into the small parking lot and dismounted, then jogged up to the clifftop of Cape Drastis. The view was incredible. He felt like he could see forever. He walked to the edge and saw that the cliff was a sheer drop of at least a hundred feet, straight down to the rocks and ocean below. He was surprised there wasn't a rope or rail. He walked along the edge, observing the rock formations, trying to identify anything that looked like a Lion's Head.

"Dylan!" He turned and saw Nels, who was holding a long, golden knife and approaching fast. *That's not just a knife*, he thought. *It looks like a dagger, like what a pirate would have.* The blade was at least a foot long and surrounded by gems.

Chapter 34

Recollection

2025

AFTER A LONG PERIOD of silence, Julian continued with his memory from forty years before. "The day started out great. It was just four guys having a fun time. We rented motorbikes, and we planned to ride around the island for the day. We drove to the Old Town so Dylan and Bull could get some local cash. Then we explored the island. We visited Achilleion, a beautiful palace from the 1800s. Then we went to the Paleokastritsa monastery. I believe it's from the thirteenth century. Dylan and Bull were having a great time. But I could tell that Nels was getting tense. I knew there was something wrong with him, but I couldn't figure it out. I was watching him closely."

Beads of sweat started to descend Julian's forehead as he spoke.

"After a trip to Kaiser's Throne, Nels insisted that we visit Cape Drastis. He was adamant. I could tell that Dylan was getting uncomfortable. I remember Bull pulling Dylan aside, and then they both came back smiling.

"If I remember correctly, it's about a forty-five-minute trip from Kaiser's Throne to Cape Drastis. At first, riding was fun. We were on proper highways, and we were racing each other. Bull took the lead. Then Dylan passed him. I remember him saluting Bull as he went by. Then I hit the gas and passed them both. Nels stayed behind. He didn't participate."

The limo arrived at the base of the switchbacks.

Julian continued, "Finally, we got to the turn-off to go to Cape Drastis, where we are now. It was a winding dirt road forty years ago. Now it's a nice, paved road. Try to picture it the way it was back then. Dylan took the lead. I was right behind him, and Bull and Nels were behind me. I heard a loud noise during the first switchback, but didn't think much of it.

"Then we came to the second switchback. I was accelerating into the turn when my bike jumped up from underneath me, and then I flipped over the handlebars. I saw Nels pass me as I did somersaults along the side of the road. I lost consciousness. Not sure how long I was out, but when I came to, I picked myself up and started heading up the hill to the peak. Something bad was happening, and I needed to get there to help Dylan."

Chapter 35

The Lion's Head

1983

"WHAT ARE YOU DOING, Nels? Where are Bull and Julian?" Dylan said with concern.

"Don't worry about them. It's just you and me," he said, his face contorted.

"What do you mean? What's this about?" Dylan's pulse was racing.

"The lost Irish Crown Jewels. That's what this is about." His eyes were wild.

"Why do you even care about that? You're from Norway," Dylan asked.

"My name isn't Nels. It's Günter Müller. I've been searching for the lost Irish Crown Jewels for years. And you're going to get them for me now."

"Were you in my room last night?" Dylan asked as he backed up, away from Günter and the knife, trying to buy time.

"Yes. And I know that the jewels are in a cave below the Lion's Head—from your journal," Günter said excitedly.

"But I don't know where that is!" Dylan shouted as his back foot touched the edge of the cliff. He was trapped.

"Look to your left. See that rock formation about fifty meters ahead? That's the Lion's Head. I came up here with a local guide the morning I read your journal. He confirmed its location."

"Okay, but from everything I've heard, the cave below the Lion's Head is near impossible to enter."

Günter stopped and pulled a rope out of his backpack. "You're going to search the cave directly below the Lion's Head for me."

***

Bull opened his eyes. He looked around. *What happened? Oh yeah, Nels inserted a stick in my back tire's spokes, and I catapulted off the road. What a dick. He'll regret that! Thankfully, I've only fallen a few yards into a tree.* He moved his arms and legs. *Nothing broken.* He stood up and walked towards the road. *This is getting old*, he thought as he remembered going off the cliff in Cassis as well. He started to jog up the road towards the peak, but his left leg wasn't cooperating. *Nels is up to no good. I need to get up there and check on Dylan.* Bull couldn't run, but he could limp forward. He pushed as hard as he could. He could hear yelling at the top.

"Hey!" It was Julian. "Get up there and help Dylan," he said. "I'm pretty beat up, but I'll be there as soon as I can. I have a bad feeling about Nels. He seems familiar to me. I've been thinking about it all day. I think I know who he is—and he's dangerous."

Chapter 36

Identity Unveiled

2025

JULIAN LED THE GROUP from the parking lot up the last switchback to the cliffs of Cape Drastis.

"What happened next?" Lisa asked him when they reached the top.

"As I approached this peak," Julian said as he pointed up to the top of the cliff, "I saw Bull. He was ahead of me. He was about right there. He was trying to run, but his body wouldn't let him."

Lisa interrupted, "Was he okay?"

"Yeah. He was roughed up. But Bull was tough. I knew he'd make it to the top of that hill no matter what. I yelled at him to get up there and help Dylan, and told him I thought Nels had bad intentions. That just made him more determined."

Floyd jumped in, "What was your theory?"

Julian looked at Floyd and responded, "As I mentioned, I attended the Institut auf dem Rosenberg in St. Gallen, Switzerland, for most of my youth. It's a boarding school. Probably one of the most exclusive in the world. While I was there, I became friends with a guy named Günter Müller. He had blond hair like me. We looked a lot alike. People used to joke about that. He was the son of a billionaire, and he had a passion for stealing art. Initially, this was a common passion. But I quickly realized that he only stole art to sell it. That was sacrilegious to me. I turned him in. He was expelled. Günter told me he'd get me someday. I thought I'd never see him again. But I did...on that day in Corfu. He looked different as an adult, but I finally figured it out...too late."

Chapter 37

Dry Hole

1983

GÜNTER HELD THE DAGGER to Dylan's throat and ordered him to wrap the rope around his own waist. Then he tied the other end around a tree.

"It's time to do some rappelling," he said. He pushed Dylan off the cliff towards the cave.

Dylan fell quickly and then slammed into the craggy rocks. After he'd cleared his head, he realized he was right beside the opening to a cave. He pulled himself inside; it was only about four feet high. Since he couldn't stand upright, he had to crawl in. Graffiti covered the walls on both sides. He dragged himself further into the cave. It got narrower. The rope grew tight. He pulled on it and got some slack. He crawled further until he could see the back of the cave. There was no place for a trunk. This was a dead end!

"Did you find the jewels?" Günter yelled from above.

"There's no trunk—or jewels!" Dylan screamed back.

"I don't believe you," Günter whined in a sing-song fashion.

"Well, it's the truth," Dylan shouted. He turned around and headed back towards the cave's entrance. He peered out of the opening and looked down. It was a straight drop to the rocks and the ocean. His voice trembled as he yelled to Günter, "Pull me up! Let's figure out another plan."

Then he heard Bull's voice. He looked up and could see Bull moving along the edge of the cliff towards Günter, who was holding the knife.

"Hey! Pull him back up!" Bull yelled. "You're the guy who's been following us, aren't you?"

"You should have died in Cassis," Günter screamed. "Leave or I'll let him drop!"

"There must be a way we can solve this," Bull said as he crept closer towards Günter.

Günter looked at Bull and smirked. "Don't take another step. He's lying to me. If he brings me the jewels, then I'll pull him back up."

Dylan watched as Bull stepped forward toward Günter.

Günter screamed as he placed the dagger on the rope.

Chapter 38

Dylan

2025

Lisa looked at Julian and asked breathlessly, "What happened?"

"Günter threw both Bull and me from our bikes. He inserted a stick or something into the spokes. But he didn't do a great job. Both of us were able to gather ourselves and head up to the peak on foot, though at different paces. Bull was hurt, but he barreled through the route ahead of me. I could hear Günter yelling at Dylan; it was clear that he was over the side of the cliff looking in the cave. I was terrified. I knew that the cliffs were almost impossible to climb. At this point, what I am going to tell you is difficult to say. Please brace yourselves," he said as he walked to the edge of the cliff.

"Bull had made it to the top before me," he continued. "I heard a lot of yelling back and forth. It was difficult for me to tell who was speaking. Then I heard a scream...and then silence. I heard Bull yell something before another thirty seconds of arguing and grunting. Then, as I reached the cliff, I heard another horrible shriek and then silence for good."

Lisa had tears in her eyes. She asked softly, "What happened?"

Julian continued in a subdued tone. "At first, I saw no one. I was injured and could barely walk. I pushed forward toward the outcropping that I assumed was Lion's Head. Then I heard a whimper. I staggered to the edge of the cliff—where I am right now—and that's where I found Bull."

"What was he doing?" Lisa asked breathlessly.

Floyd and Alex's eyes were zeroed in on Julian's every utterance.

"He was lying down at the edge of the cliff...sobbing," Julian said.

Lisa put her head in her hands. Floyd put his arm around her shoulders to comfort her.

Julian continued, "I walked up to him and sat down. I asked him what had happened. All he said was, 'They're both gone.' I asked him what he meant, and he told me that the blond man—Günter—had dropped Dylan off the cliff. So, I asked what happened to Günter. Bull sat up slowly, looked me straight in the eyes, and said with authority, 'He fell off the cliff...with a little help.' Then I noticed that Bull was bleeding, and next to him was a curious, long, jeweled knife covered in blood. He had been stabbed by Günter Müller, my old classmate from boarding school.

"I later found out that Bull suffered no significant injuries. Like I said, he was tough. The local police showed up later that afternoon. They interviewed Bull and me. They didn't want this to gain any publicity. They quickly concluded it was two accidental falls, and told us to collect our things and leave Corfu and not talk about it, or they'd charge us with a crime, which I believe now was an empty threat. They just wanted to sweep it under the rug and avoid any impact on their tourist trade. You can look for yourself: the police report was one page long, and there was no mention of this in the local paper."

"Did they find the bodies?" Floyd asked.

"They found Günter. But Dylan's body was never found. All that was ever recovered was his money belt, which was returned to Bull," Julian said with his head bowed. "Günter's parents also saw this as a potential public relations nightmare, so they never challenged the police's version of events and moved on with their lives. Do you know what your family was told?" he asked Floyd.

"Basically nothing. My grandparents were told that Dylan had fallen into the ocean. An accident. That's it. And my understanding was that Bull was traumatized and never spoke about it," Floyd said. He was struggling to come to terms with what Julian had said. "So, you're telling me that you believe Dylan was murdered?"

"Yes. There was a rope tied to a tree." Julian pointed at a thick pine in the distance. "And it snaked to here at the edge of the cliff, where it was clearly cut. Günter cut the rope, and Dylan fell into the sea. Bull confirmed it to me."

Everyone was silent for several minutes, staring over the cliff down at the sharp rocks and the rough ocean.

Finally, Floyd asked, "Do you know how we got Dylan's belongings?"

"Yes. Bull and I went to Corfu Old Town, because that's the only place that had public telephones on the island. He called Dylan's parents from a phone booth. I was standing outside, and after a few minutes, I saw Bull's back slide down the side of the booth. I opened it and found him sitting on the ground with his head in his hands. I helped him up. Bull told me it was the hardest thing he had ever done. He told me he'd promised them that all of Dylan's belongings would be returned, and he was determined to get them immediately."

Julian sighed heavily. "Bull and I rode back to Hotel Nikos and collected all of Dylan's things. A lovely American woman they had met in Florence, named Melinda, was waiting there for him. Apparently, she had told Dylan she'd try to meet him in Corfu. We had to break the terrible news to her. She was devastated. The whole thing was horrible. Bull sent most of Dylan's belongings to his family by mail but he insisted he would personally take back the guitar, journal, and money belt because he knew they were very important to Dylan, and he didn't want them to be lost or damaged."

Alex looked around the table and said, "I feel terrible about this. If I hadn't given that key to Dylan, he would never have been pulled into this nightmare."

Julian looked at her. "I've had a lot of time to process this. I also felt guilty for a long time. I'm sure Bull did as well. It changed me. This event made me into a different person. There is no way you could have known what would happen."

Adriana chimed in, "Yes, Julian was a shell of himself for a long time. When he finally came out of it, he was a more sympathetic and sincere person."

They all stood and looked over the side of the cliff. No one talked for several moments.

Alex pointed to a cave below the cliff's edge. "Is that where Dylan was forced to search?"

Julian responded, "I believe so. From what I could tell, Günter directed him to climb inside, but he didn't find anything. I was so traumatized about it that I left the island as soon as I could and never came back."

Chapter 39

The Disappearing Cave

2025

"I'VE BEEN THINKING ABOUT the final clues," Lisa said, "especially the poem from Kaiser's Throne. There was a reference to the word 'sunken.' I think it may mean 'underwater'—not simply in a cave."

Julian chimed in, "You and I are thinking alike. Before we left Kaiser's Throne, I asked my driver to check on some things for me. Please follow me."

Julian and Adriana took the lead, and the others followed. They entered the limo, and it charted back down the switchbacks. As they reached the shore at the base of the cliffs, a tour boat with the name *The Pirate* was waiting for them. A local captain was smiling and said in broken English, "My name is Caspian. You want a tour of Cape Drastis from the ocean?"

Julian responded, "Yes. Do you know this area well?"

"I have been sailing this area since I was a boy. No one knows it better than me."

As *The Pirate* left the dock, they could hear sirens in the distance. It was the local police. When the convoy arrived, a man jumped out of the lead car and began yelling.

Caspian looked at Julian and said, "You want me to stop?"

Julian responded quickly, "No. Go!"

The captain smiled and said, "As you wish." The boat accelerated so quickly that everyone fell onto the seats surrounding the bow.

Julian yelled over the noise of the motor and wind, "Is there a cave that is submerged directly below the Lion's Head?"

The captain looked at Julian and frowned. "Yes, there is a narrow cave there. It is only tall enough for a man to crawl into. It is so small that you cannot wear scuba gear. It is very unsafe."

Julian turned to the group. "Sounds like the perfect place."

Floyd asked the captain, "Is it possible to enter?"

The captain responded, "Only at low tide, and then only for ten minutes. If you are in there for any longer, you will drown when the tide returns."

Adriana asked in her charming way, "When is low tide?"

The captain glanced at his watch, then looked up and shook his head.

"When is it?" Floyd yelled.

"It is in five minutes, but it is a death sentence. I will not allow you to go in there."

Floyd began removing his shirt, pants, and shoes, and said to the captain, "Take us there immediately. I'm an excellent swimmer, and I'm willing to take the risk."

Lisa looked at him. "No, don't do this. Haven't enough people already died?"

"I have to see for myself. I'll be in and out in ten minutes, I promise. Besides..." He smiled and looked directly at Lisa, "you inspired me, and I've been working out."

Lisa blushed, and then her face again showed concern.

Floyd turned back to the captain. "Do you have a flashlight?"

The captain opened a small compartment next to the steering wheel, fumbled around for a few seconds, pulled out a small black metal object, and threw it to him.

Suddenly, they heard sirens again. The police had commandeered a boat, and it was heading their way.

Floyd said, "We have no time. I have to do this now."

The captain pulled up to the cliff and pointed to a small hole in the rockface. Floyd dove into the water and swam effortlessly to the narrow cavity, which had been temporarily exposed with the low tide. He turned on the flashlight, set a timer on his watch, then slid his body into the crevice.

He entered the narrow tunnel cautiously. Even with the flashlight, he could only see maybe two or three feet ahead. He contorted his body to place his hands above his head so he could gain traction and move himself forward on his stomach. He turned his wrist and looked at his digital watch. Only nine minutes to go, and he had barely gotten past the entrance. He grabbed a slimy rock protruding from the wall in front of him and pulled his body deeper into the fissure. He stretched his arms out in front of him so he could propel himself another body length forward when he felt a large opening to his right.

Pointing his flashlight into the opening, he was surprised to find that he was looking into a cavern the size of a living room. Excited, Floyd pulled himself forward, squeezed through the opening, and down into the compartment. He was able to stand. The opening was chest high. He looked at his wrist. Seven minutes to go. Water started to drip into the opening from the tunnel he'd just left. *The tide is beginning to rise*, he thought. He surveyed the area with his flashlight. It was just a dark cave. Maybe he should have kept pushing into the tunnel. *No time for second-guessing*, he told himself. The walls were damp; the ground was slick and spongy. There was no indication that a person had ever been here before. He studied the edges of the room with his flashlight. Nothing. The water started to enter the cave more quickly. Only six minutes to go.

***

The police boat pulled alongside *The Pirate*, its lights flashing. A voice yelled, "We have been telling you to stop. I am going to put you under arrest for resisting an officer."

Julian calmly walked to the edge of *The Pirate*, looked directly at the policeman, who was panting and sweating, and said, "We have done nothing illegal. How can we help you?"

The policeman said, "I...I...told you to stop."

"As I said, we are doing nothing wrong. Unless you can give me a better reason, I suggest you leave us alone. I will speak to the lieutenant about this later."

"The lieutenant is the one who asked me to observe you." Then the officer noticed light coming from the slowly disappearing fissure in the cliff. "What is going on?"

"Someone is in there," Julian said softly.

"What?" the policeman screamed. "He will die. We must get him out."

The captain of *The Pirate* inserted himself into the conversation. "At this point, we can only wait and see what happens. There is very little time left."

They all turned and looked at the rapidly disappearing cave. Lisa walked to the back of the boat, out of sight of the others, and prepared to enter the water.

***

Four minutes left. The water was filling the bottom of the room. *I have to leave now. Damn!* Floyd kicked the wall below the opening with frustration. It caved in. He was puzzled. It was supposed to be solid rock. Reaching inside with his hands, he touched the sides of the new opening. It was perfectly flat on all sides. Man-made. Then he felt something that didn't belong. It was a trunk.

***

Lisa looked at her watch. Three minutes left. She couldn't just stand there and do nothing. Without hesitation, she jumped into the water and swam to the rapidly disappearing cave.

***

Floyd reached in and pulled out the trunk. Though it wasn't large, it was going to be a formidable task to get it through the opening of the chamber, through the tunnel, and out of the cave in less than three minutes. He lifted it and pushed it through the opening into the tunnel. However, it was blocking his ability to get himself out.

Two minutes.

He jumped up and pushed the trunk with all his might. It moved six inches. He jumped again and shoved as hard as he could with both hands. Six more inches. It was stuck. The water was rushing in now. He was running out of time.

Suddenly, the trunk moved. *What's happening?* Floyd thought.

Then he heard Lisa's voice. She said something that he couldn't understand, and the trunk began moving quickly towards the cave opening, as water rushed toward him. Floyd pulled himself back into the tunnel. It was almost impossible to keep his head above the water. He pushed himself forward. The water was rising fast. Within seconds, the cave would be completely submerged. He took a deep breath, forced himself forward, and began to swim against the rushing water towards the entrance. He couldn't tell if he was moving forward or not due to the strength of the water...and then he saw the light ahead.

***

All of the passengers aboard both boats were intently watching the vanishing cave. *The Pirate's* floodlight shone on the opening.

"Hurry!" Alex screamed.

"Look!" Julian said.

Lisa's feet protruded from the cave, followed by the rest of her body.

She was holding something in her hands.

Alex looked at Julian and exclaimed, "It's a trunk! Could it be...?"

Then the cave's opening disappeared under water.

"Oh no," Alex cried, and she put her face in her hands. "Floyd..."

Julian pointed and yelled, "Wait. Look."

Floyd's head suddenly emerged from the ocean, and his arm shot in the air in a gesture of pure triumph.

Chapter 40

The Return

2025

JULIAN WALKED TO THE podium in the Auditorium Vasari, deep in the Uffizi gallery complex. He looked out over the audience. In the first row, he observed the prime minister of Ireland. Next to him sat Floyd, Lisa, Alex, and Adriana. Behind the prime minister, he saw Lieutenant Papadopoulos and another man he didn't recognize, who must have been from Corfu. It was a packed house.

Julian paused for effect and began his speech. "Thank you for joining me in the Uffizi, here in Florence, Italy. It is my pleasure to inform all of you that we have recovered the Irish Crown Jewels. This has been verified by our art historian, who is considered one of the best in the world. But, to be conservative, we had the Vatican's authentication expert appraise the jewels as well. She agreed with the assessment. It has been my passion to recover these jewels since I was a college student more than forty years ago. They have been missing since 1907, more than a century.

"In the summer of 1983, I followed two American boys—Dylan Stone and Bull Eastland—through Europe as they collected clues pointing in the direction of the lost jewels. I got to know them briefly. They were great young men. Unfortunately, they became entangled in something that turned out to be very dangerous. Tragically, on June 29th of that year, Dylan and another young man ended up going over the very cliff where the jewels were hidden, and the experience forever changed the late Mr. Eastland and me.

"I have to give credit to Dr. Alexandra Morana, for she is the person who found the initial clues to the existence and location of the jewels back in 1983. Please stand, Alex."

Alex stood to a large round of applause.

Julian continued, "I also want to acknowledge Floyd Stone, Dylan's nephew, and Lisa Eastland, Bull's daughter, who, along with Alex, retraced the footsteps of Dylan and Bull and uncovered the clues that brought us to where we are today."

He motioned for Floyd and Lisa to stand. They rose, looked at the people clapping enthusiastically, then sat back down. Lisa placed Floyd's hand in hers. He looked at her in surprise, and she gave him a subtle wink.

"I want to tell you the story of Molly O'Leary. According to Dr. Alexandra Morana's research, Molly was a rambunctious and bright college student in Dublin. She became friendly with Arthur Vicars, who was notoriously lax in his responsibility to protect the Irish Crown Jewels. Molly took the jewels initially as a joke. She just wanted to see if she could do it. However, she quickly realized that she would be prosecuted if she returned them, so she left school and Dublin and moved to Europe. With the assistance of her on-again, off-again boyfriend, she was employed as a nanny to Kayleigh Kelly, in Cassis, France. The boys met Kayleigh, her husband Dan, and her granddaughter, Shannon, during their 1983 trip. It was during that stay at their B&B that the boys found their first real clues, seventy-year-old letters that pointed them forward in their search. By the way, Shannon is here tonight."

He pointed to Shannon, who stood up shyly, acknowledged the applause, and quickly sat down.

"Molly also spent time in Figline Valdarno with Giovanni and Sofia Luigi. Sofia later took a pregnant Molly to Velletri, where her family had lived for generations. They welcomed the young woman and helped her through the pregnancy, when that was a controversial time for a Catholic family in the early-twentieth century. It is in Velletri where she became a mother to the renowned Cormac Martinelli, the CEO of Martinelli Vineyards—the only winemaker I know that does not drink wine." Julian smiled and nodded towards the audience.

Everyone laughed, and Cormac quickly stood, waved, and sat back down.

"Molly and Cormac moved to Corfu, thinking it would be a safe place. And it was, for a while. The two explored the island and met many people, including the famous Kaiser Wilhelm II, who became a good friend. But when the island's population quadrupled during World War I, due to the Serbian evacuation to Corfu, it became a dangerous place for a young mother and her child. Molly became ill and decided to hide the jewels for safekeeping during the occupation. She had a friend who was an oyster diver, and he hid the jewels for her in the special cave at the base of the Cape Drastis cliff. Sadly, Molly and her diver friend both passed away within a year of the jewels being hidden. He died in the war, and she died due to an illness. Cormac was then returned to Velletri, where the Martinelli family raised him as one of their own. As a result, the secret remained hidden for more than a century.

"Molly's intention was for the jewels to be found. She left clues in her letters. She was hoping that her boyfriend, Cillian, would figure out the hint, collect the jewels, and return them to Ireland. However, due to his preoccupation with the war and its aftermath, he never put the pieces together or returned to Europe to try to solve the mystery. We know all this now because she explained it in a letter found with the jewels. But it took seventy years for Alex to uncover the initial clue – the key to the trunk holding the jewels. Then Dylan and Bull spent their summer traveling through Europe and investigating the tips that they obtained along the way—meeting with Shannon in Cassis, Luigi Rossi in Figline Valdarno, and Cormac in Velletri. It's incredible what they were able to pull together. When I met them, I was struck by how down-to-earth and pleasant they were—just great human beings. I tried to protect them, but I failed. It has haunted me ever since. It took another forty years before Floyd, Lisa, and Alex followed the clues to their conclusion. I'm so glad that I have been able to get to know them and consider them my friends.

"In the end, Floyd and Lisa both risked their lives to find the treasure, diving into a cave that is only accessible for ten minutes at low tide. I'm so glad they are okay. We are eternally grateful to all of them for solving this mystery and returning these jewels to Ireland. I'm proud to say that the jewels will be displayed here at the Uffizi for three months, and then they will be returned to Dublin."

After the ceremony ended, Floyd, Lisa, and Alex pulled Julian aside. They were in the process of thanking him for his beautiful words when the Corfu police lieutenant walked up and politely interrupted them.

He said, "I want to formally thank you all for what you have done." He then looked at Floyd and said, "I also want to apologize for the way Dylan's disappearance was handled in 1983. We should have done a better job for your family." He nodded at Lisa and then said, "Please let me introduce you to my friend, Damon Petrus, the famous author and director-general of UNESCO. Though he now spends much of his time in Paris, he hails from Corfu and is a world-renowned author..."

It was at this moment that they all noticed the man standing next to the lieutenant. Floyd looked at Lisa with wide eyes, then glanced back at the man. He was slender and fit, maybe five foot ten, with neatly trimmed gray hair and a tight gray beard. Dressed in a blue sports coat, khaki slacks, and running shoes, he somehow looked familiar, but his age was hard to determine given his excellent physical condition. He could be as young as fifty or maybe older than sixty. However, the striking aspect about him was that he had one green eye and one black eye.

Epilogue

Two Years Later – Hamer, Texas

Thanksgiving

Leaves floated in the breeze as they started their journey from the live oaks towering above the bungalow toward the lake far below, which looked like glass, still and calm. The sky was navy blue, and the air carried a hint of coolness, typical for this time of year.

Without using his arms, he rose from the faded olive Adirondack chair, which was a challenge due to its permanent state of recline, and stepped toward the guardrail. He rocked the sleeping child on his shoulder as he took in the peaceful view. He felt happy. Maybe happier than he had ever been.

"Hey, Uncle Dylan," Floyd whispered as he slipped through the sliding glass door and onto the deck, "I think you're the baby-whisperer. She was out of control until you took her."

Dylan Stone, known as Damon Petrus for the last forty-four years, gazed at the sleeping child and said, "I've always had a way with children. I have three of my own, you know, as well as six grandchildren."

He was a handsome man, slender, with short, silver hair, an attractive, though slightly crooked smile showcasing straight white teeth and a neatly trimmed beard. What stood out the most were his eyes; his left eye was black, and his right was pale green. This distinctive feature had revealed the mystery of his past. A past that had eluded him for more than four decades.

He looked at Floyd and said, "Being here at this house in Hamer is triggering, in a good way. Just now, as I was rocking Clare, memories of my father flooded back as if they never left. I remember sitting on this deck with him while he sipped coffee from his old tin cup, the one he'd purchased in Italy. He would put his arm around me and invent silly stories about the local animals. Sometimes he would tell me about his travels abroad as a young man. Looking back, I'm sure that's what inspired me to backpack through Europe. He also had a great ear for music. We'd discuss everything from the blues of Robert Johnson to the influence of the Beatles on contemporary music. Did you know he took me to my first concert? It was Rush. Can you picture your grandfather and me rocking to the '2112 Overture'? I also recall sitting on this deck, watching sailboats and water skiers while listening to the muffled sounds of music echoing up the cliffs from their stereo speakers. Dad could always name the song first. Sometimes it only took one note. Drove me crazy. And when the wind was just right, you could hear a conversation happening on a boat half a mile away."

"Yeah, Papa was the best. I have similar memories," Floyd said.

"When you opened the door just now, I smelled Lisa's cooking, which reminded me of your nana. She was truly one of a kind and kept the whole family together. I'm heartbroken that I missed the last decades of their lives. But I'm especially sad when I think of them mourning their supposedly dead son and having to live with that for the rest of their days."

The child started to stir. She raised her head briefly, like a turtle, looked around, then buried her face in Dylan's shoulder and closed her eyes again.

"But I'm so happy to be here and to get to know you and Lisa…and now Clare Torry Stone."

Lisa and Alex joined them on the balcony. Lisa walked straight up to Dylan and hugged him. She was carrying a small box in her hand. She kissed Clare on the head, then walked over to Floyd's side and handed him the box. She winked at him and then looked back at Dylan and said, "I'm so glad you could make it. Just think: your first American Thanksgiving since 1982."

"It's great to be here. I wish my wife could have met you all. Once she got over the shock of everything, I know she would have loved you," Dylan said.

Alex, who had flown in from California for the occasion, chimed in, "Please tell us about her."

Dylan ran his hand through Clare's hair and paused for a moment, then said, "Therese was my physical therapist. She helped me regain my strength and eventually taught me the language. After the incident, I woke up in a hospital in Athens. I had no idea who I was or how I got there. I had no memories of my past life. She nursed me back to health, and we fell in love along the way."

Clare looked up, saw her mother, and raised her arms towards her. She had dark hair, blue-green eyes, and a dimple on her left cheek. Lisa took Clare from Dylan and cradled the baby in her arms.

Dylan looked at Lisa. "When we have time, I want to hear everything you can tell me about your father, Bull. After reading my journal several times—thanks for sending it to me, by the way—I have regained memories of my childhood with Bull. I also remember much of our trip through Europe. He was a great friend. Like a brother, really." He then looked at Floyd and said, "And I want to hear about you. What are you up to these days?"

"As you can imagine," Floyd responded, "after finding the lost Irish Crown Jewels, Alex, Lisa, and I got a lot of press. We started receiving calls the next day with a variety of requests. I'm now a private investigator, and I love it. And it turns out I'm pretty good at it. Lisa and Alex are part of the team, but they also have other priorities."

"My focus is on Clare and my personal training business," Lisa said. "But I can't help getting involved in the interesting cases."

"And I still live in California," Alex said. "Our European adventure inspired me to dive back into research, and I teach some classes as well. Interestingly, I've supported Julian in several of his searches for other lost artifacts. We correspond regularly."

"Have you thought about moving back to the States?" Floyd asked Dylan.

Dylan looked at the lake for a moment and then turned to Floyd and said, "I love my work with UNESCO. I currently split my time between Paris and Corfu. However, since Therese passed away, I have been lonely. My children have grown up and moved away. One is in Athens, another in Florence, and one in New York. I'm now at a point where change is possible, I suppose. And, I have some ideas for my next book. Let's enjoy our time together, and we'll see where it goes."

"You're always welcome to stay with us," Lisa said, "We have an extra bedroom and would love to have you."

"We have something we want to share with you," Floyd jumped in. He placed the box on the table between them and took a step backwards.

"What's this?" Dylan asked.

"I found this in the attic of my mother's house a few weeks ago," said Lisa, "under some of my dad's old legal papers. It easily could have been lost forever. But I saw your name, and I just knew it was something important."

Written in large block letters were the words, FOR DYLAN STONE'S EYES ONLY.

"We knew you were coming to visit, so we saved it for you," Floyd said.

Dylan studied it. He sat down at the table and ran his hand across the letters. He looked at Lisa. "What do you think it is?"

"I don't know. And it's killing me. I've almost opened it several times," Lisa said with a smile.

Dylan slowly removed the lid. Inside was an old cloth bag with a drawstring. He pulled the bag open, inserted his hand, and felt inside. His eyes lit up, and he looked at Lisa, Floyd, and Alex. "It's a book."

He pulled out a small journal. The cover was a pale, age-stained yellow, and it was empty except for the words "For Dylan—The Rest of the Trip—1983," handwritten in small print across the front. He opened the book to the inside cover. It looked very much like the journal he had kept more than forty years before. It listed dates and places, starting with Athens, Greece, on July 3, 1983, and ending in Amsterdam on July 22nd.

Dylan thumbed through the pages. He didn't recall Bull being much of a writer, but it was clear he had put some effort into this chronicle of the trip. There were many entries, and he noticed references to dates and people, and even drawings—all in Bull's precise script.

He turned to the first page and read aloud.

July 3, Athens

Dear Dylan,

Though I personally heard you fall off the cliff, and the police told me there's no way you survived, I choose in my heart to believe that you're alive...somewhere...somehow. I've decided to complete the trip just as if you were with me. I'll record the journey in this journal, just as you would. I hope we'll meet again someday and that I can share this with you.

"This is great; it's as if he's talking to me," Dylan said. He studied the next journal entry and began reading to the group. It was brief and written with urgency.

July 4, Athens

Dylan,

You're not going to believe this. I just now jumped on the subway as the doors closed. I'm leaving the city as fast as I can. The police are after me! Man, I could use your help.

Dylan looked at Floyd. "I think I'll stay for a while."

About the Author

In the summer of 1983, W. D. Nelson and two buddies set off on a trek across Europe with no agenda other than a return ticket from Amsterdam fifty-six days later. He brought a backpack, a guitar, and an empty journal. Two months later, he returned home a changed person, with long hair, a smashed guitar, and a journal filled with stories. That trip sparked a lifelong love of travel, and writing, that has since carried him to more than forty countries. Nelson splits his time between Houston and Canyon Lake in the Texas Hill Country. This is his first published novel. Connect with him at wd-nelson.com, on Instagram at wdnelsonauthor, or on Facebook at W. D. Nelson Author.